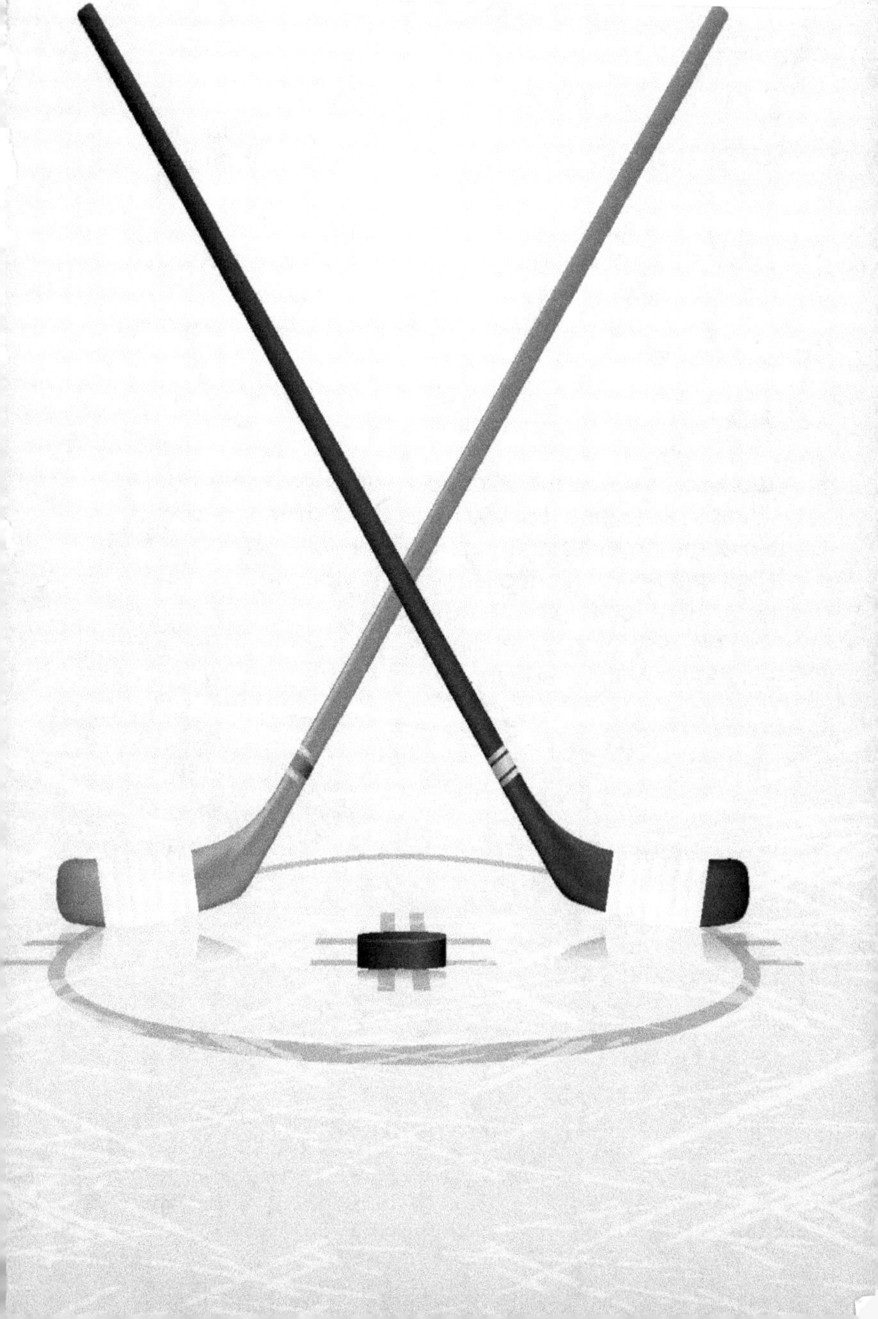

MADE FOR ME

Chase

Everyone expected me to play hockey.
I was good at it, but I was better at being a doctor.
So, I hung up the skates and joined Doctors Without Borders.
But there is no place like home, so now I'm back.
And instead of being on the ice, I'm behind the bench as the team physician.
After years of playing cat and mouse, it's time to admit it.
She's mine.

Julia

Working as a social worker was a dream come true.
It wasn't easy, and it made me shut off my heart to love.
No commitment. No strings. No promises.
Until one fateful night changes everything.
He is there for me like no other one.
The biggest thing is I let him.
Maybe he is just made for me!

BOOKS BY NATASHA MADISON

Made For Series
Made For Me
Made For You
Made For Us
Made For Romeo

Southern Wedding Series
Mine To Kiss
Mine To Have
Mine To Cherish
Mine to Love

The Only One Series
Only One Kiss
Only One Chance
Only One Night
Only One Touch
Only One Regret
Only One Mistake
Only One Love
Only One Forever

Southern Series
Southern Chance
Southern Comfort
Southern Storm
Southern Sunrise
Southern Heart
Southern Heat
Southern Secrets
Southern Sunshine

This Is
This is Crazy
This Is Wild
This Is Love
This Is Forever

Hollywood Royalty
Hollywood Playboy
Hollywood Princess
Hollywood Prince

Something So Series
Something Series
Something So Right
Something So Perfect
Something So Irresistible
Something So Unscripted
Something So BOX SET

Tempt Series
Tempt The Boss
Tempt The Playboy
Tempt The Ex
Tempt The Hookup

Heaven & Hell Series
Hell And Back
Pieces Of Heaven

Love Series
Perfect Love Story
Unexpected Love Story
Broken Love Story

Standalones
Faux Pas
Mixed Up Love
Until Brandon

SOMETHING SO, THIS IS ONLY ONE & MADE FOR FAMILY TREE!

Hockey Series
SOMETHING SO SERIES
Something So Right
Parker & Cooper Stone
Matthew Grant (Something So Perfect)
Allison Grant (Something So Irresistible)
Zara Stone (This Is Crazy)
Zoe Stone (This Is Wild)
Justin Stone (This Is Forever)
Something So Perfect
Matthew Grant & Karrie Cooley
Cooper Grant (Only One Regret)
Frances Grant (Only One Love)
Vivienne Grant
Chase Grant
Something So Irresistible
Allison Grant & Max Horton
Michael Horton (Only One Mistake)
Alexandria Horton
Something So Unscripted
Denise Horton & Zack Morrow
Jack Morrow
Joshua Morrow
Elizabeth Morrow
THIS IS SERIES
This Is Crazy
Zara Stone & Evan Richards
Zoey Richards
This Is Wild

Zoe Stone & Viktor Petrov
Matthew Petrov
Zara Petrov
This Is Love
Vivienne Paradis & Mark Dimitris
Karrie Dimitris
Stefano Dimitris
Angelica Dimitris
This Is Forever
Caroline Woods & Justin Stone
Dylan Stone (Formally Woods)
Christopher Stone
Gabriella Stone
Abigail Stone
ONLY ONE SERIES
Only One Kiss
Candace Richards & Ralph Weber
Ariella Weber
Brookes Weber
Only One Chance
Layla Paterson & Miller Adams
Clarke Adams
Only One Night
Evelyn & Manning Stevenson
Jaxon Stevenson
Victoria Stevenson
Only One Touch
Becca & Nico Harrison
Phoenix Harrison
Dallas Harrison
Only One Regret
Erika & Cooper Grant
Emma Grant
Mia Grant

Parker Grant

Matthew Grant

Only One Mistake

Jillian & Michael Horton

Jamieson Horton

Only One Love

Frances Grant & Brad Wilson

Stella Wilson

Only One Forever

Dylan Stone & Alex Horton

Maddox Stone

Maya Stone

Maverick Stone

Made For Me

Julia & Chase Grant

Made For You

Vivienne Grant & Xavier Montgomery

Made For Us

Arabella Stone & Tristan Weise

Penelope

Payton

Made For Romeo

Romeo Beckett & Gabriella Stone

Mine to Take

Matthew Petrov & Sofia Barnes

Mine To Promise

Stefano Markos & Sadie

Copyright © 2022 Natasha Madison. E-Book and Print Edition
All rights reserved. No part of this book may be reproduced or transmitted in any form or by any means, electronic or mechanical, including photocopying, recording, or by any information storage and retrieval system, without permission in writing.

This is a work of fiction. Names, characters, places and incidents are the product of the author's imagination or are used factiously, and any resemblance to any actual persons or living or dead, events or locals are entirely coincidental.

The author acknowledges the trademark status and trademark owners of various products referenced in this work of fiction, which have been used without permission. The publication/ Use of these trademarks is not authorized, associated with, or sponsored by the trademark owner.

All rights reserved

Cover Design: Jay Aheer

Editing done by Jenny Sims Editing4Indies

Editing done by Karen Hrdicka Barren Acres Editing

Proofing Julie Deaton by Deaton Author Services

Proofing by Judy's proofreading

Formatting by Christina Parker Smith

MADE FOR ME

NATASHA
MADISON

One

Julia

TWISTING THE WATER bottle cap off, I bring the plastic bottle to my lips. "I wish this was something stronger," I mumble to myself before the cold water hits my dry mouth. My stomach lurches, and I lean back against the counter in the staff kitchen. After six years of doing this job, you would think I would be used to this, but nothing—and I mean nothing—can prepare you for it.

"Hey." My boss, Rosalind, sticks her head into the kitchen, her black hair pushed back by a headband. "Monica is in your office." The minute she says those five words, the water wants to come back up. "Let me know if you need me."

I huff out a big deep breath. "Will do." I nod at her, and when she leaves, I let my head hang forward. "Here we go." I push my sandy-blond hair behind my ear, walking to my cubicle I call an office.

"Don't touch that, Penelope." I hear Monica as I make the dreaded walk toward the voice. Every step feels like my feet are getting heavier and heavier. "Why can't you ever freaking listen?" I hear her hiss. "Come here."

I stand at the cubicle entrance, watching her as she grabs Penelope by the wrist and pulls her toward her, picking her up and placing her on her lap. "Be good, and when we leave here, I'll get you candy."

"Candy?" Penelope looks up at her mom, and my heart breaks for what is to come. I swallow down the lump.

"Hey," I say, walking into the cubicle and going to sit in my chair. The desk is against one wall of the cubicle with the chair Monica sits on right beside it. "Thank you for coming." I turn my chair to look at her. My chair, not very far from hers, as I grab her thick manila folder. I try not to make eye contact with her and shut myself off.

"It's not like I had a choice," Monica huffs, and I look at her now. Her bleached-blond hair is down to her shoulders, but her black roots are half of her head. "You said it was mandatory."

"All meetings are mandatory," I inform her. "This isn't new." I look down at the notes even though I know this whole file by heart. "How are things going?"

"As they always are," she huffs out. I look down at Penelope, who just looks at me, her brown hair tied in a lopsided ponytail. Her blue eyes are so crystal that you can see through them. She's wearing little blue jeans and a pink top.

"How are you, Penelope?" I look down at the two-year-old little girl who says three words, mama, bobba for bottle, and candy.

She points behind her. "Mama," she tells me proudly, and I smile at her.

"So what am I really doing here, Julia?" Monica asks as the diaper bag on her shoulder falls down to her elbow.

"Well." I fold my hands together and place them on top of the folder. "As you know, the last couple of visits haven't exactly been okay." She rolls her eyes at me, and I want to think she is listening to me, but at this point, I have no idea if she's even listening at all. But the rolling of the eyes pushes me over the edge. "And I gave you enough warning for you to shape up."

"What are you saying?" She sits up when she hears my tone.

"I hate to say this," I say, and the stinging comes to my eyes, "but we have decided to place Penelope."

I can see her expression change the minute I say that. Her arm wraps around her daughter, and I know deep down she loves her daughter with everything she has. But she's a child raising a child, and I am not one to judge anyone, but she didn't exactly have the best parental role models. "You can't do that," she says, and her lower lip quivers.

"You left us no choice." I look at her and see the tears roll over her lower lashes. "You failed the random drug test."

"It was a mistake. I didn't know." I almost roll my

eyes. "By accident, I put a molly in my Tylenol bottle. I swear I haven't touched anything since then." Her voice goes high and trembles. "Please, Julia, give me another chance." Her hands even shake a bit with nerves.

"I've given you chance after chance after chance, Monica," I remind her softly. "You think this is what I want?" I shake my head, trying to keep things as calm as I can. I've been doing this a long time, and there have been times that taking away a child has put me in the middle of danger. I had a father pull out a knife and threaten to slice me open and eat my insides. I mean, he was high on meth, but it will stay with me forever. "You've been in my case file since you were fifteen, and now you're almost twenty-one."

"I swear, Julia, I'm trying," she whispers. "I swear if you give me one more chance, you won't regret it." I look down, and my head is screaming no, but then I look up at her. "I swear, I just need one more chance. If I fuck up again," she says, and her hands circle Penelope's waist, "then you can take her from me."

"We aren't taking her from you." I try to say it as delicately as I can. I love my job, I really do, but days like this… Days like today when I have to take a child from their parent, I really rethink what the hell I'm doing this for. "We are helping you get everything you need to help with Penelope."

"What she needs is to be with her mother," Monica pleads. "I know I haven't always been on the ball with some of her things. But I'm learning." My stomach flips. "I swear to God, Julia, if you give me one more chance, you won't regret it."

I tap my finger on the papers, knowing I should just take Penelope and turn away, but I also know this might just be the wake-up call Monica needs. Knowing she is one step away from losing her little girl might be the kick in the ass to straighten her up. "You know if I give you this one last chance, I'm putting my neck on the line," I say honestly.

"I swear, Julia, you won't be sorry," she assures me, and I believe her. At least I believe she wants to be a better parent.

"We meet again in two weeks. If anything, and I mean anything, comes up..." I don't finish my sentence because she jumps up. I pop up at the same time as she does.

"I promise you, Julia." She turns Penelope around so she can sit on her hip. "You won't be sorry."

"I want you to call me every other day," I say. "And I want you to have a job in the next two weeks."

She nods at me and turns around, walking out faster than ever, for fear I'll change my mind. I sit back down in my chair and put my head back. "How did it go?" Rosalind asks, and I turn to look at her.

"She has fourteen days to straighten up," I inform her. "I know we said that—"

Rosalind holds up her hand to stop me from talking. "This is your case, and you know best how to deal with it. I haven't doubted you once since you've been working here."

I take a deep inhale. "Thanks for the vote of

confidence," I say as she walks away laughing. "When does this get easier?"

She stops walking and turns around. "I've been doing this for over twenty years, and I still ask myself that every single day." She shakes her head. "You will have good days and bad." She smiles at me. "Cherish those."

"Thanks," I say as my phone vibrates on my desk. I turn it over to see Jillian, my twin sister, is FaceTiming me.

Pressing the green button, I see the circle going around while it says connecting. "Hello," I greet, and my face lights up when I see my six-year-old nephew, Jamieson, on the screen. "Well, isn't it the most handsome man in the whole world?" I love three people more than anything in the world, and those three people are my nephew and my two nieces. I would lay down my life for any of them. I put the folder away, looking down at my watch and seeing it's just after five o'clock. I get up, grabbing my purse and the canvas bag I got when I started working here. It had my information package in it, and since then, it's been with me. I know it's silly, but the bag has a sentimental part to it being as it holds everyone's story.

"Auntie Juju," he says softly. "Mommy said I can't have the cookies you bought me." I can tell this little man is playing me.

"And why did she say that?" I ask as I walk into the elevator and press the P button. "Mommy wouldn't say no unless there was a reason."

"No." He shakes his head, and his black hair falls on his forehead. His baby-blue eyes look full of mischief, and I can't wait to hug and kiss him. "I did nothing."

I roll my lips because his face is so angelic-looking. "Let me ask Mommy," I say, walking out into the parking garage. The clicking of my heels fills the empty garage as I grab my keys and unlock the car doors. I get in, putting the phone in the holder as I start the car, and Jamieson calls Jillian.

She comes to the phone and grabs it from him. "Did he call you?"

I try not to laugh as I pull out of the garage. "Um, I refuse to answer that question." I chuckle. "Why can't he have a cookie?" I ask, and she turns and glares at Jamieson. I mean, glare is too strong of a word. She gives him the mother look that means watch out.

"Did you tell Auntie Juju why you can't have a cookie?" she asks him, and I can hear my nieces yelling in the background. "Today, Mr. Horton called one of his friends a small dickhead," she shares, looking at him, and he just looks down at the floor. "And then told him he was going to cut him."

I roll my lips, trying not to laugh. "I mean, not that I'm saying it's right or not, but…" She now glares at me. "Did this little boy do something to bother him? There are always three sides to every story."

"Julia." She says my name between clenched teeth. "That is not the point. We don't attack other people."

"Are you alone?" I ask, and she nods her head.

"Michael is gone for two days," she says of my brother-in-law. The two of them met seven years ago and ended up having a one-night stand. She had no idea who he was, and five months later, their paths crossed again. Not only was she pregnant with Jamieson but she also found out he played hockey in the NHL and came from a hockey royalty family.

"Why didn't you tell me?" I ask as I make my way over to her house. "I'll be there in twenty minutes, depending on traffic."

"You don't have to do this," she huffs.

"Please, it would be my pleasure, especially after the day I've had," I say. "Why don't you order food and I'll be there to help give the girls a bath."

"Is everything okay?" she asks. Over the years, I've shared a couple of things with her, but mostly it's all private and confidential, so I can't disclose certain things. But when a case gets to me, she can feel it. My mother calls it the twin intuition.

"Just a hard day, that's all." I shrug. "But now I get to spend time with my favorite people." I smile at her. "See you soon."

Two

Chase

"TWO MINUTES TO go!" the coach shouts from the bench, and I look up at the Jumbotron. "I'd like to get on the plane with at least one win." I lean against the side of the wall, just out of the way, folding my arms over my chest. "Stone!" he yells for my cousin, Dylan, to get his ass on the ice. Dylan jumps up and throws his leg over the bench getting on the ice and in the middle of the play.

I watch the Jumbotron, seeing them score in the empty net. Clapping my hands, I turn around and walk back to the small office they gave me when I got here. As a visiting team, they give you the bare minimum, just enough to get your stuff set up. I pack up the medical bag I travel with as I hear the players start to walk back into the dressing room. "Bus leaves in one hour!" I hear someone yell, and I smile, knowing I'll be sleeping in my own bed tonight. Not all teams carry their own doctor to games. Some just use the doctors the other teams have, but not Nico. Nope. He doesn't want anyone touching his guys but the best.

Forty-five minutes later, I'm shrugging on my suit jacket and walking out of the office with my bags packed. I place my bags on the trolly at the same time Cooper, my older brother, comes from the dressing room. His hair's still wet from the shower, and he holds his tie in his hand. "Don't you look all Rico Suave." I roll my lips to stop from laughing as he glares at me.

"This coming from the walking, talking *GQ* model." He points at me. "Your ponytail is crooked."

"It's called a bun." I wink at him. "And the girls love it." We walk toward the bus side by side. This is another reason I took the job here. When Nico offered me the position two years ago, I laughed it off, but then I kept coming to Dallas more and more to see my brother, Cooper, who plays with the team, and my two cousins, Dylan and Michael, who also play for the team. I liked the weather, and it made me want to finally plant roots. "Just the other day, Erika was running her hands through it." He stops walking and just glares at me. He'll take any joke, but you bring up his wife, and all bets are off.

"I will put you through a fucking wall," he says between clenched teeth, and I just laugh at him.

"I'm a good forty pounds heavier than you." I turn around, walking backward. "And it's all muscle."

He just shakes his head as we walk up the steps to the plane. Most of the guys are sitting in their seat quietly, just waiting for us to leave. The time after the games on the road hit differently, especially games when we know we are going home. After day one, everyone is itching to get home. "I'm starving," Michael states when he sits behind me on the plane.

"The question is, when aren't you starving?" I ask him, taking off my suit jacket.

"Is there food?" Michael looks at Cooper and asks him. "On the plane."

"There should be." He shrugs off his own suit jacket. I undo the buttons on my button-down shirt and roll up the sleeves.

"I'm going to go ask them." Michael gets up from his chair.

"Why don't you just press the button?" Dylan suggests, sitting down next to me. "Nora will come see what you need."

"Oh, good call," Michael says, pressing the button. A ping sounds, and the light goes on. Everyone gets comfortable. Most of the men have their suit jackets off, and none are wearing a tie.

Nora comes over, and when she sees it's Michael, she laughs. "Let me guess, you want to know what I have to eat?" The four of us can't help but chuckle. "We have chicken breast, steak, and salmon."

"I'll have the steak," Michael states and then looks at me. "Are you eating yours?"

"It's eleven o'clock," I look at my watch and inform him.

"Well, we all didn't stand around looking like Thor."

He scoffs at me. "Some of us actually worked."

"I'll remember that when you come crying to me because you have a boo-boo on your finger." I sit down, facing forward, and he pushes my chair.

"I thought he broke my finger. He slashed me so hard," Michael defends, and I snicker at him. Then he looks at Nora. "I'll take one of each."

"I'll get that to you as soon as I can," Nora says. She walks back to the front, and they start to prepare the plane for takeoff.

I close my eyes for the one-hour flight, and when we land, I'm one of the first ones off. "See you guys tomorrow," I mumble over my shoulder as I head to my Range Rover.

Michael and Dylan get in the same car since they live two seconds away from each other, and Cooper gets into his alone.

The drive is a quick twelve minutes from the airport to the parking garage. By the time I'm unlocking my door, it's just a touch after one in the morning. I toss my keys on the glass table at the front door, kick off my shoes, and walk down the white marble hallway to the open-concept living space.

The white U-shaped couch faces the fireplace and ninety-inch big screen. The only light on is the lamp on the side table. The moon provides the rest of the light through the wall of windows. There is a reason they call this the penthouse.

Walking to the kitchen, I pull open the fridge and grab a bottle of water before heading over to the big island and seeing my mail left by the fruit platter. In the past week, I've only been home two days before turning around and getting back on the road again. Let me tell you, this is not how I thought my life would be.

When I turned eighteen, I didn't think I would ever end up here. Fuck, I thought I would follow in the footsteps of my grandfather and father and be playing in the NHL. But the summer before I was scheduled to attend Michigan State University, my aunt Denise asked me to spend the summer volunteering at the children's oncology department. It took me less than a week to know what I was meant to do, and all my plans changed. I attended Michigan State getting my undergraduate before I applied to Harvard Medical School. I was happy I kept up my four point zero GPA average because getting in was easy. I should also thank my father for pushing me to take advance science courses so I already had the prerequisites.

Telling my father I was not going to play hockey was another story, but he wasn't upset. He supported me during the four years of med school. When I sat down with him and broke the news, he wasn't surprised, but he was less than thrilled when I told him I wanted to join Doctors Without Borders. Being so far away from home, and with him not able to control what happened, had him pulling out his hair. I mean, I would come home every six months, more or less, until things were a little bit crazy. It was a rush, that is for sure, going into a situation and being the only one who can either save them or not.

Going to work every day now was less stressful than

before. I'm lucky I'm able to pick up four shifts a month to work in the ER when I'm not traveling, and the team is off. Then, I'll head back to New York and work with Denise during the summer.

Picking up my bag at the front door and walking back into the bedroom, I press the button to close the shades at the same time as I turn on the lights. The room is exactly like it was when I moved in last year. Actually, everything in the apartment is the same. Before I lived here, my cousin Michael lived here for a bit. It belongs to Erika, who keeps it for visiting family members after she moved out. The only things in this house that show I live here are my clothes hanging in the closet and the family picture in the living room. Dumping my bag in the walk-in closet, I pull off my shirt and pants and head straight to the shower. I shower in the dark, and when I slide into bed, it takes me two seconds to fall asleep.

The ringing of my phone wakes me from my dream, and I lean over to grab it, only to come up empty. I get up on my elbows and look around the room to see where the sound is coming from. It's coming from the closet, which makes sense since I just dumped my pants in there. I throw the covers off me and get up, following the sound of the ringing when it stops. I'm about to go back to bed when there's a knock on the front door right before it opens. "Chase?" I hear him call my name.

"Dad?" I say, not sure if I'm dreaming or not. When I walk out of my bedroom, I see him standing in the entryway, looking toward the kitchen. He turns his head when he hears me. "What the hell are you doing here?"

"Jesus Christ, Chase." He puts his hands on his hips. "Why are you always naked?"

"I'm not always naked." I laugh, turning to walk back into my bedroom and grab a pair of shorts. "I'm in my house!" I shout and hear him walking to the kitchen. I go to the bathroom before walking out to the kitchen, where I smell coffee. "Morning," I mumble and walk over to him.

He puts his hand around my neck and brings me in for a hug. He's been hugging me the same way since I was a little boy even though I'm a touch taller than him now. "Hi." He walks over to one of the stools and sits down.

"What are you doing here?" I walk toward the cabinet where the mugs are kept and take out one, then head over to pour myself a coffee.

"You literally texted me last night and said you wanted to come work out with me," my father reminds me, and I just look at him like he has two heads.

"I did?" I take a sip of the hot black coffee. "Are you sure?"

He just glares at me. "Of course, I'm sure," he hisses, grabbing his phone from his back pocket.

"I mean, I'm not saying that I didn't text you." I hide the smile behind the mug. "I'm just saying you have sometimes not read the whole thing."

"Chase fucking Grant," he snarls with his teeth clenched together, "do not fucking play with me."

"I mean, last time I asked you to grab me a latte," I remind him, "and you grabbed me a ladle."

"That was your mother's fault." He points his phone

at me. "She read it wrong."

"Okay, but you didn't think to yourself, wait, what the hell would he need a ladle for?" I ask him, and he just shakes his head.

"You could have been making soup!" he shouts and throws up his hands. "Regardless, this is the text you sent me."

"Read it," I urge him and he looks down and squints. He moves the phone farther away from his face. "Hey, Dad, it's Chase." He reads the first line and then looks at me. "I also have caller ID." He makes a face at me, and I can't help but laugh. "Are you going to work out tomorrow? If you are going after ten, let me know. I'll come, and you can pick me up…" His voice trails off. "Well."

"So I guess that…" I push away from the counter and just stare at him. His look is the same one he used to give me when we were growing up. It's the look kids hate to see on their parents' faces. It's the look that says, "Don't play with me." "I'm going to go change and be ready."

"Good idea," he says, getting up. "Great idea."

"But just so you know, I said if you go after…" I say over my shoulder, and just like that, I feel something hit my head.

When I look back at him, I see an orange lying on the floor. "Still got my aim." He folds his arms over his chest. "Now, hurry up."

Three

Julia

I HEAR THE sound of feet running toward the bedroom, and I turn off my phone, placing it on the side table. I pull the covers up to my neck and close my eyes, pretending to be asleep. I hear the door opening, and then they try to whisper. "We have to be secret," Bianca says.

"I know," Bailey replies even louder than Bianca. I hear their feet getting closer and closer to the bed, and when I feel them close enough, I jump out of bed and roar, scaring the shit out of them. Their eyes go big, and their hands rise to the sky as they scream at the top of their lungs and run from the room. "She's a monster!"

I can't help but laugh as I get off the bed and grab my phone, then walk out of the bedroom. "What the hell is wrong with you?" Michael says, holding the twins in his hands. "They are shaking."

"What's wrong with me?" I point at myself. "What's wrong with you standing in front of me half-naked?" My face grimaces. "You need to respect the common areas, Michael." I walk past him and go down the stairs.

"What common areas? This is my house," he calls down the stairs. "Jillian!" he yells for her, and I hear her mumble to shut up.

"Daddy," Bailey says, "is she a fucking goof?" I can't help but snort and look up the stairs at him.

"Fucking goof," Bianca repeats.

"Jillian." I sing her name. "Michael taught the kids a bad word."

Michael gasps. "I did not." Then he looks at the girls and says, "I told you guys that is a bad word. Mommy is going to put soap in all our mouths."

"I'll start the coffee," I offer. "Who wants pancakes?"

"Me," Bailey says, squirming to get out of Michael's arms, followed by Bianca.

I wait for them to walk down the steps, one of them on each side holding on to the railing. When they first bought this house and had Jamieson, Michael thought he should put in a slide for when he got older. The first time the boy fell down two steps, Max, his father, came in and checked to see if they could put in an elevator. Needless to say, Jillian was able to talk them off the ledge. "Auntie Juju," Bailey shares, "you aren't a fucking goof."

"Thank you," I say, holding out my hand. "But that is a really bad word, and it hurts people's feelings." I squat down in front of her. "So how about we not say it and instead say something else?" I think about what else they can say. "Like a flying gremlin."

"Flying gremlin," Bianca parrots, and she laughs in her hand. "That's funny."

I hold out my other hand for her as I stand. "It is funny." I look up the stairs at Michael, who just stares. "You guys have one hour, and then I'm leaving."

"Promises, promises." He turns and walks back to the bedroom and closes the door.

"Okay," I say, walking into the family room attached to the kitchen. "What do you want to watch while I make food?"

"*Encanto*!" Bailey and Bianca both yell, and I groan inwardly. There is only so much *Encanto* one can tolerate.

"Great," I mumble and walk back to the kitchen. I open the shades and see it's a sunny day outside. I make my coffee as I prepare the pancakes for the girls, who are sitting side by side as they watch the show.

I make them Mickey Mouse pancakes with blueberries for the eyes and chocolate chips for the mouth. I cut up some bananas and strawberries, placing it all in each bowl. Jamieson got to spend the night with Max and Allison, Michael's parents, so it's a calmer morning than if he was here.

"Who is hungry?" I ask, and they both jump up and come to the kitchen. I put each plate at their placemat and help them get into the booster seats.

"Chocolate!" Bailey cheers, clapping her hands. "You have chocolate, Bi?" She has yet to say Bianca's full name. Bianca takes her finger and touches the soft chocolate and tastes it.

"I have, Bayey." Bianca smiles at her as she picks up a small cube of strawberry and puts it in her mouth. I sit at the table with both of them while they eat their breakfast. Jillian comes down ten minutes later with Michael following her.

"Wow," I tease, pretending to look at my watch, "that's a record." Jillian rolls her lips. "Talk about a wham, bam, thank you, ma'am."

"There is no whamming and bamming," Michael says, walking over to start his green smoothie. I watch him put a bunch of green veggies in the blender.

Jillian, on the other hand, makes her coffee and comes to sit beside me. "Your shirt is on backward." I point at her shirt, and she laughs, ignoring me.

"Did Auntie Juju make you pancakes?" she asks them, and I get up.

"Okay, I'm going to get going," I announce, walking to the sink and putting my empty mug in the sink.

"What do you mean you're going to get going?" Michael shouts over the blender.

"Well, you're home, so I'm going to not be here," I say, and his eyebrows squint together.

"It's Sunday," he reminds me. "It's family lunch." I roll my eyes. Their family lunches consist of a minimum of fifty or even sixty people, depending on who is in town, and it's just food on top of food.

"I don't have to be there every Sunday," I say as he stops the blender and pours his chunky-ass green stuff into a glass. "I don't even know how you drink that."

"It's healthy," he says, taking a gulp of his drink. "If

you don't come today, my father is just going to call you to make sure that I didn't upset you." I nod my head. "And then you will f—" He starts to say the word when Jillian clears her throat. "Then you will mess with me and get me in trouble."

"Aren't you like almost thirty?" I shake my head. "How can you get in trouble?"

"You're coming," he says, turning and walking to grab a pan. "Who wants an egg white omelet?"

"I think I'll save my appetite for lunch." I grab my mug back out from the sink and walk over to grab another cup of coffee. "I'm going to have to borrow something to wear." I look over at Jillian, who rolls her eyes, because when I say borrow, I mean take forever or until I'm done with it.

Walking back upstairs, I go into her closet and grab a pair of blue jeans and a top. "This will work," I say to myself as I head back into the spare bedroom to make the bed and get ready. When I put on the jeans, they are a loose fit and both knees have holes. I bend over and roll the bottom a bit before I slip on the black tank top with the built-in bra that pushes the girls up just enough that it's sexy. I grab my white, button-down, long-sleeve crop sweater. Putting it on, I push the sleeves up to my elbows.

When I exit the bedroom, Michael walks out of his bedroom with Bailey and Bianca dressed both the same with their hair done. "Where did you get that outfit?" he asks, and I laugh.

"Your wife's closet." I laugh at him while Jillian

comes out wearing jeans and a white sleeveless shirt.

"Whose house is lunch at?" Jillian ignores the look Michael gives her as she walks down the stairs.

"My uncle Matthew," Michael replies, and when it's time to get in the car, I decide to follow them in mine so I can get out whenever I get a chance.

The cars are piled up in the driveway, and I park two houses away. I walk into the house and hear the commotion already. Kids are running everywhere. "Hey, Auntie Julia," Maddox says, coming over and giving me a side hug. Maddox is Alex, Michael's sister who is also one of my best friends, and Dylan's son.

"Did you grow?" I ask him, kissing his head, and he smirks at me just like Max does. He might be adopted, but he's the stamp of the men who are now his family.

We walk in, and I see Allison right away, with Max not too far from her side. "There she is." Max smiles, walking to me. When Jillian found out she was pregnant, it was a shock, more so to her than to anyone else. But then we found out who Michael was, and the connection that he was my father's favorite player made a bond between Max and me. From day one, when I asked him for a hug that very first time I met him, he's treated me like I'm his daughter. "You look nice." He gives me a hug while he kisses my head. "I don't like the top."

I can't help but chuckle. "Leave her alone, will you?" Allison scolds. "How is she supposed to find someone when you want her to dress like a nun?" I kiss Allison on the cheek.

"It's called being a mystery," Max retorts, and I can't

help but laugh.

"She needs to be with a man longer than six months for her to even think about a future," Jillian states, entering the room.

"That's not true," I huff and glare at her right after. "Fine, my relationships don't last long, but that's not my fault. The last time I brought a guy with me on Sunday"—I put my hands on my hips—"Matthew came and cornered me in the kitchen and had his credit score." Max just nods his head in agreement, like it's a normal thing. "We didn't even have a drink in our hands. It was ten minutes after we got here."

"Got to love the internet," Allison says.

"By the way," Max cuts in. "There was a break-in around the block from your house last week. Are you locking your doors?"

"How do you know that?" I ask him, and he laughs.

"I have a Google Alert for your area, so I get informed of all the things," he states proudly.

"I think I'm going to get something to drink." I shake my head. "Thanks for looking out for me, Max." I get on my tippy-toes and kiss his cheek. I walk into the kitchen, and people are scattered everywhere.

"I have been calling you for the past ten minutes," Alex huffs when she sees me. The two of us became best friends when Jillian got pregnant, and besides Jillian, she knows me the best. "Where is your phone?" I touch my back pocket, feeling it empty.

"Shit, it's in my purse. Let me go get it." I turn and walk out of the kitchen toward the front door, where I dropped my bag. I'm leaned over unzipping my purse when the front door opens. I look up and see Chase walk in.

"Hey," he greets, smiling at me. I can smell his aftershave, which makes my stomach flutter the same as it always has.

"Hey," I reply, standing up as he walks to me and puts his hand on my hip while he bends to kiss my cheek. "You smell good," I compliment, and he just smirks at me. His hair is pulled back away from his face, tucked behind his ears. He is wearing blue jeans that fit him in all the right places with a white shirt that shows off his golden tan. He's wearing beaded bracelets on his left wrist next to his stainless-steel Rolex.

"You look good," he says as we walk in. Every single time I see him, I'm reminded of how hot he is. Then I have to remind myself that even though he is hot, sleeping with him is not an option, ever.

"I always look good." When I look up at him, his blue eyes light up, and I can't help but smirk. "You just never seem to notice." I tap him on his nose.

Four

Chase

"I ALWAYS LOOK good." She looks up at me, and I can't help but smile when I see the lightness in her blue eyes. Her smirk says it all. "You just never seem to notice." She taps her finger on my nose, and her eyes show she is full of mischief.

I can't help but throw my head back and laugh out loud. "Oh, trust me." I stop walking and so does she as we stand in the middle of the foyer area. "I notice."

She rolls her eyes at me. "Oh, please, save it for someone else." She slaps my stomach, and I watch as she walks away. Fuck, she's got a body you could worship, and trust me, I've seen her in enough barely there bikinis to know what type of body she has. Legs that would wrap very nicely around my hips or my neck. I shake my head to take that picture out. She's so goddamn beautiful she takes my breath away. I also know she's the most untouchable human who walks the planet. Not only is she considered family but I'm sure my uncle Max will put me through the wall if I hurt her. My father might even chip in.

"What the hell are you doing here lingering like a creep?" Cooper prods, coming in the front door holding baby Leo in his arms, followed by Mia and Emma.

"Uncle Chase," Emma says, and I hold my hands for her to jump into my arms and toss her in the air. The sounds of her squealing now fill the huge room.

"You're so strong," Mia praises while I blow kisses in Emma's neck, putting her down on her feet beside Mia. "Daddy hurt his back doing that, so we can't do it anymore." She looks at her father. "Even this morning, he came down the stairs bent over."

"I did not." Cooper gasps, and Erika just snickers behind him as she walks, holding their daughter Felicia's hand. "I got kicked in the junk by your sister," he informs her, and she just rolls her eyes at him and turns to skip away to see the rest of the kids.

"I can help fix your boo-boo, if you want," I inform Cooper.

He mouths, "Go fuck yourself."

"Be nice," Erika says, stopping beside me, and I bend to kiss her cheek.

"You look beautiful today," I say, and she just smirks at me.

"Stay away from my wife," Cooper mumbles as he pulls her to his side. "Get your own woman."

MADE FOR ME

I laugh as I follow them into the kitchen and the commotion we've all become used to. The kids run off to join their cousins, who are at the tree house my father had built for this reason. "Why does it feel like it gets bigger and bigger every week?" Erika asks.

"Because it does," Cooper confirms. Erika walks away from him to go see my sisters, Vivienne and Franny, who are sitting together at a table.

The whole island is set up like a buffet of silver trays as the chefs in the kitchen keep putting out even more food. "Where were you this morning?" I ask Cooper, who just looks at me with his eyebrows pinched together.

"In my house." He laughs. "Why? Where were you?"

"At the gym with our father." I shake my head as our father comes in from outside.

"There he is," my father says, "my favorite son." Cooper smiles at him. "Not you." He shakes his head. "Him." He points at me, and I turn and look at Cooper with a smile on my face.

"Why is he suddenly your favorite?" Cooper puts his hands on his hips. "He didn't even give you grandkids."

"He is there when I need him," my father replies.

"I went to work out with him this morning," I lean over and mumble to him.

"That's right. He was there for me." My father nods.

"I mean, in my defense, I was there only because he showed up at my house." I roll my lips. "He read my text wrong."

"I told you that you need glasses," Cooper says, and my uncle Max joins the conversation.

"I told him the same," Max agrees, coming to stand next to him. "It's the age."

"You're the same age as me," my father huffs to him.

"My vision is better than yours." Seeing the two of them discuss things is like watching the Three Stooges. "We did the test the other day."

"It was fixed." My father rolls his eyes.

"Do you really think I called the optometrist before we walked in there and asked him to fuck with you?" Max asks him, and all Dad can do is glare at him.

"Yeah!" my father shouts, and we all just laugh at him.

"Dad, it's fine to admit you need glasses," I say. "Just like Cooper over here needs to admit that I'm stronger than him."

"Fuck you." Cooper pushes my shoulder. "I'll admit nothing." He walks away to join Erika at the table with my sisters and now with Jillian and Alex who have joined them.

"Did you eat?" I look to the left and see my mother coming toward me. She wraps her arms around my waist, and I kiss her head. "You should grab yourself a plate of food before it's all gone."

"You have enough food for a small island." I laugh. "But I'll grab a plate."

I walk over and grab a plate, filling it with grilled chicken and roasted veggies. I even scoop some pasta on my dish. Turning to walk out to the backyard, I see all the tables set up. I look around for a second and spot Julia sitting by herself. Shocked that she is sitting alone for once, I walk over to her. "Where is your posse?" I ask, and she looks up and laughs.

"I stayed over at Jillian's for the last two nights. I forgot all the bribe candy at home," she admits. "Kind of hard to bribe them with veggies."

Pulling out a chair, I sit down at the table with her. "Is it okay if I sit here?" I ask, and she leans back in her chair.

"If you're looking for candy, I don't have any," she jokes, and I laugh.

"Shit." I pretend to grab my plate and get up.

"Shut up." She laughs, and it fills the whole yard.

"So how was your week?" I ask her, making small talk, so we're not sitting at the table awkwardly. I mean, to be honest, it's never awkward between us. We always have something to talk about. Talking to her is easy.

"Eventful," she replies, grabbing the bottle of water beside her. "What about you?" She changes the subject from herself.

"No one lost a limb," I joke. "A couple of stitches and a couple of bruised legs, but other than that, smooth sailing."

"Sounds like as much fun as my job." She puts the water bottle down on the table and then leans forward on her hands crossed in front of her.

"Well, I get to go work at the ER for the next three days, and I can't wait."

"That sounds like more fun than the stitches," she says, and then Bianca comes up to her and pulls on her leg. She moves her hands and picks her up.

"What's the matter, princess one?" I ask as Bianca straddles her lap and rubs her eyes.

"Is someone tired?" she asks her, and Bianca shakes her head. "Well, why don't you sit with me for a while?" Julia leans down and kisses her forehead. "I missed you too much." She wraps her arms around the little girl and pulls her to her chest, where Bianca lays her head.

"And you said you need candies," I joke with her. "All lies."

"Candy." Bianca lifts her head from her chest, and Julia glares at me.

"I don't have any candies, my love," she says. "Uncle Chase is Pinocchio." I can't help but chuckle when Bianca turns back and looks at me.

"Is Pinocchio." She points at me, and I smile at her and put my finger in front of my lips.

"Shh, it's a secret," I say. She smiles at me and then puts her head back on Julia's chest.

"You look good with a baby." The words come out of my mouth before I can even stop them, and the minute they do, I want to kick myself.

"Well, this is as close to a child as I'm going to get," she states, and I just look at her. She's normally stunning, but I don't know why seeing her with a baby on her lap just makes her go to the next level.

"Why do you say that? You'd make a great mother," I assure her, and she just shrugs.

"I've seen too many things in my job to even attempt it." She rocks side to side with Bianca. "Besides, coolest aunt is a much better role than mom." She smiles. "When are you having your own?"

I chuckle. "Not sure," I say honestly. "I guess when it's meant to happen, it'll happen."

"You know you need to date in order for it to happen, right?" She winks at me. "The last time you brought a date was…" She looks up like she is thinking. "Is never."

I shrug. "I haven't connected with anyone," I share, grabbing my own water bottle and drinking a sip. "Besides, if I'm going to introduce anyone to this bunch, I have to make sure she is the right one." I put my bottle down. "I just haven't found her yet." *Or maybe you have and you haven't admitted it,* my head screams.

Five

Julia

"GIVE ME A kiss." I squat down in front of Bianca. "Auntie Juju is going home."

"Why?" she asks, whining as she plays with my hair around her finger. She always does this when she sits with me.

"Because Daddy is home, and I have to go make sure my house is okay," I say, pulling her to my chest and kissing her neck. I kiss Bailey next as I walk from the house. The sun is just setting as I walk to my car and get in. Starting the car, I roll down the windows and make my way home.

I leave the windows down the whole way as I listen to the radio and let my mind wander. Pulling into my parking space, I make sure to roll the windows up before turning off the car. I stop at my mailbox before I walk up the ten steps to my second-floor apartment. After eating all that food, I should take a walk. Stepping into my apartment, I can feel the stuffy air from not being in the house the past two days. Plopping my purse at the door, I walk in the kitchen and dump the mail and my bag on the small round dining table before walking straight to the patio door and opening the shades. I open the patio door just a touch, letting in some fresh air, before turning and walking to my bedroom. I've lived here for the past ten years. When I signed the lease on the two-bedroom apartment, my goal was to get a roommate, but that never happened. I kick off my shoes before going to the bathroom and starting the shower. After undressing, I take a quick shower and slip into the most comfortable pair of pjs I have. I walk back out and close the patio door, grabbing the big thick, knitted throw blanket Allison bought me for Christmas before sitting on the couch.

I lie down, checking my DVR to see what I'm going to watch, when my cell phone rings from my purse. I get up, walk over to it, and pull it out, seeing it's Colin. I smile as I press the green button. "Hello," I greet, walking back to the couch.

"Hey," he says as I sit down, and I can tell from his tone this is not a booty call.

"Hi," I reply, my stomach sinking when I hear people shouting in the background for him to back up and give them some room.

"Um, by any chance." He starts to talk, and I hear the sirens in the background get louder and louder. "Does the name Monica Whitehorse mean anything to you?"

I close my eyes for a second before my body flips into autopilot, and I rush off the couch and toward my bedroom. "Where is she?" I ask, knowing he's arrested her for something, and now I have to go down there and take away Penelope.

"We are at the corner of Pine and Maple," he informs me. "I would get here as fast as you can, and I didn't call you."

"Thank you," I say, pulling on my jeans before putting on my white bra and a white sweater. I grab my bag as I slip my sneakers on and rush out of the apartment.

I punch the streets into the GPS and see I'm about ten minutes from there. The whole time I drive there, I'm filled with anger. Mostly because I gave her one more chance. Knowing I shouldn't have and knowing that I'm going to probably get an "I told you so" from Rosalind. I can see the police lights from two blocks away. The sound of an ambulance comes from my side, and I give them the right-of-way. I pull over and park a block away, putting my cell phone in my back pocket. The whole time, I hope I'm not too late and that I get there before they book her. The whole time I actually pray she didn't have Penelope with her so taking her won't be traumatic. I think about placing a call to my emergency foster parents, but I wait to see before I call them. Wanting to assess the situation before starting the phone chain.

The nerves hit my stomach as soon as I start running toward the scene. A group of people has started to line up to take it in. It confuses me for a second until I see what they are looking at, and my heart stops in my chest. In the middle of the street is Monica's car, or should I say the remains of what is her car. It's even on a weird angle. I look around to see if I can spot her anywhere, but I don't see her. I get to the cop, who is stopping people from going forward, as I see the fireman bring out the saw. "You can't come past here," the cop tells me.

"I'm her caseworker." I point at the car, and he looks over his shoulder. "I got called." That's the only thing I say. It's not like I've never been called to the scene before.

"You need to stay out of the way," he tells me, moving to the side, "until they clear the scene." I take a couple of steps as I look for Colin.

He is at the side, waiting by the ambulance. I rush over to him, my heart beating so fast in my chest. "What is going on?" I look back over when I hear screaming from the fireman. "Where is she?" I look around, wondering if she's already been taken to jail.

"How long have you had her?" he asks. I see he's wearing jeans and a white T-shirt. It's his off-duty attire, so I'm confused as to why he got called in. It should just be a uniformed officer who should be here with her. I look around at the people rushing to and from the car, not sure what the fuck is going on, or maybe I'm just blocking out the bad that I know is coming.

"Since she was fifteen," I say, looking back to the car and seeing the smashed windows. I can't even see in the car because of the way the windows are damaged. "Did she have Penelope with her?" I look around, getting ready to snap as the guilt sinks in. I spot the ambulance and see the paramedics are waiting by the car with a gurney, and then I look back at Colin, the heat rising to my neck.

"I don't know how to tell you this," he says and looks around to make sure we are alone. "She's DOA." The minute he says those words, my knees give out, and he lunges forward to catch me before I hit the pavement.

"No." I shake my head, the words coming out in a whisper. "No, there is a mistake." I turn to look toward the crash site. I take a step toward the car when he wraps his arm around my waist, pulling me back to him.

"You can't go there," he says softly to me. "They are trying to get the door open to get the baby."

My head is spinning. "Is the baby?" I can't even say the words before the lump gets stuck in my throat. My stomach feels like someone just kicked me at the same time that pressure is now forming in my chest. I've been doing this for long enough to block it off, but nothing, and I mean nothing, prepared me for this.

"Not sure yet," he states, and I put my hand to my stomach, thinking I'm going to be sick. "Not sure of her injuries." He lets go of me when he knows I'm not going to run off. "She's got cuts all over her face from the broken glass on the other side."

"What the fuck happened?" I ask, looking toward the car now. I put my hand on my head, ignoring the way it's shaking.

"From what we got from a couple of bystanders." He motions to four people on the other side near a policeman as they watch. "She was swerving down the street, going fifty to sixty miles an hour."

"What the fuck?" I say, shaking my head.

"She then ran a red light, and a car hit the driver's side of her car." He points at the skid marks. "Then she must have turned her wheel because she hit the pole with the passenger side of the car. Someone said it looked like a pinball game."

"Did you see her?" I ask, and he nods.

"I was on my way to the station to start my shift, but they called me when they couldn't find a pulse, so I came right here." He puts his hands in his back pockets. "I don't know what the toxicology is going to come back with, but she reeks of booze."

"Fuck, fuck, fuck." I put both hands on my head. My hands shake, and my feet move as I do a circle while I try to comprehend what he is saying. She was sitting in front of me two days ago, alive and well, and now she's here dead, and all I can do is hope Penelope pulls through.

"We tried to get to the baby, but her car is sealed shut, so we called the fire department to cut her out," he informs me when we hear shouting coming from the firemen.

"We have a pulse," one of them says, and I can't help but squat down and put my hands to my mouth. I see a couple of the firemen reach in, and then all of a sudden, her whole car seat is taken out.

"Colin." I look at him, and he nods his head as he puts his hand on my back and ushers me forward.

The paramedic wheels the gurney toward the scene.

"She's going to escort her," Colin says, and the paramedic looks at me. I look at the car seat, seeing Penelope with her face riddled in blood and glass all around her head. She looks like she's sleeping.

"I'm from CPS," I tell them, and they give me a sad smile. "She is already in my case file," I share with them. Then I make the mistake of looking back at the car. I can see her silhouette hunched over the steering wheel, and my heart breaks. "Is someone going to stay with her?" I look at Colin.

"I'll stay until she's out of the car," he tells me. "The coroner is on his way. We can't take her out before he gets here." I look over at the firemen, who are all looking at the little girl who has captured them.

"We have to get her out of that seat," I say. "She's getting cut."

"We need to take her vitals," the paramedic says as they start rushing toward the waiting ambulance. "We don't want to move her until they assess her."

They lift the gurney into the ambulance, and one of them holds out their hands for me. I put my foot on the step at the back of the ambulance and climb in. They point at the side, and I sit down, watching them try to take her vitals. My hand moves on its own as I place her small hand in mine, feeling it's cold. "She needs to be covered. She's cold," I say, my body numb as I pray she wakes up. I pray to hear her little voice, even if it's to ask for her mom.

"We are going to secure her neck, and then we'll take her out," the woman explains as she reaches over and grabs the white and blue neck collar. She takes her scissors out to cut the safety harness so she can move her gently. She doesn't even groan. "Her blood pressure is stable," she states as she takes her pulse and then cuts the belts around her legs. The car seat I bought with her mom when she grew out of the infant carrier. Monica picked it because she liked the little butterflies on the seat cover. "I'm going to move her, so watch the glass," she tells me, and all I can do is look at Penelope.

Her face winces when she is moved, but her eyes fly open as she whines right before she starts to cry. The relief of her cry fills me as she looks around and pushes the hands away from her, and then I lean in. "It's okay, baby," I say, blinking away my own tears now. "They are going to fix the boo-boo."

She moves away from the paramedic, and I jump in. "I'll hold her," I tell them as they look at me. "She knows me. Just tell me what to do."

They share a look, and then one just shrugs. "Try not to move her too much," they urge. I put my hands under her arms, and she screams out in pain. I stop moving her, afraid I'm hurting her, but the paramedic tells me to take her out.

"She might have a laceration on her back," one of them says, and I take her out slowly as she whimpers. The glass falls from her to her seat, and you hear the clinking as some of it hits the metal floor.

"It's okay, baby," I soothe her and bring her to me, turning her to sit on me. Her head falls to my chest as I look at the paramedic to see if she is bleeding.

"No blood," he says as he takes the seat and puts it in the corner of the cab right before he gets out and shuts the doors before jumping in the front.

"You have to place her on the gurney," the woman says, and I nod and lean over to place her back on the gurney. She fights me for a couple of seconds before I kiss her bloody forehead.

"It's okay, baby. I'm right here," I comfort her and hold her hand. She looks at me, and her eyes flutter closed.

The ambulance moves, and the only thing I can do is keep my eyes on Penelope while the question runs in my head over and over again. *What did I do?*

Six

Chase

"DR. GRANT." JACKIE, one of the nurses, calls my name as I walk from an exam room. "We have incoming. Child, two years old. Not sure what injuries she has. Car accident." I listen to her as I put the chart away and then walk toward the glass door where we wait for the ambulance.

"Is she the only one coming in?" I ask her as I look around to see if I can see the blaring lights. "Or is it multiples?"

"They just said one so far," Jackie replies. "Not sure if there will be more."

I see the flashing lights coming in the distance, and I start to almost bounce on my feet. I can't explain how it feels when you know that you get to work on a new person in a couple of minutes. As they get closer, I can hear the sirens, and I clap my hands together. "Game time." I look at Jackie, who just smirks at me.

"I don't know anyone who gets so excited about working this shift like you do," Jackie says as the ambulance turns into the long winding parking lot. When the ambulance stops moving, I walk over to the back and wait for them to open the door.

Nothing can prepare me for the scene when the ambulance door opens. My whole body feels like it stops when my eyes land on Julia. Her face is white like a ghost, and her eyes are filled with tears. She wears a worried expression as she looks at me, and for a second, it looks like she doesn't recognize me. "Julia," I whisper, but then I hear Jackie from beside me.

"What are her vitals?" Jackie asks, and my eyes go to the stretcher. For a split second, I'm relieved it's no one I know. The other paramedic jumps into the cab to help bring down the stretcher.

"Two-year-old." I listen as they start to move and wait to hold my hand out to Julia, who grips my hand harder than she ever has. "Blood pressure is…" He starts to say numbers, but all I can do is look at Julia.

"Are you hurt?" I ask, looking down at the bloodstained shirt.

"I'm fine. Take care of her." She lets go of my hand as her eyes fly to the stretcher. I can see her hands are shaking, and I've never, ever seen her so unhinged before.

"How long has she been unconscious?" I ask, turning

and jumping back into action.

"She came to for a bit," they say, while we rush through the glass doors, "then drifted back."

We wheel the gurney into one of the rooms off the emergency desk. "On my count," I order, grabbing the right side of the sheet. "One, two, three," I count out, and we transfer her from the gurney to the hospital bed. "What's her name?" I look over at the paramedics.

"Her name is Penelope," Julia says softly, standing in the doorway. Her hands are in front of her as she tries to keep me from seeing that they are shaking. "She turned two three weeks ago. She is up to date on all vaccines."

I look back at the girl as Jackie cuts her pants off. "Any allergies?" I ask Julia as I take my stethoscope from around my neck and check her chest.

"None that I'm aware of," she says, and Jackie just gives her a look I want to snap at her for, but I don't have the chance to because Julia does.

"I'm her caseworker, not her mother," she explains, and Jackie just nods her head.

"Who's on call for pediatrics?" I ask after I look down and see her leg is definitely broken. I don't even want to touch it.

"Jenny," Jackie informs me, and I nod at her as she cuts off Penelope's top while I grab my little flashlight. I open her eyes to see if her pupils respond.

"Penelope." I say her name softly to see if she stirs. "Pretty girl." I look in the other eye, and I see they do respond, so I let out a little sigh of relief.

"We need to get a CT scan," I start to say when

I palpate down on her stomach, and it feels like it's swelling. "We need to do an ultrasound." Then I look at her shoulder, seeing that it's hanging awkwardly, so I know it's dislocated. "Her collarbone is broken, I think."

A nurse comes in with the ultrasound machine beside me as Jackie starts her IV. I'm waiting for her to get up and scream bloody murder, but she doesn't even flinch. I look up at the door and see Julia standing just inside against the wall, out of the way. Her face hasn't gained any color, and her eyes look like she's a blank shell. I take the white squirt bottle and squeeze some of the gel onto the girl's stomach. I grab the top of the handle and press down on her stomach. "Her spleen is ruptured," I say, moving the machine around. "Everything else looks normal." I wipe her stomach down. "Take her down to the CT scan and call surgery. I'll be down in a minute." Jackie nods her head as she and the other nurse wheel the bed from the room.

I wait until they are out of the room before walking over to Julia. "Are you okay?" I ask softly, and she just shakes her head. "Where is the mother?" I ask, and I can see her eyes gloss over.

"Dead at the scene," she says, and her lower lip quivers. "What's wrong with Penelope?" she asks as she wipes away the tear from the corner of her eye, trying not to show emotion. I knew she had a crazy job. I knew it was one she never really talked about, but I knew from experience and dealing with other people her job is the one that never gets the respect it merits.

"From what we can tell, her spleen needs to be

removed," I inform her, and she just stares blankly at me. "She can survive without it. Her leg is broken, her shoulder is dislocated, and her collarbone is cracked." She closes her eyes and leans her head back against the wall. "I'll know more after the CT scan and the X-rays."

"Thank you," she says, and I just nod at her.

"I'll keep you in the loop," I assure her. As I walk from the room, I look over my shoulder to see her head fall forward, the defeat all over her body. I even see her shoulders shake and wonder if leaving her is a good idea. I'm about to turn back when I see Jackie rushing down the hall, so my attention turns to her. "What's wrong?" I ask as she turns back, and I can hear the wailing of a child.

"She woke up and threw up," Jackie reports to me. "Probably has a concussion."

"Most definitely," I confirm as I walk into the room and see Penelope fighting to get away from Tracy, who is trying to calm her down. She cries out for her mother, and at that moment, my heart breaks for this little girl whose life will be thrown upside down.

"Call Irvine," I tell Jackie, needing the anesthesiologist. "Tell him to meet me in OR room two." She nods her head at me as I take my phone out.

I search my contacts for the name and press the phone button, not sure she will answer since she isn't on call. "Hello?" Christine greets on the second ring.

"Hey, it's Chase Grant." She starts to laugh when I say that. We went on a couple of dates, but it was clear we were not ever going to be more.

"The one and only," she jokes with me, and now it's my turn to smile. "It must be my lucky night."

"I don't know about that." I look down the hall toward the room where Penelope is. "I need a favor," I say, looking around to see if I can spot Julia. "A little girl was just brought in."

"I'm not on call," she reminds me of something that she knows I already know.

"I'm aware of that, but"—I look down and then look up again—"she needs the best."

"Oh, come on, you can't flatter me with words," she huffs, and I can hear movement from her side.

"She's two years old," I say, hearing rustling. "Mother died at the scene." All of a sudden, all noise from her side stops.

"Fuck you, Chase," she says, and I know I got her. "You fucking owe me dinner."

"Now, that would be my honor," I say softly.

"Oh, it's going to cost you," she huffs. "I'm talking lobster. King crab. Caviar."

"Whatever you want." I will agree to whatever she demands to get her here.

"I'll be there in fifteen," she informs me as I hear her car door slam shut. "What am I looking at?"

"From what we saw"—I put my hand on the back of my neck—"ruptured spleen. Broken collarbone, along with leg and dislocated shoulder. CT scan results should be out soon."

"See you soon," she says, and she disconnects as I walk back into the room where Penelope is lying down sleeping again.

"The results from the X-rays just came in," Jackie says, and I walk over to the wall as she hands me a scan.

I turn the light on, seeing her leg is broken in two spots. "That had to hurt," I say, looking at the next one that shows the collarbone snapped in half and her shoulder definitely dislocated.

"I think she may have also fractured her wrist," Jackie shares, and I look at it.

"A cast will help that. It's the growth plate. I broke that when I was in the fifth grade," I say. "My brother threw me down the hill, thinking it would be fun." I shake my head. "It was not to my parents."

She laughs and shakes her head, looking back at Penelope. "OR is going to be ready in five." I nod at her.

"Christine is on her way in," I say, and her eyebrows shoot up.

"Called in the big guns," she jokes with me, turning around and walking over to the gurney as she pushes Penelope toward the operating room. "You joining us?"

"In a bit," I say as I walk out of the room and go to find Julia. I look into the room where we originally brought Penelope and find it empty. I walk toward the waiting room, and my eyes find her. The room is filled with brown chairs with two vending machines and one coffee machine. She paces the room, walking from one wall to the other until she finally sits down. Her legs start moving uncontrollably as she looks at the phone in her hand. She must feel me watching her because her eyes fly up to mine.

She gets up, or at least she tries to, but then she sits back down again. I walk to her, sitting in the chair beside her. "Is she…?"

"She's going into surgery now," I reply, and her eyes well up. She lifts one of her hands, and I can see it shaking. My hand reaches out to grab hers. Her hand is ice cold as I hold it in mine, willing her to take my heat and strength. "Are you all right?"

Seven

Julia

I WALK THE white-tiled floor twenty steps to one wall, then twenty to the next until I think I'm going to collapse. My stomach is in my throat, and my whole body shakes from my nerves. I sit down in the chair, my legs shaking without me even doing it. I look down at the phone in my hand, knowing I have to call Rosalind. I spring back up on my feet and start pacing the room again. I shake my hands to stop them from trembling.

My body feels like it's turning to ice, and I start to shiver. I wrap my arms around myself and feel eyes on me, so I look up and see Chase standing there. The last thing I expected when the ambulance doors opened was for him to be standing there in blue scrubs wearing a white medical coat. His hair in a bun on top of his head. I search his eyes, hoping he isn't coming to tell me she didn't make it. I don't think I'll be able to hear that right now. Actually, I know I won't be able to. I search his eyes to see if there is something there. His eyes stare into mine, but I can't see what he's thinking.

He walks over to me. With every single step he takes, I hear my heartbeat echoing in my ears, louder and louder. I don't think I even breathe while I watch him. It's like everything is in slow motion, and the five steps he takes to me feel like forever. I get up, or at least I try to, and then my knees buckle, so I just sit back down again. He finally sits down in the chair next to me and the only thing I can ask is, "Is she…?" I swallow the rest of the question, not sure I want to finish it, not sure I can hear the words.

"She's going into surgery now." The only thing I process from that is she is still alive. The relief runs through me as my nose stings, and I can feel the tears ready to escape. Tears I've fought back from the minute I walked into the scene. I lift my empty hand, and I can't keep it from shaking. His hand comes out to grab mine, and the heat radiates through him and into me. "Are you all right?"

I laugh bitterly. Instead of sobbing, I shake my head furiously. "Not even a little bit," I admit honestly, surprised I'm even telling him this. When push comes to shove, I always, always put up a wall and a brave front. I wait until I'm in the comfort of my home to have my breakdown. And trust me, after doing this for so long, I've had my own share of breakdowns but never in front of anyone. Those moments were my burden to keep.

"I'm going to go into surgery," he says softly. "I just wanted to let you know." His voice trails off, and his hand squeezes mine just a touch.

"Will she make it?" I swallow down the lump forming in my throat as my eyes search his for a second before I feel the tears ready to escape my own eyes. I watch our hands as the first tear escapes and drips onto mine before it slides off and runs down his hand.

"So far, it looks good," he replies, rubbing my hand with his thumb. "But we won't know until we get in there."

I look up at him, bringing my hand up to wipe away the lone tear running down my cheek. "Then you should get in there."

He tries to smile at me, but it comes out forced. "I'll come and get you," he assures me.

"Don't worry about me," I say when his hand lets go of mine, and I want to bring it back to mine for the support. For the comfort. For the heat. For the strength. "Just make her better."

He nods at me and stands. "Do you want me to call anyone?" His eyes search mine, and the only thing I can do is shake my head.

"I have to call a couple of people," I say, my stomach sinking when I think about the phone calls I have to make. He just stands in front of me, and I blink away the tears. "I'm fine. Go." I motion with my chin, and he puts his hands in his pockets, taking one look at me before he turns around and heads down the hallway.

My legs start to move up and down as I look at the

phone in my hand. I take a huge inhale and press the side button. The phone screen lights up, showing a picture of me with Jamieson. I swipe up and go into my favorites, seeing Rosalind's name at the end, so I press her name. The call connects right away, and I bring it to my ear, hearing the phone ring. She answers after two rings, and I can tell I woke her up.

"Hello," she says, her voice a bit groggy.

"Hi," I greet as I blink away the tears threatening to escape. "It's me."

"Julia." She says my name, and I hear the rustling of covers on her end. "Is everything okay?"

"No," I reply, my voice shaking, and she gives me the time I need to say the rest. "There was an accident." My voice is low as I look around the empty room. I hear talking off in the distance, and I feel as if the room is spinning.

"Are you okay?" she asks in a panic. I can tell she's moving around, probably getting ready to come to me.

"I'm fine," I reassure her right away to stop her from rushing to me. "It's not me."

The movement on her end stops. "It's Monica." I say her name, and the pain in my chest fills me, and when I close my eyes, I can see her smiling at me. The tears escape the corner of my eyes.

She huffs, asking me, "What kind of trouble is she in now?" I can even picture her rolling her eyes. I know she isn't expecting what comes out of my mouth.

"There was an accident." I say the words, and I have to take a second before I say the next. "She didn't make it. She was DOA." Rosalind gasps, and the tears just come now. Even though I rush to wipe them away, I can't do it fast enough.

"Oh my God," she says in a whisper. "What about…?" Her voice trails off, not saying her name.

"She's in surgery," I say, and she sighs in relief. "She's got a couple of broken bones." I close my eyes, thinking of the little girl in an operating room, knowing her whole life will be thrown for a loop.

"Do you need me to come?" she asks. "I can be there in twenty."

"No," I say, shaking my head. "I'm fine." But I'm absolutely not fine. Nothing about this is fine, nothing. "I'll stay here until she comes out and then sit with her." The overwhelming sense of guilt fills me, even if I tell myself that it's not my fault.

"Okay, I'll make some calls, and we'll speak tomorrow," she informs me, and I just look ahead. "Call me if you need me."

"Thank you," I respond, my body feeling numb as I disconnect and sit in the chair. My eyes focus on the spot I last saw Chase.

I close my eyes for a second, and all I can see is Monica's smile. From the minute her file landed on my desk, I felt something for her. Just two months ago, I bent over backward to get her an interview at a dry cleaner.

"I got you a job interview." I looked at her. "It could be really good for you."

She just stared at me, waiting. "It's at Around the Corner Dry Cleaner."

"How could that be good for me?" she huffed while Penelope tried to get off her lap.

"Well, for one, it means you will have a steady income," I told her. "And then it will mean you can slowly get yourself on your feet and off assistance."

"You don't think I want that?" she said softly, and she looked down at Penelope. "The last thing I want is to be dependent on anyone." I felt it in my core that she meant it. "I want to be better for her."

I open my eyes, and the pain in my chest gets tighter and tighter. I shake my head, hoping the fog clears as I get up and walk over to the hallway, seeing that two nurses are sitting down writing while a couple more run around. I look around, trying to see if I spot anyone I know, but no one looks directly at me. I walk over and sit back in the chair, putting my head back against the wall.

I don't even hear the noise around me. The only sounds in my ears right now are the beating of my heart and the sound of my breathing. The time goes by at a snail's pace. Every single time I look down at my phone, it moves by a couple of minutes. I walk into the hallway, looking down it at the door that says "Authorized Personnel Only." I walk over to the wall and lean against it, looking at the door, willing it to open and for Chase to come out and tell me everything is okay. I slide down the wall until my butt hits the floor, wrapping my arms around my waist.

Everything is in a daze until I look up and see him walking down the hallway, wearing a surgical hat on his head. My body goes tight as I try to stand and then slowly slip back down. He looks down at the floor, and the whole overwhelming feeling of dread comes over me.

I swallow down the lump in my throat, but my mouth feels as if I've eaten a bag of cotton balls. My eyes never leave him, and I brace myself when he looks up. He puts his hand on his neck. He must sense me staring at him when he looks at me. I hold on to the wall as I get up. "Is she…?" I ask, not finishing my sentence because I can't put the words out there.

"She's in recovery right now," he says as soon as he gets close enough to me. "She has a concussion, but she's a fighter."

I don't know if it's a sigh of relief or not. "Can I see her?" I ask, and he looks around.

"I can take you back there, but you can't stay," he says, and all I can do is nod. I follow him as he walks back through the door. He walks toward the side where I hear the sound of machines beeping. I look through the glass wall at her little body in the middle of the enormous bed. "She's going to be out for a bit," he shares softly. "Why don't you come home with me and shower?"

"I'm not leaving her," I say, shaking my head, my eyes going from his back to the bed.

"We are ten minutes away, and you need to rest." He looks around. "Trust me, if anything happens, they will call me." He looks me up and down, and I look at my clothes, which are stained with blood. "You need to take a shower."

Eight

Chase

"WE ARE TEN minutes away," I say. "And you need to rest." I look around, seeing the nurse sitting behind the desk. "Trust me, if anything happens, they will call me." I can tell she's not going to leave. I look her up and down and see the dried blood all over her clothes. Her hand comes up and touches the blood on her shirt. "You need to take a shower." I swallow again, not sure this is the right move, but knowing I can't stand the thought of her spending any more time in those clothes. "So come home with me, take a shower, rest for a bit, and then you can come right back here."

Her eyes keep staring at Penelope, who is lying in the middle of the bed. I avoid telling her that her pressure went really low, and I thought she was going to code a couple of times. "But," she says.

"I swear, if anything happens, I will get you here in under ten minutes," I assure her, and she looks like she's having an intense inner struggle. "I'm going to tell the nurses"—I point at the desk—"and I have to change."

"Can I sit with her?" she asks softly, and even though I know she shouldn't be back here, I nod my head. She walks into the room and goes straight for the bed. I wait a second before I turn and walk over to the desk.

"Aren't you looking gorgeous tonight?" I say. Emmanuelle looks up from her chart, her glasses at the tip of her nose.

"Don't you start that shit with me, Dr. Grant," she huffs. "Your charm does nothing for me." She looks back down at the file in front of her.

I can't help but laugh. "Good to know." I lean on the desk with my side, putting my arm on it. "I'm going to head out, but can you make sure I'm notified if there are any changes to Penelope?"

"That'll cost you." She leans back in her chair. "My grandson is a big hockey fan." Her eyebrows go up. Of course he is, I want to say, isn't that a coincidence, but instead, I do what I have to do.

"Well, it just so happens I have a couple of tickets to whatever game you want," I say, knowing I will have to call one of my family members and ask for them. I look back at the room and see Julia, her eyes still glued to the bed.

"I'll call you if anything changes." She smiles at me. "And don't think I didn't see you sneak someone in here." She looks over at Julia.

"Caseworker," I say to her, and she shakes her head. "I'll be out in ten minutes. I'll take her with me."

"Take your time," she says softly, pushing away from the desk. "I'll be around."

I walk down the hallway, going into the on-call room. I think about changing, but instead, I just take off the scrub hat I have on before grabbing my keys and bag with my clothes in it. I walk out, going back to her, and spot Emmanuelle talking to Julia, who just nods her head. "Are you ready?"

"I don't know," she replies softly, looking at me and then at the bed. "Maybe you can just give me a shirt."

"She's not going to be up for a while," Emmanuelle reassures her. "And I promise to call Dr. Grant as soon as she wakes up or there is a change." She looks at me, and I just nod. "Besides, no one is allowed back here, so you'll be much more comfortable than sitting on one of those plastic chairs."

Julia sighs. "Okay, but you promise to call if there is any change." Emmanuelle just nods at her as she turns and walks to me, not saying anything. I put my hand at the base of her back as I lead her from the room.

We don't say anything to each other as I walk to the elevator and press the floor for parking. "Are you hungry?" I ask, and she just shakes her head. I've never seen her like this, ever. In all the time I've known her, she has always been bubbly and charming. She's the first one with a smile on her face, and just seeing her smile, all you want to do is smile back. I unlock the car doors, and she pulls open her door, getting in. I wonder if I should maybe call Jillian, but as soon as I sit down in the driver's seat and look over at her, the answer is there for me. "I'll be fine," she says as if she knows my thoughts. "There isn't anything anyone can do for me."

"How?" I ask as I start the car.

"I've been around you and the family long enough." She puts her head back on the headrest. "The need to make anyone feel better is huge. You guys will bend over backward and make deals with the devil." I can't help but laugh because she's right. If there is one thing my family does, it's try to make sure everyone is always okay.

"I can't even argue that," I say, pulling out of the parking lot. I glance over and see her looking out the window, not saying anything else, and I give her the space she needs. It takes me eight minutes to get home since it's two o'clock in the morning. When I turn the car off, her hand grabs the handle and opens the door.

We make our way up to the condo, and when I walk in, I kick off my shoes, and she does the same. I walk in, going to the kitchen and grab a water bottle from the fridge. I turn back, seeing her look around the place. "I see you've done a lot to this place." She tries to joke with me, but the smile never fills her face, and I walk to her.

"Come this way." I motion with my head at her. I've never had her in the condo since I've been here. I know she's been here before when Michael lived here, but never since I've moved in. Actually, if I think about it, I've never had a woman who isn't a family member in this house.

I walk down the dark hallway to the master bedroom.

"I'll get you some clothes," I say as she stands in the middle of the room and looks around.

"Is this your bedroom?" she asks, and I just nod. "Different than I thought."

I chuckle at her, walking into the closet and grabbing a black T-shirt and shorts. "Here you go." I hand her the clothes. Her hand reaches out to grab them. "I'm going to shower in the other bathroom." I point over my shoulder.

"No," she objects. "I'll go in the other room."

"Don't worry about it," I say, walking from the room before she fights me. I walk into the spare bedroom, going into the bathroom. Turning the water on and stepping in at the same time, I pull the hair tie out of my hair. I make the hot stream run down my back as I hang my head. What a fucking night. Never in my wildest dreams did I think tonight would end up like this.

I've seen and been to a lot of trauma scenes before, but tonight hit me different. Seeing Julia there threw me for a loop. Even with all my training of blocking everything out, the only thing I could think of was making sure she was okay. I was in the operating room assisting, and my head was wondering how Julia was coping. When I walked out, I washed my hands and made a beeline for her, thankful I wasn't going to her with bad news.

Seeing her sitting there in the hallway, my body filled with something I couldn't put words to. I was hoping she had called someone. But she was all alone, sitting down in the hallway, staring my way. All I could think was to get her the fuck out of there. I turn the water off and dry myself, grabbing the pair of boxers I pulled out and slipping the shorts on after.

I run my hands through my long hair and pin it back up in a bun. I walk out and head down to the master bedroom, listening for the sound of running water, but I stop in my tracks at the doorway when I see her.

She sits on the bench in front of my bed wearing nothing but her bra and panties, holding the shirt with the blood in her hands in front of her. I clear my throat to make sure she knows I'm here and not to just surprise her, but she never looks up. Her eyes remain fixated on the shirt.

I stand in front of her. "Julia." I say her name softly, but she doesn't move. I squat down in front of her and see her hands are wet from the tears she is crying. "Hey." She finally looks up at me, and I see that she's in shock.

"I did everything," she says, her voice in a whisper, her eyes fixated on the shirt. "Every single thing I did was…" Her shoulders shake as the tears fall. "Every time, every single step, it was just to help her." She shakes her head, and I get up, leaving her for a minute.

I walk into the bathroom, turn on the bath water, and check to see the temperature before walking back out. I see her in the same spot. The only thing moving is her shoulders as she silently sobs. I get in front of her again. This time, I put my hands on her and feel that she is ice cold. "Julia." I say her name softly, hoping she snaps out of it and looks at me, but all she can do is look at the shirt with blood on it. When the adrenaline runs out, the shock comes in, and for the first time in a long time, I feel like I was at the right place at the right time. "Julia, sweetheart," I whisper softly. This time, I move my thumbs on her hands.

"She's gone," she says. "She's gone, and I couldn't save her." Her voice cracks, and I can't even imagine the guilt she's feeling. My hands move to cover the shirt, hoping she focuses on my hands instead. I wait a couple of seconds before I move one hand under her chin. I slowly lift her head and see her eyes glazed over, the tears rolling over the bottom lids as they fall on my hand still on top of hers.

"Hey, you did everything you could," I say quietly. She looks at me, but for some reason, I feel like she's not even seeing me. "Let's get you in the bath." I stand and pull her up with me. The shirt falls from her hands to the floor as she starts to shiver. "We'll get you in a nice warm bath." I move one step at a time with her. "It's going to be okay," I say once I get her into the bathroom, the tub almost full.

"She's all alone." She stops by the tub as she looks down at the water. "She died alone with no one."

I swallow down the hiss that wants to come out. I swallow down the anger raging through my veins. "You did everything you could," I reassure her, knowing her head is telling her the opposite of what I'm saying. "Let's get you in the tub." I turn her and unclasp her bra. My eyes don't move from hers as her bra falls to the floor. "Step in," I urge her, opting to let her keep her panties on.

She looks at me. "Why?" she asks, and all I can do is look at her. "Why?" She looks down for a second and then looks back up at me. "Why her?"

"I don't know, sweetheart." I push her hair away from her face. "No one has that answer."

"I should have…" Her voice trails off. "She could have been so much more."

The burning forms in my stomach. "Step in." I hold her hand in mine as I move a bit so she can step into the tub. She puts her first foot in the tub and then climbs in with the other foot. I get down on my knees beside the tub, pulling her slowly down with me. Her hand slips from mine as she sits in the middle with her legs folded in front of her. I get up for a second, walking over and getting a cup from the counter. "I'm going to wash your hair," I say, wanting to wash this whole day off her, wanting to get every single part of her clean. I fill the cup with water and slowly pour it over her head. "Is it too warm?" I ask. She doesn't answer, just shakes her head.

"I failed." She says those two words, and then it happens in slow motion. Her hand comes up to her mouth, and she lets out a bone-chilling sob. It's like it was ripped from her soul. Her body shakes uncontrollably, and I rise, getting into the tub with her. I sit behind her, my legs going along hers as I wrap my arms around her.

She collapses her back on my chest, and I lean back in the tub. "I've got you," I whisper into her hair as I hold her. "Let it out."

NINE

JULIA

THE SOUND OF a soft alarm fills the room, and I try to open my eyes, but they're so heavy I can't. My eyes finally flicker open, and I look up at the ceiling. I look at the white walls, and then my eyes roam the room. I blink them a couple of times as I look up at the ceiling, the soft light from the outside coming in. I feel the movement on the bed and I see his back as he leans over and turns off the alarm. *Chase,* I think and everything from last night comes rushing back to me and I sit up quickly. "Is it the hospital?" I'm about to throw the sheet off me and get out of bed.

"It's the alarm," Chase says, holding up his phone, showing me, and I lie back down in the bed, my eyes stinging and burning. "Since you're up," he says softly and I look over at him. "I'll make coffee." He gets up out of the bed and walks toward the bedroom door. "I'll be back," he tells me over his shoulder and I don't say anything.

I turn my head to the side, looking out of the window and seeing the sun coming out, but the clouds look like they are rolling in. The memory of last night comes back so vivid in my mind. Sobbing in the bath in Chase's arms. I have never lost it like that in front of anyone. I mean, I've never lost it that bad—period, forget about if I did it in front of people. I've had days where I've become withdrawn when stuff happens, avoiding phone calls or seeing anyone. However, a couple of days later, I pull up my big panties and push the bad away.

Smelling the coffee, I turn and look at the doorway seeing him come back in, holding a cup of coffee in each hand. He's wearing shorts and his hair is pushed back, but it falls forward. His chest is perfection, as always, his scruff makes you want to nuzzle in it, and his lips, let's not talk about how perfect they are. Actually, everything about him is perfect in every sense of the word. He's also the last person I would even think about crossing that line with, no matter how much we joke about it. "Oh, coffee in bed." I put on a brave face, sitting up in the bed and holding out my hands for one of the mugs. He hands me one and I grab it in both hands, bringing it to my lips and smelling it before I take the first sip. "Thank you." I look over at him as he sits in the bed with his back against the headboard. "For everything." I avoid looking at him, instead watching my hand and the coffee cup.

"How are you feeling?" he asks and I shrug my

shoulders. "Julia," he says softly and I blink away the tears that are stinging my eyes.

"I never expected to ever wake up in your bed." I look at him now, putting on the fakest smile I can give him. He just looks at me. "Last night," I start to say and my voice trembles and I take a deep breath.

"We don't have to talk about it. We can forget it."

"Oh, we are going to forget it all right," I agree, taking a sip of coffee. "But just for the next two minutes we are going to discuss it and then…"

"Then we will pretend it never happened," he finishes and I look over at him as he brings his cup to his mouth. The hands that rocked me side to side while I wailed, the same hands that dried me off and dressed me. The same hands that picked me up and carried me to bed, tucking me in.

"I am not usually that bad," I start, but then he puts his hand on my leg and I look up at him.

"We don't even have to talk about it, nothing happened."

"Well, you finally saw me naked," I joke with him, swallowing the lump that is forming in my throat, because instead of making me talk about it and making me feel all vulnerable, he is changing the subject.

"I've seen you naked before," he declares and my eyebrows pinch together. "The first time we were on vacation with the family. We left the bar and I was trying to put the moves on you, but instead, you decided it would be better to strip on the beach in front of my parents' villa." I open my mouth in shock now. "And then you said, 'Surprise, Shorty' while you ran into the water."

I can't help but throw my head back and laugh. "That did not happen."

"Oh, but it did, my mother came outside and called me a Peeping Tom." I put one hand in front of my mouth. "While my dad hit me in the back of my head and told me to get away from you."

"How do I not remember that?" I look over at him. "I do remember your mother coming to get me with a towel."

"Yup." He smirks. "Then Michael came and threw you over his shoulder." He tries not to laugh. "But he didn't know you were naked under it and then you said, 'There are two moons out tonight.'" I slap my leg now laughing. "It's a good thing it was my father who found us and not Uncle Max. He would have shot me in the foot."

"Oh my God." I gasp. "I guess after that I lost my shot." I smirk at him and he doesn't answer me. "We should get going," I say, getting out of the bed. "I want to make sure if she wakes up, I'm there so at least she can see a friendly face."

"I'll get you something to wear," he tells me, getting up.

"Yes, because your clothes will fit me so well." I put my arms out and he can see the way the T-shirt just swallows me.

"I have some clothes Vivi left here the last time she was in town," he throws over his shoulder. "Hopefully, it's nothing too—"

"Pretty," I fill in the word for him.

"Pretty and revealing." He winks at me, walking from the room. I shake my head going into the bathroom and closing the door. The white towel he dried me off with sits on the counter. His wet shorts he was wearing when he got in the tub with me are in the sink, along with my thong.

"I put the things on the bed." I hear him from the bedroom. "I'm going to grab some clothes and get dressed in the other room and meet you in the kitchen."

"Okay," I say to the closed door and let out a breath I didn't know I was holding. When I close my eyes, all I can see is Chase sitting me on the toilet seat while he dried my feet off. I was in a daze, if that is even a good name for it. My eyes were open and I saw everything he did, but I wasn't really here.

I open my eyes now and wash my face, walking out and looking on the bed where I see black pants and a white shirt. I just look at the closed bedroom door. "He really is a catch," I say to the empty room. "He's going to make one girl really happy someday."

I get dressed, and when I walk out of the room and meet him in the kitchen, I stop in my tracks. He's wearing blue chino pants, which aren't supposed to be sexy at all, with a white and blue button-down shirt he rolled up to his elbows. His silver Rolex on his wrist, his hair falls to the front reaching his chin, but with soft curls, and it just makes my hand itch to touch and see if it's as silky as it looks. If he was any other guy, I would definitely be making him my friend with benefits. "Hey," I greet and he looks at me.

"I just called the hospital," he says and the smile fades from my face. "She is still under. She woke up for a minute and then went right back to sleep."

I nod at him, not sure I can say anything over the lump in my throat, so all I do is nod my head. We walk out and go to the car. I am so nervous my whole body feels like my skin is going to come off it. I get in the car and my index finger taps the door. "You okay?" Chase asks from beside me, and for the first time I don't pretend to be okay.

"Not even a little," I admit as I look out the window. He doesn't press me for more, he just leaves me with my thoughts. When we get to the hospital, I get out of the car and wait for him.

"Did you even have to come in today?" I look over at him and he takes his cell phone and puts it in his back pocket. His dress shirt pulls against his chest.

"No," he replies, not even trying to lie to me. "I did my shift for the week," he tells me as we walk across the parking lot and into the hospital.

"Well then, I guess I really owe you," I say, looking around and seeing that there is no one here. It's only when I look at the clock on the wall do I see it's a little after seven.

I fold my arms as I follow him back to where Penelope is. When the doors open to the ICU, all I hear are the sounds of the machines beeping. My eyes roam the room and I see Emmanuelle getting up from the desk.

"Well, well, I was just about to call you," she says to Chase and I gasp out loud. "She's fine." She takes her glasses off and they hang around her neck on a silver chain. "She woke up about thirty minutes ago."

My feet walk to the room where she is at and I see Abigail, Chase's cousin and Dylan's little sister, sitting beside Penelope. "What are you doing here?" I ask her.

"I showed up to volunteer." She smiles at us. "I got in a little earlier than expected"—she looks down at Penelope—"and they asked if the baby whisperer could come down. So I came down and we had some Jell-O and some apple juice." She smiles at me and then looks back at Penelope as she leans down and kisses her head. She is in her last year of high school and she is in some program that allows her to spend time volunteering in the hospital. Her goal is to become either a nurse or a doctor. If you ask me, she's going to be amazing in whatever she decides.

"Hi," I coo to Penelope when I get close enough and she looks at me.

"Mama," she says, pointing her finger to the door and I can't help the tear that escapes and runs down my cheek. I don't have a chance to say anything to her when I hear a commotion going on outside.

"Where is she?" A woman raises her voice. "You tell us right now where she is or so help us…"

"You need to calm down," I hear Emmanuelle start to say and my feet move to the entrance of the door.

I look over at the woman who is standing there in yoga pants and a tight shirt, her bleached-blond hair pinned on top of her head, but you can see the growth under it. She must sense me watching her so she turns around. The short balding man stands beside her, I take three steps toward them. "Hi," I greet and neither of them looks like they remember me. "I'm Julia." My eyes go from hers to his to see if saying my name might ring a bell, but neither of them say anything. "I'm Monica's social worker."

"You," her mother accuses, her voice filled with disgust, taking two steps toward me. Her finger comes out as she points at me. "You did this."

Ten

Chase

FROM THE MINUTE these two come into the room I can tell there will be trouble. They walk in like they are supposed to be here. They walk in even though it said "Emergency Personnel Only."

"I'm sorry, can I help you?" Emmanuelle asks her and the woman just ignores her and continues walking until Emmanuelle steps in front of her. The short man in the back is letting the woman do all the talking.

I take a step toward Emmanuelle and stand behind her. "I'm looking for my granddaughter," the woman says, looking around the room and I know right then and there who they are looking for. I don't know why but the hair stands up on the back of my neck. "Where is she?" The woman raises her voice. "You tell us right now where she is or so help us…"

"You need to calm down." Emmanuelle tries to be calm. "You don't have authority to be in here." She walks around the desk and I know in two seconds she's going to pick up the phone. Emmanuelle gives zero fucks if you are the President of the United States or the Queen, you raise your voice and make a scene, she'll get your ass tossed to the street.

"Like fuck I don't," she hisses, and my eyes go to the room where I know Penelope is in. I see Julia start to walk out and my body goes on alert. I make sure I'm in the middle of the woman and Julia as she takes three steps toward them. She walks with her shoulders square and her head high. "Hi," she says softly, "I'm Julia." She looks at them for a second before she continues, "I'm Monica's social worker."

"You," the mother says, her voice filled with venom. Her hand flies up and her finger comes out and my feet are moving at the same time as hers. "You did this." She shakes her head. "You and all your bullshit lies you fed her. You did this to her." She roars out, "You killed her!"

My heart speeds up and my hands fist at my sides, I don't even take a second to assess the situation before Julia can say a word. "If you don't calm down." I step in front of Julia to make sure she can't see her. "We are going to call security and you'll be escorted from here." My voice stays tight as I ignore the way the burning in my stomach is building. If it was up to me, I'd throw their asses out in a blink of an eye.

"Pfft," the woman says, "and I'll call the police and say you are hiding my grandchild from us."

"Stacey," the short balding man says from behind her. "Calm down."

"Shut up, Stanley," she snaps at him and all he can do is look down. "We have a right to see our granddaughter."

"And no one will stop you." My voice stays calm, even though my body is shaking with nerves. "But if you are going to come in here and disrupt things, then we will have no choice."

"Show me where my granddaughter is." She folds her arms over her chest. "Or else I'll call the news, or better yet." She takes her phone from her pocket. "I'll record you stopping us from seeing our grandchild after our only daughter died."

I feel Julia's hand on my arm. "Chase," she says softly, "it's not worth it."

The door opens and I see two security guards come in and I look over at Emmanuelle, who just nods at me. "Now we can do this the easy way or the hard way." She walks toward the security guards. "You can act calmly and we will give you five minutes with your granddaughter," she informs them and the woman opens her mouth, but Emmanuelle holds up her hand to stop her. "Until she is transferred to her own room, or"—she looks at the guards—"you will be escorted out of here without seeing her, and only be able to see her when she is transferred." She takes a step toward the woman. "And I would hate for paperwork to take longer than it should," she warns, her voice low. She looks at the man. "I suggest you talk to your wife and choose option A."

"I don't want that bitch anywhere next to her." She

points at Julia and I'm about to go Hulk on her. I have to swallow down the rage and look down at the floor. I don't even know why, but heat fills my body while anger fills my veins. I want to roar out but Julia doesn't give me a chance.

Julia steps in front of me now. "I'm her caseworker," she responds, her voice tight and strong. "You can throw insults at me. You can stomp your foot and throw hissy fits until you are blue in the face. At the end of the day, Penelope is my main concern." She stands tall. "I look forward to the home visits." She turns to the security guards. "There is no father listed on the birth certificate, so unless he comes forward, this is her next of kin." She looks at the man. "You have five minutes."

"Fucking bitch," the woman mumbles as her husband ushers her forward.

"Wow," Emmanuelle says, shaking her head and walking with them.

"You okay?" I ask when it's just the two of us.

"I've been called worse," she tells me, not looking at me. "Abigail is in there." She motions with her chin. I look at her, not sure I understand what she said when I look at the room and my cousin Abigail comes out.

"Jeez," she exhales, looking over her shoulder. "She has hair just like Grandma Parker. I wonder what Sunday dinner is like at her house."

"Did she say anything to you?" I ask her and she shakes her head.

"No, Emmanuelle told me to leave, but while I was leaving, she told Penelope her mother is dead." She closes her eyes. "All Penelope said was mama."

I don't have a chance to say anything because the grandparents come out of the room. "Watch yourself," Stacey tells Julia right before she walks away from her.

Julia doesn't say a word to either of them and only when the door closes behind them does Abigail say something. "Eat glass," she spits, turning around going toward Penelope's room.

I look over at Julia and see her shoulders slumped a bit as she shakes her head, looking down and laughing. "Are you okay?" I take a step toward her, my hand coming up to hold her elbow.

"You mean, did what they said hurt?" she asks. "More than I will let them know. But I have to focus on Penelope now."

"You know there was nothing you could have done," I assure her, and I'm about to say something else when the phone rings in my back pocket. I pull it out and see it's Anthony, the equipment manager. "Hello," I say when I slide the button right.

"Hey, we need you at the rink," he replies, and I look at my watch to see it's close to eight. "Tristan got here early and decided that he was going to go on the ice by himself. Idiot pulled something and was screaming for help."

"I'll be right there," I say, disconnecting the phone. "I'm sorry. I have to go."

"Go on. I'm going to be here for a bit. Knowing Stacey, she is going to file for emergency custody before she asks how her daughter died."

The pit of my stomach hurts when I nod at her. "Will you call me if you need anything?"

She shakes her head no and I roll my eyes. "Listen, what you did last night was a lot more than you needed to do."

I put my hands in my pockets before I do something stupid like touch her face. "What happened last night?" I ask her, playing dumb.

"Don't you have to go put on your cape and go save someone else?" I can't help but laugh at her. "Go." She moves her head toward the door.

"I'll call you later," I say and instead of walking out right away, I take one more look at her and then leave.

I get into the car and make my way over to the rink, the whole time my head is still on Julia. I park the car at the same time Cooper parks his truck. I get out and look over and see the passenger door open and Dylan steps out. Michael gets out of the back door and I just shake my head.

"It's like a car of clowns." I clap my hands. "Is Wilson in there?" I move my head to the side and wonder if the other door will open.

"Wow," Cooper says, walking around the car and he looks at me. "You look like proper shit."

I can't help but laugh. "Is that so?"

"You look like Thor on a bender," Dylan declares and we turn to walk into the arena.

"I was on shift at the hospital," I remind them.

"Oh, did you bring home a nurse," Michael says, "to kiss your boo-boo?" I push his shoulder and he smashes into the wall.

"You're the only one who gets a boo-boo that needs to be kissed," I say, and the three of them head into the locker room while I go down the hall toward my office. I toss my keys on the desk and then walk over to the treatment room.

"Okay," I say, walking in and seeing Tristan sitting on one of the examination tables. He's out of his hockey gear and in team shorts and a shirt. "Who has the big boo-boo?" I joke with him. Tristan is one of the rookies on the team, drafted by Dallas two years ago, he just started playing with the team this year. "So, tell me what happened." I walk over to the sink and wash my hands.

"I was on the ice, just going around in a circle, and then it's like something pulled in the back of my leg," he explains and I sit down on the little rolling chair.

"Straighten your leg," I urge him and he winces. "Was this the leg that got slashed the last time?" I ask him as I touch his knee and I'm happy he isn't wincing. I move my hand to the back of his leg and then he yelps. "Lie on your stomach." He gets up and he lies down and I see the big bruise on the back of his leg. "You have a big bruise." I touch around the big purple mark. "My guess is you have a pulled hamstring."

"Fuck," Tristan curses. "What does that mean?"

"It means, depending on the next couple of days, you can be out three weeks or you can be out three months," I say and his head whips around.

"Are you fucking with me, Doc?" he asks and I have to laugh.

"I never fuck about injuries or dates. I'm going to call Bruno and we can go over exercises."

"This means I can't play tonight," he pouts, sitting down.

"This means you can definitely not play tonight," I confirm and he just puts his head back.

"I was on a points streak," he groans in frustration.

"If I send you on the ice like this, you'll last maybe a shift," I say. "And you might give out and then they can score on us and it'll all be your fault."

"Wow, talk about kicking someone when they are down." He gets up. "You didn't even try to give me a pep talk."

I can't help but laugh. "Just keeping it real," I say and Tristan walks from the room. I take my phone out of my back pocket and text Bruno, the team trainer. As soon as I'm done, I pull up Julia's number.

Me: Hey, just checking in.

I press send and then wonder if I should have called her instead.

Me: How you doing?

"Good God." I shake my head. "You sound so stupid."

I look down at the phone, seeing the gray bubble pop up.

Julia: Leaving the hospital in the Uber, headed to work.

My heart skips a beat and my hands get sweaty. I look around to see if anyone notices what is going on, not sure I could explain it.

Eleven

Julia

I LOOK OUT the window of the Uber as he makes his way over to my car. Only when I walked out of the hospital did it dawn on me that I didn't have a car. My heart speeds up as we make our way closer and closer to the scene. I wipe away the tear that escapes, even though I fight it off. The yellow tape is still up and you can see the glass scattered on the street.

"You can stop here," I tell the driver and he just looks at me. "My car is right there." I point over to the side. He stops the car and I get out, trying so hard not to look over at where the car was last night.

I walk with my head down toward the car, pressing the button and getting into the car, letting out a big breath. I put my hands on the steering wheel and my head falls on it, the tension in my body is off the charts. I feel like any second, I'm going to snap and fall into a downward spiral. I put my head back on the seat, closing my eyes as I try to steady my breathing when the phone rings from my bag.

I fish into the bag and take it out seeing that Jillian is calling. "Hello," I answer, putting the phone on speaker.

"Hey," she says and I can hear from her side that she is in the car. "What's up?"

"Not much," I reply, looking down at the phone, wondering if Chase said anything. "On my way to work."

"Oh, good, are you coming to the game tonight?" she asks.

"No," I say right away, "I'm going to have to pass, just got another case on my desk." I beat around the bush. "And…"

"And you'll be elbows deep in reading," she fills in. "Are you okay, you sound weird?"

"Yeah." I know that if she was in front of me, she would know in a split second I was lying. "Just, I lost one of my girls last night."

"Oh, fuck, you should have called me."

"I was at the hospital all night," I say.

"Still, you shouldn't have been alone," she says, and it is at this moment I should say that I wasn't alone. This moment is the perfect opportunity to say Chase was with me, but something stops me from telling her, and for the first time in my life, I keep a secret from my sister.

"Anyway, I'm on my way to work. I'll call you tonight or tomorrow," I say. "Kiss the kids for me."

"Will do," she confirms and I disconnect the phone. I

start the car and make my way over to the office.

Even when I step into the elevator, I know I shouldn't be here today, but I need to just get everything down, and in the file, just in case. I walk to my desk and Rosalind comes out of her office. "I didn't think you would be here," she says, walking toward my cubicle.

"I just left the hospital. Monica's parents showed up." She just looks at me with her mouth open. "I guess they had to alert the next of kin."

"How was that meeting?" Rosalind asks, folding her arms over her chest.

I lean back in my chair. "Well, for one she didn't even recognize me." I roll my eyes. "Even though I showed up at her house when Monica first ran away. But when I said my name, she called me a bitch."

Rosalind pffts out, "You've been called worse."

"I think she's going to go for emergency custody," I say, and she shakes her head.

"She'll get it since there is no father on the birth certificate. I'm going to see if I can get into her place and see if she has anything in there." I pick up the file I know is hers.

"Why don't you go home and rest for the day?" Rosalind suggests and I nod at her.

"I'm going to make some notes in here." I open the file. "Make sure I wrote everything I need to down." My chest hurts now. "I can't believe she's gone." I shake my head.

"It never gets easy. Let me know if you need anything from me."

She walks away from me and I stare at the file in front of me. A picture of Monica is stapled right next to a picture of Penelope. I start reading notes from when the high school contacted us about her. She was suspended for skipping school and her mother came to get her and basically threatened to beat the principal's ass if she bothered her anymore. She ran away two days later and I got called in, the school thought her mother did something to her. That wasn't the case, Monica had moved in with her boyfriend, who was ten years older than her. I shake my head as the memories come back. The tear falls in the middle of the paper as I reach over and grab a tissue. She was so stubborn sometimes, or better yet, every single time.

I flip the page over and see the word pregnant circled five times.

"I have something to tell you," she said as she sat in front of me at the park. She had called me to tell me she needed to talk, so obviously I went to meet her. She had just gotten out of the system. "You can't freak out." I waited, not saying anything, we had just gotten her a job. "I'm pregnant."

"Oh my God," I said out loud. "What? How?"

She laughed at me and the sound of her laughter fills my ears even now. I blink away the tears that sting my eyes. Closing the file, I put it away in my bag and get up. "I'm going to head out," I tell Rosalind, who just nods her head at me.

The hot air greets me right away, and I'm walking to my parking spot when a black car stops in front of me.

I look when the driver's door opens and Colin gets out. He's wearing jeans and a white shirt. "Hey," he greets, putting his glasses on top of his head. "Just the person I was looking for."

"Well, you found me," I shoot back, trying to smile but it just takes so much effort.

"How you doing?" he asks, walking to the trunk of his car.

"I've been better," I admit to him, watching as he opens the trunk and grabs the green diaper bag. My heart shatters in my chest and I try my best not to hyperventilate. It was a gift I bought her right before she gave birth.

"We found this in the car." He grabs the bag by the two handles and picks it up. "Dusted off all the glass," he says, shaking it just to make sure. "Figured you might want it for the baby."

My hand lifts as I take it in my fingers, gripping the handle. "Thank you. I'll make sure I get it to Penelope," I say and the sound of his trunk closing makes me jump.

"Why don't I give you a call tonight, take you out for a drink?" Colin suggests with a smile.

"Yeah, that sounds good," I say, but what I don't add is it's not going to happen. He gets in his car and drives away. My eyes linger on the bag for a lot longer than I want to admit. I walk to my own car and open the trunk, putting the bag in there.

When I get into the car, instead of heading home—where I should go—I head to the hospital. My head is so messed up it's only when I'm halfway inside do I remember I forgot the bag. I think about going back but just decide I'll get it later. I walk into the hospital and head over to the information counter. "Hi, I'm looking for a patient named Penelope Whitehorse." She types the name in the computer and then looks at me.

"I'm her caseworker with CPS," I inform her and she nods her head.

"Fourth floor, room four twelve," she says.

"Thank you." I walk toward the elevator and press the button. There are so many more people now than this morning. My head is spinning as I step into the elevator and press the four.

I stand in the corner with my head down, not sure I want to see anyone I know. I'm at the point of the day where I just want it to be over. I'm going to check on Penelope and then I'm going to head home and have a very stiff drink. The elevator pings on the fourth floor, and I walk out, looking at the arrows to find where I should go.

I walk down the white hallway, going for the nurses' station instead of just to the room. The lady behind the desk looks up. "Hi, I'm Julia. I'm with CPS and you have a Penelope in room four twelve." I look toward where the door is. "I'm just here to check in."

"Go in, she was with a volunteer before, but no family members have stopped by yet," she reports. "I was going to call you guys to see if you were sending someone down."

"Let me check on my end," I say as I turn and walk to the room, seeing Penelope sleeping in the middle of the bed. I walk over to the bed, sitting on it as I take her in.

There is going to be two parts to her life from now on: before her mother died and after her mother died. Either way, in my heart I know I'll never not follow her path.

"What the fuck are you doing here?" I hear from behind me and look over to see Stacey. This time she is dressed in blue jeans and a shirt. "Get the fuck away from her," she snaps and Stanley comes in wearing a suit that looks like it's two sizes too big on him.

"Stacey," he says between clenched teeth.

"I want you to get out of here," she tells me, her voice rising so much the nurse comes. "And this time you can't kick us out because we got an emergency order of custody," she says, smiling as if she won the game.

"So we don't need your kind here. Not now, not ever." I don't bother telling her that isn't how this works.

Instead, I try to get her with kindness. "I'm happy she has someone who is going to be here for her." She laughs bitterly. "I'll be in touch," I state, going to walk out and she snags my arm.

Everything inside me goes cold, and I mean everything. "You'll get what's coming to you," she sneers at me.

I want to rip my arm out of her reach, but instead I stare into her eyes and then mine go down to the hand on my arm. "If you don't get your hands off of me, I'll be filing a report of assault." I smile at her as she glares at me. "And I have witnesses to corroborate."

Stanley pulls her away from me, not saying a word to me. I step out of the room. "Your name is on file," the nurse says under her breath. "I'll call you if anything happens."

I nod at her, not sure if I talk right now anything will come out. I go through the whole motion of getting in the car and then getting home. It's only once the door is closed behind me my legs finally give out.

TWELVE

CHASE

***ME: JUST CHECKING** in to see how your day went.*

I look down at the phone, seeing if she'll answer me, but nothing comes through. My finger taps the screen a couple of times, my mind so focused on Julia I don't hear the truck arriving next to me nor am I ready for the knock on the window that scares the shit out of me. I jump in my seat, making Cooper's laugh fill the garage. "What the heck are you doing in there?" I look over and see his face out my window and all I can do is give him the finger.

I close my phone and open the driver's door. "Stalk much?" I ask him, getting out and opening the back door to grab my suit jacket.

"What are you talking about?" Cooper says, watching me. "I called your name four times." I slip the jacket on, placing the phone in the inside pocket. "I thought I heard Celine Dion singing 'All by Myself' as I got closer and I could swear I thought you were crying."

The chuckle comes from me, even if I don't want it. "I was not crying. I was focused on something."

"I know, at one point I thought you were watching porn and taking care of yourself." I look over at him with my mouth open. "Now, that would have been weirder than you crying. Can you imagine me calling Dad and being like 'Hey, so I caught Chase whacking the mole in the parking garage.'" He motions with his hand in front of his pants and if I had my phone out, I would have snapped a picture and sent it to the family group chat. "I should have had him on FaceTime." He puts his hands on his hips and looks up at the sky, as if he missed his big opportunity. "Dammit."

"Aren't you going to be late for the game?" I ask him, knowing he's always the first one who shows up.

"I've got loads of time to spare." He puts his hands in his pockets. "What's up with you?"

My heart speeds up with that question. "What do you mean?"

"You are out of it. I mean, more so than regularly. You haven't started that plant diet again, have you?"

I shake my head, laughing as we walk toward the arena. "It's called plant based and it's healthy."

"You were grouchier than normal," Cooper declares. "You didn't even try to get naked once on the beach during that time." I open the door and all I can do is put my head back and my laughter fills the garage. "I'm not kidding, imagine not having your brother's dick and balls swinging." He slaps me on the back. "It was magical." I put my hand to my stomach laughing. "Even the kids wondered if you were sick."

The door opens and we stop walking to look back and see Michael and Dylan coming in. "What happened to you?" Dylan asks.

"What the hell is wrong with me?" I ask them. Okay, fine, I feel a little bit out of sorts, but I was blaming it on the fact I didn't sleep. Even though my head knew that wasn't the case.

"You look like someone kicked your dog," Michael observes, "and then came back and kicked you in the nuts for good measure."

"Oh my God," Dylan says from beside him, laughing and then stops abruptly. "Jesus, you aren't on one of those diets, are you?"

"Goodbye," I say, walking away from them. Even though I want to pull Michael aside and ask him if Jillian is coming, but it's going to come out of left field since I've never, ever asked him that in my life.

I walk toward my office, the phone rings in my pocket and I'm not even going to lie, I stumble to get it. Never have I wanted my phone to ring in my life. My heart speeds up a touch when I look down and see it's not who I want it to be. The number is not even stored in my phone, but I answer it anyway and the automated person on the other line wants to sell me an extended warranty for my car.

I hang up the phone and take off my suit jacket

because it feels like it is strangling me. I hang the jacket on the hook by the door when I look up and Nico walks in. He smiles at me. "If the team ever gives in and does a calendar for charity, we are putting you on the cover." I can't help but laugh.

"Over Cooper or Wilson?" I say. "Michael and Dylan?" I ask him. "Let's not forget Tristan, who people are calling 'the rookie bachelor of the year.'"

He laughs. "You going to sit in the box with Tristan tonight?"

"I wasn't going to." I tilt my head to the side. "Should I?"

"I think it would help." He looks at me and then looks around to make sure no one else is around. "The news hit him pretty hard that he couldn't play tonight."

"He'll be fine in a couple of weeks," I say and he shrugs.

"Young kids never like being told no." He laughs. "Trust me. I have kids. They changed something in my iPhone that switched no to yes." I roll my lips to stop from laughing. "I didn't even know you could do that. Took me five minutes on YouTube watching instructions to change it back."

"I'll go sit with him," I assure him, also knowing that going into the box I might get a glimpse of Julia if she is here.

"Thanks, Chase," he says, ducking out of my office. I walk into the examining room and make sure I have everything I need in case someone gets hurt. I take my phone from my pocket, seeing she hasn't answered my text. I tap my finger on the screen for a couple of beats, and then I just press her name at the top and hit the phone button.

It rings four times before being sent to voice mail. The message is automated and instead of hanging up I actually leave a message. "Julia." I say her name, looking down and then up. "It's Chase, just calling to see how you are." My heart speeds up nervously. "That's all I guess."

I chuckle. "This is the weirdest, saddest fucking voice mail I've left in my whole adult life. Call me, so I don't have to leave another awkward message." I press the red button to end it and I think of her listening to this and laughing at that last part. The need to see her fills me, and when I walk up to the box, my eyes roam the room to see if she's there. There are people all over in the room since the box belongs to the Dallas organization, so usually the wives and kids come up here. Since tonight is a midweek game, the wives and kids don't usually come. But if this was a Saturday game, it would be filled up.

I spot Tristan sitting down on one of the stools at the high-top table that faces the ice. I walk over, sitting down on the stool next to him. "Hey," I greet, and he looks up from his phone.

"Hey," he says, his voice low. He looks around, his leg shaking with nerves.

"If you think this is bad," I say, looking around the room, making sure Julia isn't here. "Wait until something happens on the ice and all you want to do is help, but you can't do anything."

He just stares at me with his mouth open. "Jesus Christ, Dr. Grant, it's a good thing you aren't a motivational speaker."

I can't help but laugh at him. "Just keeping it real, Tristan." The door opens and my eyes fly toward it, seeing it's just Nico and Manning who come in. Manning was a big part of the team when he was the captain. When he retired, Nico brought him in as the GM of the team.

"Gentlemen," Manning says, coming to sit down. The guy is massive at six foot five and built. He sits down next to Tristan and they spend the night watching the game. The two of them talk about the plays that will happen or should happen.

When the third period is almost over, I get up and make my way back to the locker room. It's been a quiet night over all, and I've only had to go down and check on things a couple of times. I sit down on the bench, taking out my phone, while I wait for the buzzer to tell me the game is over. My fingers move to the Instagram app, and when I open it, the first thing that pops up is Jillian's name. The picture there is of Julia looking at Bianca with a huge smile on her face, their noses touching. The caption reads "Thick as Thieves." I can't help but smile at the picture and then instead of just double tapping it to like it, I zoom in on Julia's face.

The buzzer sounds and I can hear people walking down the hallway toward the dressing room. I turn off the phone and get up, making my way into the hallway. I always stay until after the last person leaves, just in case they have ailments after the game.

When I get into the car and pull away from the arena, I see it's just after ten thirty. My car heads in the direction of my condo, but at the last minute I drive by it. I don't even give myself time to think about it before I'm parked in front of her apartment building. I get out of the car and stare at the building, I've picked her up before, so I know the building but I don't know which apartment is hers.

I walk over to the front of the building, seeing the six doorbells for the tenants. I go down the list, trying to see if I can find her name but it's not there. I walk again to the front of the building, making sure I'm in the right spot. I look down at my phone and then up again at the building. There are six balconies but not one light is on. The only light I see is the fairy lights on one of the railings that barely give out any light.

I think about just getting back in my car and getting the hell out of here. But instead, I stand here in the middle of the sidewalk looking around. The street is so quiet, there is no noise. It dawns on me at that moment if someone looked outside their window, they might think I'm trying to one, either break into an apartment, or two, stalking someone. Either way, none of it is good.

So I take one more stab at it and call her. I put the phone on speaker as I look up to see if maybe a light comes on. I'm not really expecting her to answer her phone, and after the fifth ring I'm about to hang up when I hear the sound of her voice. "Hello."

Thirteen

Julia

I THINK ABOUT letting the call go to voice mail. I didn't even hear the last message he left me. I know, after everything he did for me, the least I could have done was answer him.

The whole night I've been lying in bed trying to forget the last two days. After walking in, I spent an hour on the floor with my back to the door sobbing, until it felt like I had no more tears left. I didn't turn on a single light, walking straight to the bathroom, and soaking in a bath until the water ran cold. I grab my white and pink tie-dye shorts set, slipping it on.

I didn't even have the energy to cook nor did I have the appetite to eat. So instead, I slipped into bed and turned on the television. Finally, after the fifth ring my finger presses the green button. "Hello," I answer softly, bringing the phone to my ear as my hand slips under the covers.

"Julia." I hear his voice and my eyes close for just a second, and for the first time tonight my body relaxes. "Where are you?" His voice is so soft and low, I can't help but blink away the tears that are threatening to come again.

"I'm home," I say and hear him huff out. My eyes focus on the television and not on the way my heart is beating faster because he called me again.

"I'm outside your building." His words shock me and I hold my breath, not sure I heard him properly.

"What?" My eyes fly open and I toss the covers aside, getting out of bed, and walking to the bedroom window. I push the curtain to the side and see him standing there looking up at the building. *What the hell is he doing here?* I ask myself. I mean, it's not like he didn't know where I lived. He's picked me up a couple of times and even dropped me off, but he's never, ever been here.

"I came to make sure you're okay?" he admits, looking up at the building. "I tried to ring your bell but I didn't see your name."

I walk away from the bedroom window and step out to the living room, making my way over to the patio door. I move the curtains to the side as I bend and unlock the bottom lock and then the top lock of the door, opening it. I step out into the warm air. "I'm Suzie Wong."

"What?" he asks, confused. "Why?"

"Max." I try not to laugh. "He said it wasn't safe to have my name out there, so he made me change it."

I mean, he didn't make me change it; he gave me the option of either him changing it or me changing it. I took longer than a day, so he did it for me.

"To Suzie Wong." He shakes his head and I walk to the railing, looking down. "Obviously he would." His eyes find me. "Of course you would have the fairy lights." He laughs and I see the phone in his hand as he talks to me.

"What are you doing here?" I ask him the loaded question. I stand here with the phone still stuck to my ear, and I'm not sure if I should hang up or not.

"You never got back to me," he states as he looks up at me. He is wearing a blue suit I've seen before. I know it fits him like a glove. I know that when he raises his hand to run it through his hair, the material pulls tight on his arm. "So I was stopping by to make sure you were okay." His eyes find mine in the darkness.

"I'm alive"—I wave at him—"as you can see." I hope now that he's seen I'm okay, he will turn around and just get back in his car and leave.

Then he says the words that let me know he is not going to leave. "Now is a good time for you to invite me up."

My heart clenches in my chest, and I ignore it, pushing it away as fast as it came. "Now is not a good time," I reply, hoping he just takes it as I need alone time and walks away. "I'm not up for company." *Not even yours*, I say in my head.

But I should have known better, considering who his father is. Considering who the whole family is. "We don't have to talk." When the words come out of his mouth, my stomach gets tight.

"What else is there to do if we aren't talking?" I smirk at him and his eyes never leave me.

"Why do you do that?" he asks, and the lump builds in my throat.

"Do what?" I ask, knowing full well what I'm doing, but shocked he picked it up.

"You are avoiding everything with jokes." He points out exactly what I was doing.

"I was not." I try to sound offended. "I was just wondering what we would do if we can't talk." I shrug. "But, I mean, if you want to come up, we can see if we can do other stuff."

"We can't cross that line." For the second time in two minutes my stomach gets tight again, but this time for a whole different reason.

"We can't cross that line," I repeat his words because every other single word is tied up in my tongue. I want to ask him why we can't cross that line.

It's like he can read my mind because he answers my silent question. "It would be complicated."

"It would be complicated." I emphasize on the words would be. "The lines would totally be blurred."

"The lines would be very blurry." He repeats my words as the two of us have a face-off in the warm night air. His neck is cranked back looking at me.

"Well, then, you came here to see me." I put one hand on my hip. "Did you bring food?"

"No." He laughs and shakes his head, and the sound of his laughter makes my stomach lurch up as I let my guard down for a minute to admit I like the sound. It only lasts a minute before I put it back in the box and lock it up. It's a box in my mind, where I keep my most prized possessions. It has memories of my father smiling. It has memories of meeting Max for the first time and then him hugging me. I swear it felt like my father was right there. It had the first time I held Jamieson, Bianca, and Bailey in my arms. The way my hand tingled the first time I shook Chase's hand and now his laugh. "I don't have any food."

I gasp out, "You show up at my house"—I put my hand on my chest—"in the middle of the night, and you don't even bring me doughnuts or, I don't know, cookies. Ice cream, anything that you are supposed to bring a woman who is having a hard day. I thought you knew better, Chase."

His laughter fills everything in me. The coldness that was in my veins starts to warm. "It's not even eleven, I don't justify this as the middle of the night." He finally hangs up this phone as he puts his hands on his hips. "I can order whatever it is you want." I want to roll my eyes at that but I don't. "What did you eat for dinner?"

"Nothing," I admit honestly. I don't put in that I didn't eat because I was too busy having a mental breakdown in my bath. "I wasn't hungry."

His head snaps back as he looks up at me. "Maury said, that's a lie." The minute the words leave his mouth, I can't help but throw my head back and laugh.

"God, you act like just because you've known me for five years, you know me," I huff.

"It took five minutes with you to know you never pass up eating," he jokes with me.

"Oh my God, are you ever going to let me live that down?" I put my hands on my head.

"You grabbed the burger from Jamieson and ate it," he reminds me.

"I was checking if it was too hot for him." I roll my eyes. "And he wasn't even hungry."

"He went to Michael and moaned that you stole his food." He laughs now.

"Anyway," I try to change the subject, "I wasn't hungry, so I didn't eat."

He just nods his head and looks down at his phone. His fingers are doing something and from this height I can't see what it is. He presses the buttons and then looks up at me. "Food is going to be here in twenty minutes." My mouth hangs open in shock. "So do you want me to wait out here until the food comes or are you going to let me up?"

"Wow. I never saw how annoying you were." He chuckles.

"What's it going to be, Julia?" he asks, and if I was closer to him, I would be able to see the lightness in his eyes when he laughs.

"Fine," I huff, trying to be annoyed, "but I'm watching *Sister Wives*."

"I was hoping you would say that," he fires back and turns to walk to the front door of the building, and I hear the buzz come from inside.

"Did you just ring my bell?" I ask shocked, and he

presses the button again.

"No," he says. "I rang Suzie Wong's bell."

I shake my head as I walk back into my apartment, closing the door behind me. The doorbell buzzes again as I make my way to the speaker. I press the button at the same time that he buzzes again. "Who is it?" I ask and then press the listen button.

"Chase Grant," he says his name.

I shake my head. "Sorry, I don't know anyone by that name." I roll my lips as I hear him groan.

"Fine, it's Thor," he jokes with the nickname I gave him the first time I met him.

"Did you bring your hammer?" I can't help but fuck with him.

"If you don't let me in, I'm calling Max and telling him I can't get in touch with you." He knows he just won this game. "Then I might even call my dad and say." He trails off.

"Ugh," I groan. "Fine, you win." I press the button to let him up and I unlock the door. I open it and step out into the hallway and can hear him walking up the stairs. He gets to the top of the stairs as he looks right and then left. He does a chin up when he finally sees me standing here. I fold my arms over my chest as he walks to me and I ignore how much better I feel with him here. "That was a low blow," I accuse when he's close enough to me that I don't have to raise my voice and wake up my neighbors.

"It wasn't a low blow." His voice is low. "It was the truth." When he gets within a foot of me, I smell his cologne.

"You would not have called them." I shake my head. "You would have called Michael for sure."

"Negative. He wouldn't even answer my call. Besides, when you want things done, you call in the big guns."

"Oh, good God," I huff, turning and walking into my apartment, feeling Chase right behind me.

"It's so dark in here," he observes as he closes the door behind him. I walk to the wall and turn on the light. I look back at him as he stands there in my entryway taking up so much space. I've never had anyone in my space before. It's my safe place and I keep it drama-free, which is why I never invite anyone over. "Are you okay?"

I think about lying to him, but instead the word comes out before I can stop it. "No."

Fourteen

Chase

I WATCH HER turn and walk into her apartment and I follow her. "It's so dark in here," I say as I close the door behind me. She walks over to the side where she turns on a lamp. The soft yellow light fills the small entryway. She stands there with her hair tied on top of her head, wearing shorts and a long-sleeved shirt. Her nose is red and her eyes look like she's been crying. "Are you okay?" It's a loaded question and I wonder if she'll be honest with me or try to sugarcoat things.

"No," she answers me honestly, and I don't know why, but I want to lean in and grab her in my arms and say it's going to be okay. She turns around and walks into the apartment, I follow her as she passes a small round table with four chairs. The living room is to my right as she moves down another small hallway. She turns and I stop at the doorway, watching her walk toward her bed. The king-size bed fills up most of the room with a white side table on each side. I spot the flowers on the side table where she sits, wondering if she is actually dating someone. It's not as if she announces when she dates anyone. My stomach knots at this thought, and all I can do is watch as she pulls the white cover onto her legs.

She looks over at me. "Are you okay with me coming into your bedroom?" My whole body feels as if I've taken five scoops of pre-workout. I don't want her to feel like I'm intruding in her space.

She laughs at my question. "You've seen me naked." She leans back on the pillows propped behind her back. "And given me a bath." She puts her phone on the side table next to the flowers.

"This is true," I say as I walk into the room, feeling like every single step I'm making is burning my feet. *It's fine,* my head tries to calm my nerves down, *it's just Julia.*

"You are the one who wanted to come in," she reminds me as I get to the side of the bed, and I see another frame but this time on the bedside table next to me. I pick it up and it's a picture of her with Jillian and her mom, taken at her sister's wedding. "I'm not going to bite." I look at her and she rolls her lips. "I mean, unless you want me to."

I shake my head and ignore what she said. I also ignore the way my cock stirred thinking of her teeth on me. "This is nice," I compliment as I sit on the bed with my feet off it since I'm still wearing my shoes. I look around and see she has the television mounted on the wall in front of her bed. "Feels homey." I inwardly groan at how awkward my words are right now.

"You mean because it's cluttered." She points at the chair in the corner I didn't see with a pile of clothes on it. I notice the lace bra hanging on the side of the chair. It's baby blue, and if she wears it, there is nothing to hide.

"It's not cluttered." I shake my head and cross my hands, putting them over my lap so she won't see my cock is fully hard. "It's lived in."

She throws her head back and laughs, and I look over at her. "Well, if you actually lived in your place, instead of just staying in it, maybe yours would be the same."

I shrug my shoulders. "Maybe, but I'm not home long enough to do anything."

"Yes, you are." She rolls her eyes. "You just need to, I don't know, unpack your shit."

"I don't really have shit," I say honestly. "I have my clothes. I spent years living out of a backpack." I look over at her, and with only the light from the television, I can't see her eyes, and it bothers me. "Maybe, eventually, I'll feel like I'm not just crashing there and it'll look lived in."

"Or, maybe you just need to find a place that's yours and not someone else's." She points at me and I'm about to answer her when the phone rings from the inside of my jacket pocket. I jump up, grabbing it, and for some weird reason I expect it to be Max telling me to get the fuck out of her bed, but instead it's the food.

"Hello." I put the phone to my ear and whisper to her,

"It's the food."

"I'm here with the food, but you didn't put the apartment number," the man informs me, and instead of giving him the number, I walk out of the bedroom and to the front door.

"I'll meet you downstairs," I say as I open the door and jog down the flight of stairs. I open the glass door and grab the two brown bags in my hand. "Thank you." I wait for the door to click closed in front of me before turning and walking up the stairs.

"You need to just drop off the food and leave," I mumble to myself. "You came and saw she is okay, sort of." I walk up the stairs toward her apartment and my heart speeds up even faster than it did when I walked in the first time. I stand at her door for a whole thirty seconds before I grab the handle and open it up again. "Just drop the food and go," I tell myself, but then I walk to the doorway of her bedroom and see she has turned on the lights in her room.

There is what looks like a tablecloth over her bed covers. "I don't have the energy to eat anywhere else," she admits to me, patting the cloth in front of her. Walking to her side of the bed, I hand her the bags. "What in the world did you order?"

"Burgers, and then they had the fried pickles I know you like." She opens the bag and looks inside. "I might have also gotten some onion rings because, well, you always eat mine and they had curly fries."

She looks up at me and smiles, and I know I'd order her the food every single day if it makes her happy. "I don't eat all your onion rings." I tilt my head to the side and raise my eyebrows. "Okay, fine, I let you order them in case I don't like them." She takes a container out, opens it, and squeals, "Stuffed mushrooms." She puts it down on the bed. "Take your shoes off." She looks at me.

"You can eat on your bed, but you draw the line at my shoes." I shake my head, and instead of slipping out, I walk to the other side of the bed, kicking off my shoes. I shrug my jacket off me and place it at the end of the bed.

"Do you usually eat after the game?" she asks as I sit down and wait for her to open all the containers.

"Not usually, depends on how the game is, to be honest."

"Michael eats as soon as he gets home," she shares and I laugh.

"When isn't Michael eating?" I ask her. "He eats as soon as he gets to the rink. Then he makes the peanut butter and banana toast before he suits up."

She hands me the foil-wrapped burger. "He also stays up until like midnight sometimes." She unwraps her own burger and takes a bite.

"It's the adrenaline." I unwrap my burger and take a bite of it. "So how was your day?"

She grabs a packet of ketchup and opens it on the foil while she dips one of her fries in it. "Pretty shitty," she says softly.

"Did you go see Penelope?" I ask her, and she nods her head as she chews another bite of her burger.

"I did"—she grabs a stuffed mushroom—"and her grandparents got emergency custody of her."

I watch her as she eats. "Is that a good thing?" I ask her, not sure what the circumstances are.

"Time will tell, I guess." She shrugs and puts down the burger on the foil in front of her. "There is no father listed on the birth certificate, so they were going to get custody anyway." She grabs an onion ring and takes a bite, tossing the rest of it on her foil. "It is what it is." Her voice trails off and she gets out of the bed. "Do you want water?" she asks, and I nod at her before she walks out of the room. I look over and see she's barely made a dent in the food I've ordered. I ordered everything I know she likes with the hopes she would devour it.

She comes back and hands me a bottle of water as she slips into bed on her side. She leans back and doesn't touch anything in front of her. "Are you not hungry?" I point at the containers in front of her. All of them are open as the food stares back at her.

"My eyes say yes." She looks over at me and I can see she's exhausted. Her eyes are less red now, but when she blinks it takes her a couple of seconds before she opens her eyes again. "But my stomach says I've had enough."

"When you don't eat for a couple of days, it's usually recommended to start slow with soup," I say as I finish my burger.

"Is that so, Dr. Grant?" She smirks at me as she puts her water bottle on the bedside table as she wraps up all the food. She places the food in the brown bag. "Do you want to take the leftovers home?" I shake my head as she walks from the room and I hear her in the kitchen.

"It's time for you to go," I say to the empty room.

Instead of getting up and grabbing my jacket, I stay in my spot. My head knows I need to leave, my body—on the other hand—is staying exactly in this spot.

She walks back into the room, grabbing the tablecloth off the bed, rolling it into a ball. "Are you tired?" I ask her and she shrugs.

"I'm exhausted," she shares as she tosses the ball in the corner of the room before walking to her side of the bed. "Mentally and physically." She gets into the bed, turning the light off. "Emotionally."

She grabs the remote from the side and presses play, and the sound from the television fills the room. I lean back on the pillow behind me, stretching my legs on the bed. She takes a couple of pillows from behind her and tosses them at me in the middle of us. I grab them and tuck them behind my head. She lies down and watches the television. I know I should leave but something inside me stops me.

I'm going to go when she falls asleep, I tell myself. I don't know how long I lie here, but when I hear the sound of her softly snoring, I look over and see she's sleeping. My chest contracts for a second as I watch her. "Time for you to go," I say softly to myself, "she'll be okay." It's almost as if I have to convince myself. My head tells my body to get up, but my heart says just one more minute. It takes two more before I drift off to sleep beside her.

Fifteen

Julia

THE SOFT SOUND of bells chiming fills the room and my eyes slowly drift open. I blink for a second and the weight of his arms around me makes me want to drift back to sleep. I snuggle deeper into the pillow and feel his heat at my back, the sound of bells goes off again, and this time I can't help but groan. I feel him pull away from me and then the sound goes off. "What is up with you and that alarm?" I ask him, and then he turns back to me and his arms go around me again.

He's still on top of the covers and I'm under so I feel like I'm pressed in. "It's my alarm," he mumbles and I want to turn around in his arms, but instead I just stay here. This is the second day I've woken up in his arms. My stomach flutters thinking about it, and all I can do is push it away. I've been in bed with men before, some even in the morning, it's not a big deal. For a minute I think I can hear my head laughing at myself.

"What time is it?" I ask him, now fully awake; there is nothing that will get me to go back to sleep, especially knowing he's in bed with me.

"Seven," he says, and then the bells go off again and it's his turn to groan as he rolls on his back and reaches for the phone on the bedside table.

I make the mistake of turning and looking at him, he's still wearing his suit pants and shirt. His hair is loose and all I want to do is bury my hands in it and pull him to me. "I think that was a sign to get up." I laugh at his back.

He turns onto his back now as he blinks away the sleep from his eyes. "I can't believe you slept in your suit."

He puts his hand on his stomach. "I didn't think I would fall asleep," he admits as he turns and looks at me. "I was waiting for you to fall asleep before I left. I heard you snoring and then I was going to head out."

I gasp out, "I do not snore."

He just smiles as he puts the hand that was on his stomach on top of his head. "Sure you don't."

"You could have gotten comfortable." I get up on my elbow. "At least gotten under the covers."

"And have you see me semi-naked." He laughs and I can't help but laugh with him.

He gets up now and looks down at me. "Everyone has seen you naked." I can't help but stare at him. "Jamieson even drew a picture of you on your wake board naked."

He claps his hands and the chuckle escapes him.

"That was funny."

I raise my eyebrows. "Maybe for you, but imagine Jillian's face when she opened the paper and saw it. He even drew your penis hanging."

"Michael wanted to kill me, it looked like I had a third leg." He turns to walk out of the room. "I'll start the coffee."

"I'm going to jump in the shower," I say, and I think he mumbles something but I just head into my en suite. I close the door and walk over to the shower, turning it on before I go to the bathroom. I get into the shower, putting my hands up in front of the water to wash my face. "How was last night?" I talk to myself. "Oh, good." I splash water on my face. "Do anything special?" I turn as the water runs down my back. "Oh, nothing really, had dinner in bed with Chase and then slept like a baby in his arms." I chuckle to myself. "Yeah, a totally normal thing to do."

I turn the water off and wrap myself in the white terry cloth robe, stepping out and smelling the coffee right away. I walk to the kitchen and then I smell bacon also. He stands in the small kitchen, his white shirt now off. His back to me, his ass making those pants look better than anything I've ever seen, and the need to sink my teeth into it makes me shiver. His hair is now pulled back and tied at the nape of his neck. "So you sleep fully clothed but cook shirtless?" I ask him as I step in and go to the cupboard and grab a coffee cup.

"I didn't want to get grease stains on my shirt," he says, and all I can do is shake my head and ignore the need to watch him.

"I will never not approve of you doing anything shirtless." I bring the cup to my mouth and take a sip of the hot coffee, hoping that I burn my tongue so I can stop fucking talking.

"Do you want to start the toast?" he asks and I put four slices in the toaster. I walk over and grab the utensils and the orange juice, placing them on the table in the middle. I place two placemats next to each other and then I think maybe I should have them face-to-face. I spend way too much time overthinking it, and when I turn around, he's walking from the kitchen with two plates in his hands. I have this crazy sense of déjà vu and I have to shake my head to stop the thoughts that are coming at me.

"I finished your eggs," he announces as he places a plate down in front of me and then another in front of himself.

"I'll grab the coffee," I say, walking away from him and the way this whole thing feels like it's a normal thing for us, because it's not. The only times we've had breakfast together is when we were on vacation with each other or if the family is having a brunch. Him cooking for me is definitely not a normal occurrence in my life.

I fill my cup with more coffee and grab the half-empty cup beside the stove, refilling it also. "You forgot glasses for the juice," he informs me when I feel his hand on my hip as he towers over me as he reaches for two glasses.

I let out the breath I didn't even know I was holding when he walks back to the table, my heart beating so fast in my chest, it's all I hear in my ears. I place the cup of coffee in front of him and slide into the chair beside him. "Thank you," he says, picking up his coffee cup.

"I think it's me who should be thanking you for making me breakfast," I reply nervously, and I swear my hands are going to leak soon they are so sweaty with nerves.

"What are your plans for today?" he asks as he grabs a forkful of scrambled eggs.

"I have to be in court at ten," I say. "Then I think I'm going to go into the office and read through Monica's file again and make sure everything is in place." I grab my own forkful of eggs. "What about you?"

"I have to be at the rink at ten, it's optional skate." He takes a bite of toast and I wonder if he is going to tell Michael about making me breakfast. "There is one of the rookies who got hurt last time and he's taking it bad. So I'm going to go in and train with him."

"You just rescue everyone." I push down the way my leg moves nervously when I think he just stayed with me to make sure I was okay. I mean, I don't even know what I was expecting. "You might need a cape to match the hammer," I joke with him and he laughs. Again, I feel like we've done this before, except this time I lean over and kiss him on his neck, right where I know his heart beats.

"I'm going to go get dressed," I state, getting up and leaving half my plate. "I'm not really a breakfast girl." He raises his eyebrows. "When I'm not on vacation or hungover." His lips roll as I grab the cup of coffee. "Finish mine." I push the plate to him. "Leave the dishes,

I'll clean them up," I urge, turning and walking away from him before I do something stupid like drop my robe and straddle him.

Closing the door behind me, I walk over to the side table and grab a pair of lace panties, slipping them on before I walk over to the closet where I grab a pair of cream-colored pants. I take the robe off, tossing it on the bed and seeing his jacket there. "Fuck," I curse, putting my lace bra on and just grabbing the first brown short-sleeve shirt I see. Grabbing his jacket, I rush out of the bedroom door, hoping to catch him before he leaves. Instead, I find him cleaning the kitchen. "I said I would clean," I remind him as he closes the dishwasher and turns to look at me.

This time his dress shirt is back on. "I had time," he says and he looks at the jacket in my hand. "Did you think I left without it?"

"I wasn't sure," I say as he walks to me.

"My shoes are also in there," he says, walking past me and into the bedroom. I close my eyes and try to avoid feeling like an idiot. At this point, I need him to get out of my space so I can think clearly. He walks back from the room and holds out his hand for his jacket. "May I?" he asks and I just laugh at myself.

"Sorry, I was thinking of something." I try to make an excuse. His fingers graze mine as he grabs the jacket from me. He slips his jacket on and I see the white shirt pull across his chest. "Thank you for coming over and checking on me." I look down for a second, trying to gather my words so I don't sound like an idiot. I look up and it feels like he's closer than he was when I looked down. I look up into his blue eyes. "I really appreciate it."

He puts his hand up and I think he's going to touch me, but instead he holds his neck. "Will you call me," he says softly, "if you need me?"

"Yes," I reply, and I can swear he feels as if he's closer than he was before. My heart speeds up and my mouth suddenly becomes dry when I see him moving his head toward me. All I can hear is the echo in my ears.

I can almost feel his lips on mine and I try not to move. "Liar," he says softly right before he steps away from me and walks to the door. "I'll call you later."

Only when I hear the door shut behind him do I finally say, "What the fuck was that?" I put my hands on my hips. Kissing him would be a huge mistake, huge. It's almost as if you don't know what you're missing, right? So it's better to not know at all. "You should be glad he didn't kiss you," I tell myself as I walk back into my bedroom and grab my shoes. "But why are you so pissed that he didn't?" I ask myself when I grab my purse and head out the door, locking it behind me.

I make my way to court and the whole day it bothers me that he didn't kiss me. Even when I walk in the hospital four hours later to check on Penelope, I'm still thinking about it. Like, he was in my space. I play the scene over and over again as I walk down the corridor, and then I see the man who has been all over my thoughts all day long.

He stands there wearing blue chinos and a button-down shirt, as he leans into the counter at the nurses' station. He has a smile on his face as he talks to the nurse. He must feel me staring at him because he looks up and his smile gets even bigger when he sees me.

I'm about to ask him if he's following me when I see a man step out of Penelope's room. He looks right at me. "Julia Williams." He uses my first name and I wonder if I've met him before. I'm about to say something when he holds up his hand and I see white papers in his hands. "You've been served."

Sixteen

Chase

"SO HOW HAVE you been?" I look at Marie who sits behind the nurses' desk. "I haven't seen you in a while."

She laughs and she can already smell my bullshit; the minute I finished practice I got in my car and drove straight here. Even when I got in the elevator and pressed the fourth-floor button, I was telling myself I was just doing a follow-up on one of my patients. "Since when do you visit this floor?" She shakes her head as she writes in a chart. I think about lying to her, but I don't.

"Okay, fine, you got me." I lean against the desk and smile at her. "I was just checking on a patient I had the other day." Marie lifts her head and looks at me. "Penelope." She gives me a sad smile as she reaches for her file.

"She's doing a bit better," she informs me and I can

feel eyes on me. I turn my head and see her. Julia, the woman who has been on my mind since I walked out of her apartment. When I almost crossed that fucking line and kissed her. She rushed from her room so fast with my jacket in her hand and the only thing I could see was her lips. The only thing I could think about was bending down and kissing her. The only thing I knew I shouldn't do was kiss her. The minute the door closed behind me, I practically ran out of there as if the building was on fire and I had to save myself. Only when I was in my car did I take a second and get my breathing under control. My hands gripped the steering wheel and all I could do was close my eyes, which made it fifty times worse since all I could see was her. When did she start taking my breath away? When did kissing her feel like the best idea I've ever had? When did it hurt to walk away from her and not kiss her? When did seeing her make everything better? When did it all change?

She gets closer to me and I look over at a man who looks like he's been waiting. Everything seems as if it happens in slow motion. He gets close to her and I hear his voice calling her name, I look at him and then to her to see if she knows him, but her face is filled with confusion. "Julia Williams." He holds up his hand with papers in it. "You've been served."

"What?" she asks in confusion as he places the papers in her hand. He nods at her and walks away from her toward the elevator.

Her whole demeanor changes when her eyes quickly go from her hands as she turns to look at the man, who just walked away from her as he gets in the elevator. I take three steps to her. "What's the matter?" I ask her as I get close enough to her.

"I have no idea," she says as she opens the papers that are folded in thirds. Her eyes roam the top of the paper and I see the color slowly drain away from her face. Her hands start to shake as she blinks quickly. She turns around, looking back at the elevator and then toward Penelope's room where someone has closed the door.

"Julia," I call her name, my body is so tense it feels as if my skin is crawling off me. "Talk to me." It's more of a plea than anything else.

Her eyes fly to mine as I see the tears form. "I'm being sued." She puts her hands to her stomach with the papers in them. "I think I'm going to be sick."

I take one step toward her, wrapping my arm around her waist to hold her up in case she falls. "Okay, let's get out of here." It's the only thing I can think of doing.

She walks with me, her head down the whole time. "Let's get you in the fresh air." I talk to her calmly, explaining to her where we are going. I get in the elevator with her as she leans against the back wall. "We need to get you some water," I say and she just stares at me and I swear it's like she's not even here. I can't even imagine how she is feeling, I also know I would take whatever she is feeling for her not to go through it. My head goes around and around as if it's going through a tornado as I think of what to do.

The elevator pings and I slip my hand into her empty hand, the other one still gripping the papers in her fist.

"I'm parked right outside," I say and she just follows me.

Taking my keys from my pocket, I unlock the door and open it for her. I sit her in the passenger seat and squat down beside her. "Hey," I say, wanting her to look at me, but when she does, everything in me stands still. The emptiness is a look I've never seen on her, it's a look I never want to see again. "It's going to be okay," I assure her and all she can do is swallow. I close the door of the car and pull out my phone.

I press the button and he answers after one ring. "Hey," I greet as soon as I hear his voice.

"You miss me already," he teases, and just hearing his voice makes me feel better. Even though the two of us have butted heads most of my life, there is no one else I would turn to for help. I know without a doubt, that no matter what, he would be in my corner, ready to fight my battle with me and for me.

"Dad." I say his name and he must sense something is off with me. I look around the parking lot, trying to think of what to say. I think about the need to protect Julia and I know whatever is in those papers, she is going to need someone in her corner. I also know it's not my place to say what is going on. "I need you" are the only words that come out.

I can hear him cover the speaker on the phone as he yells something. "Where are you?"

"About to get on the plane to head back to New York," he says, and I can hear the car door shut. He was in town for a couple of days and was leaving today.

"Can you be at my place in ten minutes?" I ask him.

If he says no, I honestly have no idea what the fuck I'm going to do. I'm going to have to call Michael or even Max. I just know I need to call in the big guns.

"I'll be there in ten," he assures me, disconnecting the phone. I put it in my back pocket, close my eyes, and look up at the sky. I take a couple of seconds to catch my breath before I open the driver's door. I reel in the part of me that is my father and just wants to grab the papers and read them. I try to ignore everything that is going on in my head, she needs a friend, nothing more.

My stomach gets tight when I pull open the driver's door and see her sitting there, looking down at the papers in front of her. "I need to call my work," she whispers as I start the car. "I have to." Her voice trails off as she flips the papers to the second page and then the third.

"I think you need to contact a lawyer," I suggest, pulling from the parking lot. "Can I?" I ask her, and she holds out her hand to me with the papers in her hands. The minute I see the top of the paper, the blood in my veins boils. I read the name of Penelope and then her grandparents' names and then I see Julia's name and my hand wants to fist the papers in it. They are suing her for reckless endangerment. "Oh my God." I don't mean to say the words, they just slip from my mouth.

"Ten million dollars," she says, almost in a whisper. "Emotional distress of a minor." The two tears roll down her cheeks. "Ten million dollars. I will never, ever be able to pay that. Not even if I spend my whole life working for it." She closes her eyes and she puts her hand on top of her head. "I can't believe this." She puts her head back on the headrest. "All I've ever wanted was to make a difference." She wipes away a tear from her face. "After all the shit I've put up with over the years, all I've cared about is making a difference."

My heart breaks for her as I throw the papers down and take her in my arms. "We are going to get through this," I say and she just shakes her head.

"All I've ever wanted," she repeats again as she wipes the tears off her cheek, "was for Monica to be better. Was for Penelope to have the life she deserves. That is all I've ever wanted for her. That is all I've ever tried to do for her."

"You don't have to tell me that." I grab her hand in mine. "I know all you ever want to do is help people."

She looks at me. "It's why I do this job. It's not for anything else, but if I can make a difference in one person's life." She turns and looks out the window. "If I just help one person, that is all that matters." Her voice trails off. "And now they are saying all these lies about me." She rests her head on her fist as she looks out the window. "My whole career is going to be picked apart." I don't say a word, instead I just make my way over to my house as fast as I can. "In the blink of an eye, everything is gone." Her voice is but a whisper. "Everything is gone."

Seventeen

Julia

I CAN'T EVEN breathe properly as I look at Chase, who again is here for me when I'm at my worst.

I look at him. "It's why I do this job." I swallow down the lump in my throat. "It's not for anything else, but if I can make a difference in one person's life." I turn and look out the window, watching the world go by me. "If I just help one person, that is all that matters." My voice trails off. "And now they are saying all these lies about me." I put my elbow on the door, making a fist with my hand and leaning my head on it. "My whole career is going to be picked apart." I close my eyes and the only thing I can see is the amount of money they are suing me for. I will never be able to pay off a debt like that. "In the blink of an eye, everything is gone." My voice is but a whisper. "Everything is gone."

He pulls into the underground parking lot and I don't even know what is going on. He holds my hand as he walks to the elevator, never once letting it go until he unlocks his door. "What are we doing here?" I ask him as he tosses his keys on the table.

"Waiting for the cavalry," he says, and I have no idea what he means. Instead of asking him another question, I walk into the apartment. I walk straight to the kitchen and open the cabinet Michael used to keep the booze in. I grab the bottle of scotch and walk over to grab a crystal glass.

I open the bottle and pour myself a shot, ignoring that the tears are just pouring out of me. I don't think I can stop them if I wanted to. "I shouldn't drink this," I mumble, "I have to go to the office."

I look at him as he stands there in the middle of the living room, looking at me. "I have to call the union," I finally say. I swear, it feels as if I'm on the highest roller coaster ever built, sitting at the top—then suddenly dropped—except I'm not wearing anything to protect me from flying out.

The sound of the front door opening and shutting makes my eyes fly to the hallway. I wonder if he called Michael and I know I have no choice but to say something at some point. I thought having Michael come would have been hard on me. Instead, it's the last person on earth I ever want to let down. Max.

He follows Matthew, and the minute I see him I can't help but put my face in my hands and cry. I stop the sobs from ripping through me, but I can't help the way my shoulders shake.

"What happened?" Matthew asks and I can't even look up. The thought of him being disappointed in me is just too much to bear. Thinking he is going to think less of me, all I can do is hide my face.

I can hear footsteps get closer to me and then I feel his arms take me in them. "It's okay," Max whispers to me. "Whatever it is, it's okay." I can't help but wrap my arms around his waist as he holds me. "Oh my God," Max says. "Did you hurt her?"

"Oh my God." Chase's voice goes louder. "Really, Uncle Max?"

"Is she?" I hear Matthew now talk. "Is she pregnant?" I look up now, seeing Matthew glare at Chase. "Chase fucking Grant," he grinds out between clenched teeth with his hands on his hips. "What is wrong with you?"

"I'm not pregnant." I finally find my words and Max lets me go, but keeps his arm around my shoulders.

"Thank God," Matthew says and then looks over at Chase.

"Seriously, Dad, out of everything in this whole world, the only thing you could think of was she was having my baby?" He holds his hand up and then looks at Max. "And you think I put my hands on her?"

"What was I supposed to think, she's in your house drinking and crying," Max explains. I step forward now to stop whatever is happening before it gets too much.

"I need to go to the bathroom," I say softly, "and when I come back out, I'll tell you why I'm crying."

"Do you want something to eat?" Max says softly. "I

can order the fruit basket you like."

I shake my head no and I look at Matthew. "Thank you for coming," I say, and I can't even look in his eyes because I'm afraid I'll see disappointment in them.

I walk with my head down to the bathroom, and I'm about to close the door when I feel a hand slap the door. "Are you okay?" Chase stands there asking me silently.

"Remember when you brought me home two days ago?" I ask him and he just looks at me. "I thought I wouldn't survive that night." The words don't stop there. "I think this is even worse than the last time."

"Do you want me to run a bath for you?" he asks and I gasp.

"Your father is here with Max," I whisper-yell. "They already thought you knocked me up."

"Only my father thought that." Chase puts his hands in his pockets. "Max thought I hit you."

"I just need to splash water on my face and I'll be out," I assure him and he just looks at me. "I might even throw up, depending on how the next two minutes go."

"I'll be outside waiting for you," he says and steps out of the doorway and closes the door with him. I don't bother locking the door, because let's face it, the three of them can smash down the door with one hand.

Walking over to the sink I turn on the cold water, avoiding looking at myself in the mirror. I can't even imagine how I look. I cup my hand under the cold stream of water, waiting for my hands to fill up, before splashing the water on my face. I repeat it three times before I turn the water off and look at myself in the mirror. For the first time I look how I feel, destroyed. I grab a towel and dab my face before I take a huge deep breath and walk out.

I don't know what to expect, to be honest, and when I walk in, the three of them are sitting on the couches. Max and Matthew sit on one couch facing Chase, neither of them says a word. The bottle of scotch is in front of Chase with the glass I poured and never drank, beside it the folded papers I was served. My stomach spins, and I think I'm going to be sick, but when I see Chase stand, all I can do is walk over to him. "We should get this over with," I say, sitting down and putting my hands on my knees, ignoring how much they are shaking. "Wow, I thought this would be easy." I laugh but a sob comes from me and I put the back of my hand to my mouth. "Sorry," I say, shaking my head and Chase gets up, walking into the kitchen. He grabs a water bottle from the fridge. He comes back, sitting next to me, and hands me the bottle of water. "Thank you," I say, and he waits for me to take a sip. The cold liquid hits my mouth and it takes everything to swallow past the lump. I put the bottle on the table in front of me, next to the white papers.

Matthew leans forward. "If someone doesn't tell me what the fuck is going on…" He looks at Max. "How are you so cool?"

"I'm giving her a second to compose herself." Max smiles at me. "Take your time."

"I mean, there is no good way to say this," I start to say, and I feel Chase put his hand on my back. "Last week I had a case where I was supposed to take away the little girl from the mom." I try to keep it as simple as possible, without telling them any confidential information. "She was with me for a while. She was twenty-one, her child was two."

"Fuck," Matthew curses, sitting back on the couch and my legs start to shake up and down.

"Yeah, more or less," I try to joke, but a tear escapes me. "Bottom line, I gave her one more chance." My stomach tightens. "Sunday night I got a call that there was an accident." My hands start to shake on my legs. Chase slides his hand between both of mine, the heat from his hand fills my whole body. I look over to him and offer him a smile, but nothing comes. All I can do is blink as the tears escape my eyes. I look back at Matthew and Max and it takes everything inside me to continue. "She died at the scene." My voice cracks and I bend my head, and I can't help the way my body shakes with tears. Chase takes his hand from mine and wraps his arm around my shoulders, pulling me to him.

"It's okay," he comforts, kissing my head. "It's going to be okay."

"Take your time, sweetheart," Max says and I look over at him. He's not sitting with his back to the couch anymore. He's sitting at the edge of the couch, his hands in the middle of his legs, folded. "Just take your time."

I nod at him. "The baby survived." The minute I say the words, Matthew hisses and I look over at him. He avoids looking at me, instead he looks off to the side. *I probably disgust him. I need to get the hell out of here,* is the only thing I can think of now. "There is no father in the picture, so the grandparents got emergency custody of the child."

"Where is the child now?" Matthew looks at me and I can see the tears in his eyes.

"In the hospital," Chase says for me. "She came in with her on Sunday. She has a couple of broken bones and needed surgery."

"Today I went over there to see how she was doing," I continue the story, "and I was served with papers."

"What papers?" Max says. I lean forward and pick up the white folded papers that will change everything. "They are suing me for emotional distress of a minor." Even saying the words now, it feels surreal. As if I'm watching a movie about someone else.

"What. The. Actual. Fuck." Matthew looks up to the ceiling.

"That," I say, "and ten million dollars." I shake my head and start to stand. "I have to go call the union rep." I put my shoulders back as Matthew and Max just share a look. I wipe my eyes and bend to pick up the papers. "Then I'm going to head to work." I look at Chase, who stands next to me, his hands still on my shoulders. "I know it's a lot to take in," I say, looking back at Max and Matthew. "But I was doing what I thought was right. I'm going to call Jillian and my mother after I find out more." I move away from Chase's touch, not sure how much longer I can act strong. "I'll let you know what happens." I look at Chase, who just stares at me.

I don't know if it's because Matthew and Max are here that he lets me leave, but he does. I make sure I hold my head up while I walk to the door. The minute it's closed behind me and I'm in the elevator, I let my shoulders fall.

Only when I'm in the lobby of the building do I realize that I don't have my car. I'm about to call an Uber when my phone rings. I look down and see it's the only other person in the world I can turn to. "Jillian." I say her name and my voice cracks right before the sob rips through me.

Eighteen

Chase

I STAND HERE and watch her walk with her shoulders back and her head held high. My eyes never leave her as she walks around the corner, the sound of the door opening and then slamming shut makes my chest contract. Sitting next to her while she told them the story, I wanted to grab her and hug her the whole time. I wanted to shield her from everything. The need to put her behind me so I can suffer the wounds filled my body. Nothing, and I mean nothing, could have prepared me for how raw her voice was. How she had the courage to lay out everything in front of the both of them was everything.

Having all the balls in the world to tell them what was going on with her, and then looking at the two of them not saying anything, I wanted to jump up and ask them what the fuck was going on. Why were they sitting here so calm and not burning down the house? Why the fuck was no one telling her it was going to be okay? Why the fuck wasn't my father trampling over her to get the papers? I had no idea what was going on and I hated every single second. I should have counted to ten before I turned my wrath on them, I should have done a lot of things, but I didn't. I'm my father's son after all, so I was ready to go to war with the only two people I thought would help her, yet let her leave. By. Herself. I should kick my own fucking ass for not going after her and leaving her all alone.

I whip my head around to my father and Max. "What the hell are you two doing?" I shout. "Are you just going to sit there and do nothing?" I look at both of them. Max sits at the edge of the couch while my father leans back on it, just staring at me. "You're going to let her call a union lawyer?" I can't help but lift my arms, putting my hands behind my head and crossing them. The silence is almost deafening, which makes me even angrier, so I word vomit. "You." I look at Uncle Max, who now sits back on the couch mimicking my father's stance. "You've always said that she's like a daughter to you." My stomach gets tight, the feeling going up my chest and toward my throat. My feet feel as if I'm wearing cement boots and I'm stuck at this spot. "You're just going to let her hang out to dry? They are suing her for ten million dollars. I don't know how much she makes a year, but I'm guessing she doesn't have ten million dollars saved up." I put my hands on my hips, the nervous energy coming through me like never before. I look around the room, my eyes going to the glass of whiskey she poured herself and then didn't drink it. The urge to pick up the tumbler and toss it across the room makes my hands tingle. "I can't believe this."

"I know what I'm going to do," my uncle Max says, his voice calm as he puts his elbow on the arm of the couch and leans his face on his fist. "But the question is, what are you going to do about it?" His eyes stare right into mine, neither of us looking away during the stare down.

I look at him, confused at his question. "What does that even mean?" I ask him. "Is this a code thing that only the two of you understand?" They've been each other's sidekicks for as long as anyone can remember. When my uncle Evan came into the picture, he gave them the nickname M&M. They say they don't depend on each other, but if my father is somewhere, Max is very close by and vice versa.

"I know what that means." My father gets up off the couch and then stands looking at Max. "Do I need to be here for the next part?"

"No." Max shakes his head, making my father nod his as he looks at me. He smirks at me right before he walks down the hall toward the bedroom. The only thing going through my head at this moment is, *what the fuck is going on?* I put my hands on the top of my head, speechless and feeling so helpless that I don't know what else to do. I want to yell at my father's retreating back to help me, but all the words stay jumbled inside my throat.

I sit back on the couch, as if someone cut me off at

the knees, my eyes never leaving the hallway where my father just disappeared to. "What's the story with you and Julia?" Max asks and I blink a couple of times before I turn to look at him.

"There is no story." I say the words and they taste like acid in my mouth. Everything inside me gets even tighter. As if you would take a wet towel and try to wring all the water out, that is exactly how it feels. *There is no story*, the words replay in my head, making me wonder when it fucking changed. *There is a story*, my head screams, *we just don't know it yet.*

"If there is no story." He sits forward now, his voice never going high, never going low. Staying steady and tight. "Then you should keep in your own lane."

I swallow down the lump in my throat and my legs start to shake nervously. "What does that mean?" I stare into his eyes, hoping like hell he doesn't see the bullshit I'm trying to sell him. I know exactly what he means. I also realize I don't know the answer to the question. I mean, I know the answer but it's fucking crazy, right? Like we've been friends for forever. We've been each other's wingman when we would go on vacation. We've been playing this cat-and-mouse game from day one. We've never crossed over that line, but the line is becoming very blurred on my side. Not only is it blurred, it is starting to erase and it feels like I am seeing everything for the first time.

"It means if you don't want to get into the car with her"—he opens his hands now—"then get the fuck out of the car." He folds his hands over his chest waiting for my answer. Which even if I wanted to, I can't answer.

"You hang around with my father way too much." I try to make a joke out of it, but nothing on his face says this is a joke. I pretend I don't know what he's talking about but he couldn't be clearer, basically shit or get off the pot.

"I'm not joking, Chase." There is no humor in his tone either. "If you aren't in this one hundred percent, you need to stop and get out."

I throw my hands up. "I don't know what that means." My voice goes even louder and my father comes from the bedroom.

"What's going on?" my father asks as he comes down the hallway. He looks at me and then looks at Max, waiting for one of us to answer. Nothing comes out of my mouth; I open it to say something but nothing comes out.

"Just telling Chase that if he's not in the car with her, he's got to get out," Max states and my father nods at him as if this makes perfect sense.

"Okay." I put my hands up. "I'm going to need you to talk to me not in the language of M&M and in the language of humans."

My father laughs and shakes his head. "Son, you sat there beside her holding her hand." I roll my eyes at him. "Then you put your arm around her. Protected her."

"This isn't nineteen forty-two where we are going steady because I held her hand." I roll my eyes at them. "I was comforting her." I look at Max. "Something you should have done."

"You were already doing it," Max points out to me. "Sitting down next to her, listening to her say story." He chuckles. "A story I think you've heard before, I might add. But anyway, it was fun watching the vein on your forehead look like it was going to pop."

"He gets that from me," my father says proudly as he smiles at me and all I can do is glare at him.

"Oh, I know." Max laughs at him. "It came out every time I kissed Allison for the first two years. I used to do it on purpose to see if it would explode."

"This isn't a joke," I declare. "She's going to lose everything because she wanted to give that girl a chance." I stand and the beating of my heart is so hard and strong I'm surprised it's not beating out of my chest. "She needs someone who isn't a fucking union lawyer, who is just going to treat her like she's another case file."

"I think we got our answer," my father states, looking at Max who just smirks as he gets up.

"And what answer is that?" I ask him, frustrated that no one is taking this seriously.

"The two of you," my father says. "It was fun watching the both of you." He smirks. "It's always been the two of you." He shrugs. "You just had your head up your ass." If I thought I was speechless before, I lied, this right here I have no words for.

"Did you call?" Max finally speaks, saving me from saying anything else.

"He's going to call me right back," my father tells him and then Max's phone rings and he grabs it from his pocket.

"Michael," he tells us as he hits the button.

"Hello." He puts the phone to his ear and I want to say to put it on speakerphone. "I'm on my way." He hangs up and then looks at me.

"Julia got a call from Jillian when she was in the lobby," Max shares, and I swear I feel like someone kicked me in the balls. I was so in my head about these two I forgot she didn't have her fucking car. "She just got her and she's going to her house."

"Well, it looks like you're off the hook," my father says, and the back of my neck feels like it's on fire. "Let's go," he urges Max and they walk out of the apartment, leaving me alone.

I sit down now, my legs giving out, my stomach feeling like I'm going to throw up. My head is spinning a hundred miles an hour. My hands ache from being in a fist half the time. I close my eyes and hang my head. The sound of her voice echoes, "It's going to be all gone."

My eyes flicker open and I look at the drink in front of me. I grab it and take it down in one gulp, it burns all the way down to my stomach. "What are you going to do about it?" Uncle Max's voice echoes in my ear now. "If you aren't in the car with her, get out of the car." My mind spins around as I think of the answer. My mind thinks about where she could be now. I wonder if Michael is there and then I wonder if I should go over there. I look at the crystal glass in front of me, and in the blink of an eye, I hurl it across the room at the wall. It shatters into a million tiny pieces, just like her heart did when she walked out of here.

Nineteen

Julia

I SIT ON the couch and tell Jillian and Michael the story I told Max and Matthew. This time with a couple of fewer tears because I didn't want Jillian to know just how bad it is. "They can't just sue you!" Jillian gasps and stands. Michael puts his hand in hers and pulls her back down on the couch. "They can't just come and sue her."

"They sure can," I say, "and they are." Staying strong is harder than falling apart. The minute I heard her voice, I just cracked. It took her less than ten minutes to get to me since she was downtown with Michael. I can't even tell you what we discussed in the car. All I know is I sat in the back with my eyes closed as I pushed away the pounding of my head. I heard Michael call Max and then the next thing I knew we were pulling into their driveway. The whole thing was a blur, fuck, the whole two days was a blur.

Jillian was a wreck beside me and she didn't let go of my hand for even a second. Michael looked like he was in the most uncomfortable situation he'd ever been in. His face was pale and his finger was tapping his knee as we waited for Max to get here. I thought for sure he would come with Chase following, but it was just the two of them. I couldn't even look them in the eye this time. I just told my story with my head facing down as I focused, my hand in Jillian's. "Ten million dollars." She shakes her head and then takes a deep breath. "We have to sell the house." She looks at Michael.

"What?" I gasp. "Absolutely not."

"We don't have to sell the house," Michael says. "I just need to move things around."

"Um…" I release Jillian's hand. "No one is selling any house and or moving things around, whatever that means."

"We'll be fine," Michael replies, looking at Max who just nods at him. "It'll be fine."

"Only in this family do they talk about ten million dollars like it's fifty bucks." I shake my head and laugh. "You know what I could do?" I look at Jillian. "Go on Tinder."

"You are not going on Tinder," Max and Matthew say at the same time.

"Why?" I ask, shocked, then turn to Matthew. "I might have to borrow the private plane, but then it's a given they will wire me money."

"You really need to stop watching Netflix," Michael

suggests.

"I might need a bodyguard to rough them up." I look at them and see Max looking at me and smirking and something lifts off my chest. "But then the money will just roll in."

"That's called prostitution," Jillian declares. "You think they are going to give you all this money without sex?" She huffs out, "Not a chance in hell."

"Okay," Matthew says, getting up and slapping his hands together. "This has been fun." He looks at Max. "I'm assuming we are staying until things settle." He just nods his head. "I'll have the girls fly out tomorrow."

"Already on it," Max says, getting up. "They should be here within the hour."

"I don't need all this fuss," I say, getting up. "Honestly, it'll be fine. It's too late to call anyone, so I'm going to save all that until tomorrow. But I'm sure it'll be fine."

"But what if it isn't?" Jillian asks softly. "We are going to do whatever it is we need to do for you." She gets up and puts her hands on her hips. "And that is that."

"Jesus." I throw my hands in the air. "When did this one become so sassy?" I point at her with my thumb, then look at Matthew. "Is it from you?"

"All good things come from me." He walks over to me and puts his hands on my arms, and I can already feel the tears coming to me. "We are going to get through this," he assures me softly, his eyes as warm as they were the last time he saw me. There is no judgment nor is there disappointment there. He bends to kiss my cheek. "I'll call you tomorrow."

I want to say he doesn't have to, but instead my mouth deceives me. "Okay," I say softly and he kisses my cheek and walks toward the playroom, yelling for the kids.

"If you'll excuse me," Jillian says. "The last time we left him alone with the girls, he told them to kick anyone in the balls who got next to them." She looks over at Max, who tries not to laugh. "Poor Maddox"—she shakes her head—"they both got him."

"At the same time," Michael states, getting up to follow Jillian from the room, leaving me alone with Max.

I look down and know if I don't say anything, it'll eat at me. "Max." I say his name a little higher pitched than I wanted to. I clear my throat and then look up at him. "I don't expect anyone to help me out of this mess." I try to get the words out before the lump in my throat stops anything from happening. "I just want you to know that I'm really good at my job." My hands start to shake but I hold them together to stop them. "I know it's hard to think otherwise, especially with me being sued but—" I swallow.

"Julia." He gets up and comes over to me, putting his arms around my shoulders. "You don't need to tell me how good you are at your job," he assures me. The one lone tear that I blinked away from its last-minute escape he wipes away. "Because I see how good you are. We are very proud of everything you do and everyone you try to help." He rubs down my arms and pulls me closer to him and kisses me on the head. "And we are going to help fight this because that is what family does. And you're family." I look up at him and I can't help but smile because all I see in his eyes is the warmth he always has. It's the same look in his eyes as when he found out that he was my favorite and I asked him for a hug. Okay, maybe he looked a little shocked but still the warmth came after.

"I left for two seconds and you made her cry?" Matthew says, coming into the room.

"It's good tears," I say, defending Max who stands now.

"Did you corrupt my grandkids?" he asks him and Matthew just smirks.

"It's called educating," Matthew informs him. "Now I need a meal."

They walk out of the room and the phone buzzes in my pocket. I grab it and see it's Chase.

Chase: Checking in to see if you are okay.
Me: As okay as I can be. Tomorrow is another day.

I press send and Bianca runs into the room and asks me to give her a bath. "There is nothing more I want than to give you a bath," I say, picking her up, and for the next two hours I get lost in just being an aunt.

I don't even check my phone before I collapse in the bed, and when I turn over on my back, the sun is trying to get into the room. It's the first day I don't wake up to an alarm blaring and I wonder if his alarm went off today. I blink away the sleep as I try to listen to the noise downstairs, but it's eerily quiet. Tossing the covers off me, I get up and go to the bathroom, grabbing my phone and seeing it's almost nine. I slip on my robe and slide the phone in the pocket before making my way down the spiral staircase. I hear the sound of the television coming from the family room. I walk in and see Jillian is in the kitchen cleaning up. "Good morning," I grumble and look around. "Where are my kids?"

"Your kids"—Jillian snickers—"have all gone to school. Michael had practice, so he took them in."

"But," I say, walking over to the coffee machine, "I didn't even hear them." I shake my head.

"You must have been out of it," Jillian says as she sits on a stool at the island. "How are you feeling?"

I turn with the cup of coffee in my hand and lean against the counter. "Like I've been hit with a semitruck and he brought along a couple of friends and they all ran over me." I take a sip of the coffee. "Front and back." She laughs and she's about to say something when the phone rings in my pocket. I pull it out and see it's Rosalind calling. "It's my boss," I say softly, my chest now feeling as if someone is sitting on it. "Hello," I answer it.

"Julia," Rosalind says and I can hear her voice is soft. "I just got the paperwork." I close my eyes.

"I'm sorry I didn't call you yesterday," I say softly. "It was…"

"You don't have to apologize for anything," she replies and then I can tell in her voice that something is up. "Listen, Julia, I hate to do this to you." I don't know what is coming next but my stomach sinks to my feet. I put the coffee cup on the counter, not saying a word. "We were talking and thought maybe it would be a good idea for you to take some time off."

"What?" I gasp, shocked, thinking maybe I misheard

her.

"It's not for long, only until this thing dies down," Rosalind assures me. "You know parents like this. They are going to get tired really fast." She takes a deep inhale. "They will go away soon enough." *Will they?* I ask myself. I have ten million reasons they won't.

I didn't know what was coming, but I never, ever in a million years expected this. I was wrong when I said I felt like a truck ran me over. It's more like a meteor crashed into earth on top of me. "I'm sorry, what?" is all I can say. "Nothing has been decided," I say, not sure what to say.

"I know," she replies, her voice going soft. "I fought as much as I could." I close my eyes as the tears run down my face. "We have to think of the other cases you have." I want to fight back and argue my side of it, but the lump in my throat is so big I can't talk. "What if they come in and throw all those other cases in turmoil? We just can't have that. I don't want to do this, but I have no choice." She stops talking for a second and then it's almost as if she whispers out, "Did you call a lawyer?"

"Not yet," I say, two words, just two little words. Two words are the only thing I can say.

"I would call them," she urges. "Talk soon." I don't bother to answer her. I just hang up the phone, putting it on the counter beside me.

"What happened?" Jillian asks from her stool.

I grab the cup of coffee, pretty sure I'm in the stages of shock. However, after the last couple of days I wonder if I'm not in some big nightmare. Everything I've done the past six years is going to be gone in the blink of an eye. Everything I poured my heart and soul into is going to be ripped away from me. I can't sugarcoat it, especially not with Jillian. "I think I just got fired."

Twenty

Chase

THE ALARM DOESN'T even wake me up because I've been up all fucking night. It has to have been the longest night I've had in a long time. Getting out of bed, I walk to the kitchen and start a protein shake instead of coffee. "She's fine," I tell myself as I put fruit in there and ignore the pull to pick up my phone for the umpteenth time. Placing the smoothie in a to-go cup, I walk to the bedroom and dress in a team track suit.

I wash my face and brush my teeth before I head toward the rink. I park in my regular spot and I'm not surprised to see no one is here yet. Pressing the lock button on the car, the sound fills the garage when my phone rings in my hand. My heart speeds up as I think it's her, but when I look down, I see it's my sister, Vivienne.

"It's really early," I say, putting the phone to my ear.

"Some would call it farmer time?" I joke with her. She is the only one in the family who thinks the day should start at ten o'clock and anything before should be deemed illegal.

"It's not that early." She laughs and I can hear the covers rustle from her side. "Besides, I'm calling for—"

"Oh, I know you're calling for something," I cut her off as I walk into the arena. A couple of the trainers have arrived and I wave at them as I walk to my office. "I mean, it's not like you ever call to see how I am."

"Wow." She chuckles. "Is someone feeling neglected?" It's my turn to laugh. "Does someone need a hug?"

"What do you want?" I ask her, pulling out the chair before I sit in it. "I'm assuming you do want something."

"You would assume right for once." I shake my head. "I'm coming down today," she says and my eyebrows pinch together.

"It's the middle of the week." I lean back in the chair, rocking back and forth. "You usually grace us with your presence on Friday and then leave on Sunday."

"I know," she huffs, and I hear the sound of her slippers flop from her side. "But something is going down in the family," she adds and my stomach gets tight.

"Who told you?" I ask her, not willing to say anything if she doesn't know anything.

"No one told me shit. All I know is Dad was due back yesterday and this morning, or maybe last night, Mom hightailed it out of town."

"Maybe they are just here visiting." I admit nothing.

"Negative," she replies, and I can hear the sound of her Nespresso machine. "There is something going down and I think it's big." She gasps. "What do you know?"

"I don't know anything." My palms get sweaty. "Why would I know? I always find out things in passing."

"Oh, please," she huffs.

"I literally found out that Erika was pregnant when you asked me to pass the salt," I remind her.

"That was one time." The sound of her laughter fills the phone. "Besides, you've been gone for so long."

"Oh, here we go." I shake my head, taking a sip of the protein drink. "I was gone for four years, but if you ask anyone, it's been eighty-four years. I've been back longer than I've been away."

"He needs a hug and a pep talk." She sighs deeply. "This is a lot of effort on my part to just ask if I can stay with you."

"Why don't you stay with Mom and Dad?" I ask her and roll my lips, knowing exactly why she doesn't want to do that.

"Never again in my life," she retorts, and now my laughter is filling the phone. "Who still has sex at their age? And in the middle of the day." Yup, there it is, she forgot her phone at the house and turned back and found them doing the nasty in the living room.

"What about Cooper?" I ask her.

"He's got a million kids," she jokes. "And before you ask me about Franny, I just don't want to. The two of them seem to be in a race to make it in the Guinness book of records for how much one can have sex. It's like five times a day at this point."

"Eww, there are things that you should tell me and things you shouldn't. That is one. I work with him and she's my sister."

"Well, he's very light on his feet since his balls are always empty. So can I stay with you?"

"No," I say and she laughs.

"I am going to book my flight and send you the details." She ignores the fact I just said no. "See you tonight, little brother."

She doesn't even wait for me to say goodbye before she disconnects and I look down at my phone to see if Julia texted me. I don't know why it bothers me, I'm also not in the mood to sit down and think about it. "Look who it is." I look up and see Cooper coming into the room. He is dressed exactly like me, but he has a baseball cap on his head backward. He sits down in the chair in front of my desk. "So what's new?" He leans back in his chair and I just stare at him. "Romeo."

I roll my eyes and avoid looking at him. "What did Dad tell you?"

"Dad didn't tell me anything." It's almost like he is singing the words to me. "Why, is there something he should have told me?" I can't help but glare at him. "He didn't mention you driving somewhere."

"Oh, dear God." I shake my head. "Of course you would get that logic."

"Who doesn't get that logic?" he asks, and Dylan sticks his head into the room.

"Is this a meeting?" he asks before he walks over and

sits down in the chair next to Cooper. He looks at me and then at Cooper. "What happened?"

"If I say stay in your lane or get out of the car?" I try to repeat the words Max said. I mean it's the only fucking thing I heard all night long. "Do you know what that would mean?"

Dylan scoffs at me and then it sets in. He gasps and snaps his finger. "You like a girl," he reasons, making Cooper laugh out loud. "Oh my God, you like a girl and you're stringing her along."

"Of course, he would get it." I point at Dylan who's like a mini version of the both of them.

"Who does he like?" Dylan ignores me and looks over at Cooper, who just shrugs. "Who is it?" he waits for someone to answer him. When no one does he snaps, "Oh my God, who is it?" He taps the arm of the chair. "Is it someone we know?"

"Don't you guys have to get to work or something?" I ignore his question but he doesn't take it as a *shut up*.

"How well do we know her?" Dylan looks at Cooper, who crosses his hands over his stomach, just smirking. "I mean, there really isn't anyone except..." His eyes go big and then his head snaps around to look at me. Shock all over his face, his mouth opens wide and he slowly lifts his hand to his mouth. "No," he says in a whisper, "didn't you guys bang on the beach in Hawaii?"

"That's what I said." Cooper looks at me.

"We never banged. It was all talk," I finally say.

"She wanted your hammer," Dylan goads, trying not to laugh as he puts a fist in front of his mouth and I flip him the bird. "Didn't Franny buy her a hammer for her birthday that year and she made Wilson shape the handle into a dick?"

"He nearly cut off his finger doing that." Cooper now can't stop laughing. "And it was a group project."

I get up now, not interested in talking about Julia since I haven't been able to talk to her since she left my house. "I have to get to work"—I look at them—"and so do you."

Leaving them in my office, I walk down to the gym, seeing Tristan there as he works on his stretching. "How are we feeling?" I ask him. He just shrugs, but I can see he's very frustrated with this whole not-playing thing. "It could be a lot worse," I say, and he rolls his eyes at me. "I'm not kidding."

"Are you going to say it could be a lot worse if I cut off my leg?" he asks, and I just laugh at him.

"I'm not that dire." I look around. "You could have been sent down to the farm team," I explain, and he gasps. There is nothing worse in this world than being a rookie who everyone is watching and then being sent down to the farm team. It literally fucks with their heads so much and the media makes so much fuss over it. "See, told you it could be worse."

"Do you think I'll be able to skate next week?" he asks quietly, and I just shrug.

"We can try," I say, not willing to rain all over his parade today. "Let's work out, yeah?" I urge him and we work out side by side.

It's four hours later when I finally get a break to sit

down. I grab my phone and see I still have nothing from Julia. Am I surprised? No. Does it bother me? Yes. I'm sure she is going nuts at work, especially after yesterday, and I wonder if she called the lawyer. The fact I don't know any of this burns me to the core.

Me: Hey, just checking in. Call me when you get a minute.

I put the phone down and then get up, bumping into Michael, who is walking from the locker room with his head down as he types something on the phone. "Hey," I greet and he looks up.

"Have you heard from Julia today?" I ask. I'm waiting for him to ask me why I need to speak to Julia. I also did not think this through, and if he asks this, I have no answer for him.

"She's at my house," he says, and now I'm the one who is confused.

"It's a work day," I say out loud and look down at my phone.

"Guess you didn't hear?" he says, and the blood rushes out of my body.

"Hear what?" It comes out more harsh than I want it to.

"She got fired." I don't know what I was expecting, but it sure as fuck wasn't this. "Well, they are calling it a sabbatical." He shakes his head and all I can think of is how Julia must be feeling. "I call it her being the fall guy."

I walk away from him as he's speaking, feeling sick to my stomach. I don't even know I'm headed toward the car until I'm getting in it. Instead of texting, I call her, I'm expecting her to send me to voice mail.

I'm definitely not expecting her to actually answer. "Hello."

"I just heard the news. They fired you?" I hiss between clenched teeth.

"Wow, your family is slipping." She laughs. "This happened three hours ago."

I close my eyes and lean back on the headrest. "Are you busy for dinner?" The words come out before I can process them. *What the fuck are you doing?* my inner voice screams. *What I should have done a long time ago.* "Pick you up at seven." I'm not even waiting for her to answer me. "Text me where to get you." I'm about to hang up before she tells me no. "And if you don't text me, I'll just show up at Jillian's after I go to your house."

She gasps. "See you later."

Twenty-One

Julia

"ARE YOU BUSY for dinner?" The minute the words come out of his mouth, everything in me stops. My hand even stops midway to my mouth with the cup of water in it. I don't even have a chance to replay the words in my head by the time he says, "Pick you up at seven." My mouth suddenly goes as dry as the sand in the desert on a summer day. Even if I tried to swallow, nothing will go down. "Text me where to get you." I open my mouth to speak but nothing comes out. "And if you don't text me, I'll just show up at Jillian's after I go to your house." This makes me gasp out, "See you later."

The sound of the phone disconnecting makes me move the phone from my ear, staring down at it. "Who the hell was that?" Jillian asks from beside me. We are camped out on her couch, where we have been all day long. Even Alex has joined us as she sits on the couch beside us.

"Chase," I answer, trying to wrap my head around what the fuck just happened.

"What did he want?" Alex asks.

"I think I'm going on a date with him." The minute those words are out of my mouth, Alex springs up from the couch.

"Excuse me?" She looks at me with big eyes.

Jillian's head whips around so fast I'm surprised she doesn't get whiplash. "What did you just say?"

"She said she's going out on a date with Chase." Alex says it slowly, but at the same time, she is fisting her left hand while inserting her right forefinger into it.

"Oh, no," Jillian says, jumping off the couch. "You can't go out with him."

I'm about to ask why not when Alex does it for me. "Why the hell not?"

"Because it's a horrible idea," Jillian replies, and I don't know why, but that thought doesn't sit well with me.

"Well, I for one think that it's about fucking time." Alex looks at me and smiles. "This whole tango has been exhausting"

"What tango?" I ask her.

"The two of you together have been like watching *National Geographic* and waiting for the both of you to just snap and fuck on the table." She grabs her phone and I can't help but laugh at this. She pulls up something on her phone. "You can't even deny it, look at this picture."

She hands me her phone and I reach out to grab it. I look down at her screen and it's a picture of Chase and me on New Year's Eve, sitting beside each other on the long bench against the wall. His hand is wrapped around my waist and both of us are laughing at something as we look at each other. I don't even remember what he said but all I can do is focus on him, my heart literally goes up and then down. What is happening right now?

"Alex," Jillian says, "this is Chase we are talking about." She then looks at me. "You can't treat him like the others."

I roll my eyes and lift both of my hands up in frustration. "You don't think I know that?"

"She knows that," Alex says at the same time. "It's different."

"Yeah," I say, pointing at Alex, "it's different."

"Why?" Jillian asks and all I can do is glare at her.

"It just is." I toss the blanket off my legs. "Now I have to go get showered." I turn and start to walk from the room.

"She's going to get the hammer tonight," Alex jokes, laughing while Jillian groans.

I don't bother turning around, instead I just lift my hand and flip them the bird. I walk up the stairs with my stomach in my throat. I sit on the bed at the same time the phone vibrates in my hand.

Chase: Where am I getting you from?
Me: My house.
Chase: Can you be ready in an hour?
Me: What happened to seven?

Chase: More time for you to cancel on me.

I can't help but laugh.

Chase: See you in forty-five minutes.

"Are you sure about this?" Jillian says and I look up to see her and Alex there, side by side.

"I'm not sure about anything. I started this week on a roller-coaster ride and it's been going up and down since." I think about telling her how he held me in the bath. I think about telling her how he showed up at my house to see if I was okay, but I'm not ready to share that. "But it's Chase and it's me." I shrug my shoulders. "We both know that if we cross that line, we both have to be sure."

"Well, then," Jillian says, "what are you going to wear on your date?"

"Jeans," I say at the same time Alex says, "Nothing."

"I have to go." I get up and grab my stuff. "He's picking me up in forty-five minutes."

"What?" they both say at the same time.

"He thought if he gave me more time, I would cancel." I ignore them when they both snicker with laughter. "I hate you both," I grouse, walking past both of them toward the front door.

"Don't do anything I wouldn't do," Jillian pokes and I stop on the last step.

"You slept with Michael on the first date and got knocked up," I point out to her.

"I did." She smiles big. "Good times."

I walk out of the house and get into my car. Michael

had someone pick it up and deliver it to me. I don't even ask questions anymore; I just say thank you. My mind goes around and around as I get ready for the date. When I'm slipping on my white jeans and then the pink flowered loose spaghetti strap top, I have to sit down. I put my hand to my stomach and hear the soft knock on the door. "Come in!" I yell and I hear the door open and then shut. "I'm in my bedroom."

"Um." I hear him stop walking. "Are you naked?"

"Do you want me to be naked?" I ask, rolling my lips and then I see him standing in the doorway. He is wearing blue jeans and a baby-blue polo that makes his eyes lighten up. Just seeing him makes all the nerves go away.

"Are you okay?" he asks as he leans against the doorframe, folding his arms over his chest and crossing his legs at the ankles.

"What are we doing?" I ask him and he continues his leaning stance. "Like, this whole taking-me-out-to-dinner thing." He just stares at me, somehow knowing that I'm not done speaking and it's only normal because he knows me. Like he knows, knows me. "Jillian thinks this is a bad idea."

He smiles at me and the nerves in my stomach feel like there are butterflies in there. "I'm not saying I was threatened by Michael, but I'm also not not saying it." My mouth hangs open.

"He didn't." I gasp, shocked he would go toe-to-toe with his cousin over me.

"He did also throw in Uncle Max, just for some extra

power." I shake my head laughing. "And my father."

"I don't want it to ruin what we have," I admit the truth to him. "Like, going out with you would be amazing and great. Because I'm awesome." I toss my hair over my shoulders. "But what if this goes south?" His eyebrows wiggle at that comment. "Not that kind of south."

"Nothing will ruin what we have." His voice comes out softly. "Are you ready?"

"I don't know." I stand and look at him. "Is this enough?" I look down at my outfit, slipping on my ballerina shoes. "Should I wear heels? Where are we going?"

He stands up straight, putting his hands in his pockets. "You look beautiful," he reassures me softly. I've been told that I'm beautiful all the time, but the way he says it makes me look down to hide my blush. He holds out his hand for me. "Shall we?"

I walk to him and slip my hand in his, as he pulls me out the door with just enough time to grab my jean jacket with my empty hand. He lets my hand go so I can lock the door, and the minute I put the keys away, he takes my hand back in his. "Where are we going?" I ask him again, ignoring how my hand feels in his.

"It's a surprise," he says, stopping next to his car. His hand slips from mine and he brings it up, his thumb touches my cheek. "I've missed you." His voice is almost in a whisper. To be honest, with the way my heart is beating and echoing in my ears, it's a miracle I hear him.

I look up at him smiling. "You know what I didn't

miss?" My smile goes so big it hurts my cheeks. "Your alarm blaring at the ass crack of dawn."

He throws his head back and lets out the biggest laugh. I have to stop myself from taking a step forward and kissing his neck. Instead, I open the passenger door, holding the handle in my hand. "Okay, Mr. Grant, take me on this date of yours."

"Oh, it's a date?" he asks and my eyes go big, my mouth hanging open. "I just said dinner."

"I," I start to say. "Um..." I try to think of words and then I want to kick myself for thinking it's more than it is.

He lets me hang out there for a minute before he steps even closer to me. "It's definitely a date."

"Jerk," I blurt out to him as my hand is still holding on to the handle. His chest is touching mine and my other hand comes up to touch his chest. "I know we haven't even started the date, but thank you for trying to take my mind off things."

His hand comes up again as he holds my chin in it. "Thank you." His face comes even closer to mine. "For not running."

I want to laugh but I can't because everything in me is on edge. I can almost feel his face advancing to me, every single second his face comes just a touch closer. I can literally taste the kiss. I'm holding my breath; my stomach feels like it's going through a typhoon. He's about to kiss me when out of the corner of my eye I see Colin walking down the street with an officer next to him. His head is down, and when he looks up at me, he gives me a look I've never seen before.

"Colin." I call his name when he is close enough. Chase looks over his shoulder at him.

"Julia." He says my name and I look over at the officer beside him, who puts his hand on his belt.

"Are you in the area for something?" I ask him, not sure why but I suddenly feel uneasy in my skin and I can't put my finger on it.

"We are. I'm really sorry," he says. "I'm here on official police business." The blood drains from my body as I think something happened to my mother. "We are here to take you in."

"Excuse me?" Chase says, almost stepping in front of me.

"You're being arrested for child endangerment." He says the words and I don't think it's really registering with me. This has to be a joke. "I'm going to have to read you your Miranda rights."

"This is a joke," Chase says from beside me. He takes a step in front of me, but Colin holds up his hand to Chase at the same time the officer grabs my arm.

"You have the right to remain silent," the officer recites. He turns me and I see spots in front of me and I think I'm going to pass out. "Anything you say can and will be used against you."

"Handcuffs?" Chase says, his voice going louder and louder. "There is no need for that."

I don't even hear what the officer is saying at this point as I feel the metal cuff on my wrist being snapped. Colin is saying something to the officer, who ignores him and holds on to my forearm. I feel as if my soul has left my body. It feels like I'm floating away from it all as my feet move with him toward his police car. The tears flow down my face as he bends my head to push me in the back seat.

"Don't say a word!" Chase yells as they close the door. "I'm going to get you out of this," he says into the back window. Colin stands there talking to Chase as the officer gets into the car and pulls away.

Twenty-Two

Chase

"YOU NEED TO calm down," the guy, Colin, urges in front of me, but nothing, and I mean nothing, is going to get me to calm down. "She's going to be out in a couple of hours," he says as if it's nothing. "Call her lawyer." He walks away from me and gets in his car.

My head is spinning as I look at him and then back at the police car that drove away. I don't even see it anymore. The panic sets in, and I grab my phone, it rings twice before I hear my father's voice. "Hey," he answers and the tightness in my chest comes on.

"Dad, they took her," is all I can say. "They just took her." I look around, waiting to see if this is a joke or something. Surely this isn't happening. This can't be happening. "They took her." My voice goes frantic.

"Who took her?" he asks, his voice going louder.

"Chase!" he snaps my name.

"The police," I reply, my whole body starting to shake now with so much rage I don't know how to stop it.

"Chase, I need you to focus," he redirects and I can hear movement on his side of the phone call. "Who are we talking about?"

"Julia," I say. "We were going out and they came and arrested her."

"Fuck!" my father yells. "Karrie, call Max," he says from his side. "They took Julia. Where are you right now, Chase?"

"Outside her house," I reply, looking up at her apartment with the fairy lights. "I don't even know where they took her. The guy said that she was going to be out in a couple of hours." I put my hand on my head. "Dad, I don't even know where they fucking took her."

"Chase, I'm going to need you to snap the fuck out of it," he says, his voice tight. "I'm on my way to get Max. I need you to call Michael and see if Jillian has her work number or anyone who she can get in touch with."

"Okay," I say, turning around to see if the cop is there still. I rush over to his car as he sits there on the phone.

"Where did they take her?" I ask him.

"Station 46," he answers right before he takes off.

"She's at Station 46," I tell my father. "Dad, we need a lawyer."

"We have one," he says and then I see my phone beep, telling me I have another call. I don't know why I think it's her calling me, but it's Max.

"Dad, Max is on the phone," I say, hanging up on him

and going to Max. "Uncle Max."

"What the fuck happened?" he questions, and I hear car doors slam on his side. It's only then do I put him on speakerphone. I pull up the address to Station 46, running to my car and getting in.

"I came to take her out and we were leaving when two cops came," I say.

"She doesn't have a lawyer," Michael chimes in, and I'm not surprised that they are together. "She called the union lawyer three times today and no one called her back."

"I have to call a lawyer," I say. "My dad said we have one."

"He's already on his way to the station," Max assures me. "He was on call since last night."

"You knew this would happen?" I snap, wanting to punch my steering wheel.

"We didn't know for sure, it was a possibility, we were waiting to get all the information before telling her," Max says and then I hear another door close. "I just got your father; we are heading down to the station."

"I'll meet you there." I hang up and it takes me ten minutes to get there. I can only imagine what she is going through. Scratch that, there is no way I would ever know what she is going through. I park my car and walk into the precinct, seeing two doors on each side and a desk in the middle with a man sitting behind it.

"How can I help you?" He leans back in his chair.

"I have someone who has been brought in," I say, looking around to see if maybe I can see her.

"He's here for Julia," the guy from before says, coming to me. "I got him.

"Did you call her a lawyer?" he asks and the need to throat punch him fills my bones.

"Wait a second." I hold up a finger. "Are you trying to pretend you give a shit?" I ask him. "From your tone it sounds like you are sincere, but thirty minutes ago you stood by while they put handcuffs on her."

He huffs out, "I had a job to do and I told the officer that she didn't need cuffs." He puts his hands on his hips. "Julia is special."

I'm about to say to go fuck himself when the doors open and I look over. My uncle Max walks in with my father on one side and Michael on the other. They all look around, and when they see me, they walk over. "Where is she?"

"She's downstairs being booked," the guy says from beside me. "I'll go in and try to see her."

"Don't do her any favors," I say to his retreating back and he just shakes his head. "Where the fuck is the lawyer?"

"He's pulling up," Max states.

"How was she?" Michael says and I just shake my head. "Jillian is going to lose her mind."

The door opens and I spot a man walking in. "Stuart," my father calls his name and he comes over.

"She's being booked," he says to my father and then holds up his hand to him, walking over to the desk. "You have my client in the back, and I want to see her." He smirks. "Now."

"Why are you always a pain in my ass?" the officer asks him. "Out of all people, you."

"We go way back," Stuart says when he looks at us. "Now I want to see my client."

"Yeah, yeah," the officer responds and then Stuart comes walking back.

"What is going to happen to her?" I ask him.

"She's going to be fingerprinted and"—he looks at his watch—"hopefully pass in front of a judge today, if not tomorrow."

"No way," I say, shaking my head. "No fucking way she stays in here all night." Just the thought of it is too much for me to bear. "You better go talk to whoever the fuck you need to talk to and make sure that she passes today, now, in ten minutes. Whenever." I hold my arms over my chest. "Or else."

Stuart looks at me and then over to Max and then my dad. "I'm taking it this one is yours?" My father doesn't have a chance to answer him because the guy calls his name.

"Can I come in with you?" I ask, taking a step forward. "You can say I'm your assistant."

"You look like Tarzan and you also look like the Hulk getting ready to escape." He shakes his head. "I'll be back."

I look at my father and Max. "Is he the best you could find?"

"He's the best there is out there," Max assures me. "His retainer speaks volumes."

"How much was it?" I put my hands on my hips and

he looks at my father.

"I have to go call Jillian," Michael says. "Come get me if anything happens."

He walks out and the three of us don't say a word, every single second feeling like an hour. Every minute feels like an eternity. "What the fuck is taking so long?" I hiss, looking back at the door he walked into.

"It's been four minutes," my father points out, neither of us moving. I pace the little waiting space back and forth. I have never in my life felt so useless. I have never in my life felt the pain that I am feeling right now. I have never in my life wanted to trade places with another human, until now.

The door opens and Stuart comes back out. "How is she?" I rush to him.

"In shock," he says, and I put my head back and hiss out. "Her prints are done. She knows some of the guys in there, so they want to get her out fast." He looks down and then up again. "The prosecutor knows she isn't a flight risk." I groan. "Bail is going to be set at seventy-five thousand."

"Fine. I have that covered," I state. "Should I call someone to fill out papers or something?"

"My office is working on the paperwork. I don't know how to say this, but she is going to have to stay overnight."

"No fucking way," I grit between clenched teeth. I thought I felt helpless before, I lied.

"I tried my best but the docket is closed for the day." He looks at my father. "I could call in a couple of favors but with everything she is facing with the case, I am not going to do it. The last thing she needs is to be showed favoritism."

"So we just let her rot all night in jail?" I throw my hands up, and I swear to God, I really wish I could break walls right now.

"They have her in a cell by herself. She knows half the men in the back there. She is going to be fine without being fine."

"She is not going to be fine," I say, closing my eyes.

"There is nothing we can do," Max says. "If there was, we would be doing it." He slaps my shoulder.

"I'll be here first thing tomorrow," Stuart declares. "Call me if you need me."

"What do you mean, you have it covered?" My father looks at me.

"It means that I'm going to be covering her bail," I say, putting my hands on my hips, "and her lawyer fees."

Max just pffts out, "Really?"

"Really," I say and then Michael comes in.

"What's going on?" he asks and then looks at the three of us. "What happened?"

"Julia is going to be in until tomorrow," Max says to him.

"Dad," he says, his voice filled with as much pain as I feel right now. "We can't leave her in there."

"We have no choice," Max says softly. "Bail is set at seventy-five thousand."

"It's fine," Michael says and then my father laughs.

"Yeah, Chase is covering it." My father slaps my

shoulder now.

"Why?" Michael asks, his eyes going small as he glares at me.

"Because she's my responsibility," I state, and I have never been surer of anything in my whole life.

"You haven't even been on a date with her." Michael folds his arms over his chest. "How can she be yours?"

I look down and then up at them. "She became mine when I had to hold her in my bathtub while she cried in my arms." All three of them look at me with open mouths. "She was probably mine before then, I was just too stupid to see it."

"I'll agree with that," my father says. "Now I need to know that you are not going to go nuts in there." He motions with his chin toward a door that Stuart just went into. "You are going to see her standing in front of a judge in handcuffs." The thought alone makes my body feel like someone set me on fire. "So I'm going to need you to chill the fuck out. The last thing she needs is seeing you lose it."

I look down and take a deep breath in and exhale. "I'll be fine," I lie. They all know I'm lying because each of them would be the same as me right now. "I just need to get her out of here."

"Well, we will come back tomorrow and take her home," my father declares and I shake my head furiously.

"I'm not leaving." My voice comes out in a whisper and I look at the three of them. There are no words I can say except the ones that come out. "If she's here, so am I."

Twenty-Three

Julia

I FOLLOW THE officer into the police station, never been brought in from the back. The officer, who I've never met before, holds my arm a bit too tight but the last thing I'm going to do is say something to him. The minute he lets go of my arm, it throbs. Did he really think I was going to try to run?

When we walk into the station, I see Wayne and Derrick, two officers I usually work with on cases. "Sit here." The officer points at a plastic chair beside a desk. I sit down, not saying a word, he turns and walks away.

"Julia, we are so fucking sorry." Derrick comes over to me and I just shake my head.

"Rudy," Wayne yells to the officer who brought me in, "uncuff her!"

"That's not procedure," Rudy replies, coming back

and looking at the both of them.

"She's not going anywhere," Derrick says to him, "just uncuff her."

Rudy huffs out, slipping the key into the lock and uncuffing me. My hands rub where the metal was. "You better make sure she doesn't run."

"Run where?" I ask him and he doesn't bother answering. "I think I'm going to throw up," I mumble under my breath.

"I'll get you some water," Derrick says and I look down at my hands.

"We are going to get everything moving quickly so we don't have to drag it out," Wayne assures me, and I'm done.

"I want a lawyer," is the only thing I say to him. "I want a number to a lawyer."

He nods at me and smiles sadly. "We'll get you someone."

My legs start to bounce up and down with nerves. I can feel a panic attack coming, my chest gets tight and my breaths come out in pants. Derrick comes back and hands me the bottle of water. I reach for it and take a sip, my mouth feeling dry. "We are so sorry, Julia, we tried." His voice trails off.

"You have a job to do," is the only thing I can say. It's not his fault I'm in this mess, it's my own.

"Her lawyer is here!" a man yells into the room. "And it's Stuart."

Derrick and Wayne both look at me at the same time. "Big guns," they say in unison. "Good."

"I want to meet with my client in private." The man walks in wearing dress pants and a button-down shirt. "Nice to meet you." He smiles at me. "I'm Stuart."

"Um," is the only thing I can say.

"You can meet her in room one," Derrick says.

"Thank you." He nods at him. "And where is Phillip?"

"Around here somewhere," Wayne says. "But I can call him."

"That would be great," Stuart replies. "Come with me." He motions with his head and I look at Derrick and Wayne for permission of sorts. They just nod their heads at me.

I follow Stuart to the door that says room one. He opens the door and waits for me to step in, and closes it after me. "Have a seat." He points at one of the two chairs that are tucked into a brown table in the middle of the room.

I pull out the metal chair and sit down, my hands starting to shake. "Julia, my name is Stuart and I've been hired by Mr. Grant." I look down at the brown table, the stinging in my eyes starts for a second before the tears run down my face.

"I didn't do anything," I say softly.

"I know you didn't." His voice goes softer than before.

"What's going to happen to me?" The question has been going around and around in my head the whole ride here.

"I'm going to try to get you out on bail today," he says, folding his hands on the table. "But with it being almost the end of the day, I don't know how realistic that is." My heart picks up speed at the same time I feel bile crawl up my throat. "Bail is going to be set and you are going to be bonded out."

"But I've never been in trouble before," I say, trying to grasp at everything he is saying. "Like, I work for the state."

He's about to say something when there is a knock on the door and someone comes in. "Sorry to interrupt," the man says to us. "I heard you were looking for me."

"Phillip," Stuart says his name, then looks at me. "This is the prosecutor. How fast can we get her out?"

"Tomorrow morning," he replies, looking at Stuart and then at me. "Everything is shut down for the night." My head wraps around the fact that I'm going to spend the night in jail. "We are going to have to fingerprint her." It's at that point I don't listen to the rest. I can't, the buzzing in my ears is so loud I can only see his lips move. I snap out of it when I hear, "Seventy-five thousand dollars."

"Seventy-five thousand dollars," I repeat. "I don't have seventy-five thousand dollars."

"You just need to come up with ten percent," Stuart explains to me. "Is there no way we can get her out today?" Stuart asks him and the prosecutor shakes his head, turning and walking from the room.

"What is going to happen?" I ask Stuart. "Will I stay here?"

He takes a big inhale. "They are going to fingerprint you and then take your mug shot." My head hangs down, even if I don't want it to. "Then they are going to place you in a holding cell. My guess is you'll be alone because they know you."

"And then what?" I ask him. "What happens tomorrow?" I don't even bother asking him what happens the day after that and next week.

"Tomorrow we will appear in front of the judge and you will have an arraignment hearing. The judge will read the nature of the charges against you, and you will be formally asked to enter a plea. I will speak on your behalf and we will be entering a plea of not guilty. I will have the documents ready for your bail, and once they are signed by the judge and filed, you will be free to go. I will need you to schedule an appointment with me next week so we can discuss the case."

"How much do you charge?" I ask him and he just smirks at me.

"Let's just say that it's taken care of," he assures me, getting up and I follow his move.

We walk out of the room and back to the chair where I was placed. This time Colin is the one sitting there. "I'll see you tomorrow," Stuart says. I just nod at him, watching him walk out and inwardly begging him to take me with him.

"How are you doing?" Colin asks. "I'm so fucking sorry, Julia."

"It is what it is," I reply, my body going numb.

"Let's get all the paperwork out of the way," he suggests as he gets up. "Follow me." For the next three hours I am patted down, fingerprinted, and they take my mug shot. When he walks down the stairs, I can see the bars of the cell getting bigger and bigger with each step I take.

In each corner of the room are cells with a desk in the middle of them. "Hey," Colin says to the guy sitting behind it. "Do we have an open cell?" he asks the man, and he points at the right. "She's to stay solo." The man just looks at me and then back at Colin. "This is Jeff," he says of the man. "If you need anything, just ask him."

"This isn't the Ritz," he mumbles, and Colin ignores him as he walks to the cell that Jeff pointed at.

"I'm going to go get you something to eat," he says, and I don't even bother answering him. I walk into the cell and look around; a metal bench is pushed against the wall. A sink is stuck randomly on the wall with the toilet stuck to it. The sound of the cell door clicking into place has me jumping. "I'll be back soon," he reassures me, and all I can do is walk over to the bench and sit down before my legs give out on me.

I put my head against the concrete wall, pulling my legs up to my chest. Closing my eyes, I let the tears come because at this point, who the fuck cares. I can't even imagine what people are going to think of me, let alone how my life is going to change now.

All I can see in my head is my mother crying. She probably has to put her house up for my bail and just the thought of it makes my eyes fly open. I look around, seeing no one here but me and the guy behind the desk.

Colin comes back to bring me food, but I don't touch it. He tries to sit with me to pass the time, but he's called out as soon as he sits down. I don't even know what time it is or even how fast time is going. All I know is I sit here in this cold holding cell, my eyes never closing. My body goes numb. I force myself not to have to pee, but finally I give up and walk to the toilet. There is nothing that shields what I'm doing, there is no privacy, it's for everyone to see.

I sit in the same position all night until someone comes into the room. He stops at the desk officer, who has been replaced by someone else, but I have no idea who the guy is because no one has come to talk to me. The guy points behind his neck and the man walks to my cell. "Julia Williams," he says when he stops in front of the cell door. "Time to go."

I stand, my legs shaking from sitting down all night long. "Turn and face the wall with your hands out in front of you," he demands, and I follow his order and feel the metal cuffs wrap around my wrists. "Okay," he says and I take a step forward as he opens the cell door. "Ready?" he asks, and I don't say a word because I'm not ready. Nothing, and I mean nothing, can make me ready for this.

Twenty-Four

Chase

"IT'S ALMOST TIME," my father says from beside me on the bench. I open my eyes and look over at him. He hasn't left my side for one minute this whole night. When I decided I wasn't leaving and went to sit on the metal bench, he looked at Max and then at me. It took him one second to come over and sit down next to me. Max and Michael had to go home and make sure Jillian was okay, but my father made sure that if I needed him at all during the night, he was here. I spent the whole night with my head resting against the concrete wall watching the door. Hoping that by some miracle they would have let her go. They didn't.

"Thirty minutes," I say, looking at my watch. "Thirty fucking minutes."

"We should head over to the courthouse," my father

suggests, getting up as I follow him standing up. I walk out of the precinct and head over to the courthouse. I hand my father the keys to my car, getting in the passenger side. "Did you want to stop and get something to eat on the way?" my father asks as he turns the car on. The only thing I can do is shake my head.

I've said maybe five words to him all night. I spent the first two hours freaking the fuck out that she was behind the concrete wall and I couldn't get to her. I went from sitting down to standing up and repeating the action over and over. At one point I thought they were going to ask me to leave, but that Colin dude came out and covered for me. I didn't say anything to him either. The freak-out was followed by anger. I had so much anger in me all I wanted to do was punch the concrete wall over and over again. I felt like my blood was boiling in my veins and at any moment it would explode. When it got to be around midnight, that was when the sadness kicked in, fuck that feeling of burning in your stomach because you literally can't do anything to help. The feeling of trading places with a person to shield their pain hurting your chest so much, because you can't do it. Bottom line: I have never felt so many emotions in such a short time as I did during the night. I've been to war zones to help and didn't even feel half of what I felt sitting on that steel bench. I've had to tell parents that their child wasn't going to make it. I had to tell big strong men they would never be able to walk again and watch them shatter in front of me, and still never felt what I felt at that moment.

Everything is a blur to me as I look out the window as

the trees and cars pass us by. When my father parks, I see Michael get out of his car followed by Max. I step from the car and walk up to them. "Where is the lawyer?" I look around trying to see if I can spot him. "Shouldn't he be here by now?" I ask them as I put my hands on my hips. "Like, what the fuck is he doing?"

Max looks at my father, who slaps my shoulder and squeezes it. "You need to reel all that anger in," he says calmly, "because when you see her, you are going to have to be her rock."

"If my wife is any indication as to what she went through," Michael says, his voice soft, "it wasn't good at all." I look at his face and see the same anguish I'm sure is on my face. "Jillian spent the night rocking in the same spot." His voice gets tight. "It almost felt like she was in another space."

"Zara and Zoe said it's normal," Max says to him quietly and he just shakes his head.

"I don't care what you call it," he says. "It was like she was with Julia in that cell." I swallow down the bile that rises up my throat. "If I don't bring her home, I have no idea what is going to happen."

"We are bringing her home," my father cuts in before he knows I'll lose it.

"Good, you guys are all here." I look over at Stuart, who is dressed in a three-piece suit this time, a black briefcase in his hand. "We should head in."

My father and Max walk with him. "Where the fuck did he think we were going to be?" I hiss between clenched teeth. "I know that we have to take Julia to see

Jillian." I look over at Michael. "But it's going to be a short visit."

"Is that so?" Michael says. "How sure are you about that?"

"As sure as if I'm not walking out of here with her," I say, looking at him, "I'm going in there with her."

"Don't do anything stupid," Michael warns from beside me. "The last thing we need is more people in there."

I don't say anything to him, instead I walk upstairs and toward a brown door that says courtroom number four. "Here we go," Stuart says, pulling open the door. I'm the last one to walk into the room as the four of them stand in front of me. I don't know if they are doing this to stop me from charging up there or they are looking around.

My eyes roam around the room to see if I see her and I don't. Stuart walks forward to one of the benches in the back and sits down. "What are you doing?" I ask him.

"I'm waiting for her case to be called and then I'm going up there," he states and I hear Michael behind me.

"Just sit down," he grits between clenched teeth. "All we need is you going apeshit now and postponing shit." He practically pulls me to sit in the bench behind Stuart and our fathers.

"What time is her hearing at?" I lean forward to ask Stuart.

"It can be anywhere from nine to three," he says and I sit back on the bench, my hands clenching by my sides.

I look forward at the judge sitting at the top of the

bench. A woman brings him a manila folder. "Next up on the docket," he announces and all I know is I hear her name. "Julia Williams."

Stuart stands up and the side door opens, and then I see her. She walks into court with a man holding her arm, her hands placed behind her in cuffs. Michael puts his hand across me to stop me from springing up, and my father does the same thing to Max. Max just looks down and shakes his head, but my eyes never leave her. The tightness I felt in my chest all night long gets just a touch lighter. I can even breathe a touch easier now, knowing she is there in front of me and in a matter of time she is going to be in my arms.

The man leads her to the brown table on the left, just in front of us. Stuart takes his place beside her and he leans over and tells her something, and her head nods. The judge starts reading the charges, I can't hear anything except for my breathing and heartbeat in my ears. The judge never looks up, never even sees Julia. Stuart says, "Not guilty, Your Honor." The judge looks over at the prosecutor, who for some reason I want to throat punch.

"We ask that bail be set at seventy-five thousand dollars," he says and I look up at the ceiling and I see spots of black and white.

"Bail is set for seventy-five thousand dollars," the judge mumbles as he writes something down before closing the file and taking the gavel to bang it. Stuart looks over at her and says something, and she just nods as the guard comes over and escorts her out.

"Where is she going?" I fly from my seat as my eyes

go to the door that closed on the side.

"She is going to be bailed out," Stuart explains.

"You go in there and stay with her," I say between clenched teeth and he just smirks.

"That is where I'm going, but I figured, before you got yourself held in contempt of court, I would keep you informed." He looks over at my father. "I'll see you guys outside in the waiting area."

"How long?" I ask him, bouncing on the tips of my toes.

"It depends," Stuart says and walks away before I can say anything else.

"I know that it's not the time," my father says, "and I know that you are one step from snapping and setting this whole place on fire."

"Can we not say those words in a government building?" Michael growls, looking around. "Before we all get arrested." He looks at me. "I'm going to text Jillian. Don't fuck up anything."

"Hey," my father calls me, so I look over at him. "We are all on the same side. Stuart is on her side."

"I don't know him," I say. "And he's a bit too relaxed for my taste."

"He's doing what he needs to do," Max says.

"Yeah, whatever," I reply. "All I know is that if she isn't out soon…"

"Don't finish that sentence," my father warns me. "Let's go make sure that we are there when she comes out."

I nod at him, walking from the courtroom and into

the lobby. I'm standing with Michael, leaning with my back to the wall, my forefinger tapping my leg anxiously as I wait for her. Max and my father are standing in the middle, both of them on their phones. I don't know how long we are waiting. It feels like an eternity, but then the door opens and Stuart comes out first, with her following him. I take a step toward her at the same time she looks up.

Her eyes roam the room and she spots Max first as she walks to him. In two strides, I'm by his side when I hear her voice finally. "Max," she says, looking at him, and I can see her hand shaking. Everything inside me screams for me to walk over to her, throw her over my shoulder, and take her out of here. Then she says the next words, "I'm so sorry for letting you down."

I know what she needs is everyone around her and I am just going to have to bide my time until I can take her home.

Twenty-Five

Julia

"WE SHOULD GET out there," Stuart says, as the man behind the counter hands me the bag I had on me when it all happened. "Before someone ends up in trouble."

I don't have a chance to ask him what he's talking about before he turns around, walking out of the room we just left. My head is still spinning from walking into the courtroom. I didn't look up with the fear I might see my mother and Jillian. Not sure I could have held it together if I saw them, so I kept my head down, getting up when I felt Stuart getting up. I don't even know what was said. I rub my wrists that are free again from the heavy metal handcuffs.

He pulls open the door and steps out. I take a step forward, my head down. Only when I feel the eyes on me do I look up. I'm expecting to see my mother and Jillian here waiting for me. Instead, all I can see is Max there with Matthew. I walk to him. "Max." I look up at him, and the tears well in my eyes. I hold my hands together to stop them from shaking. The lump in my throat is so big I don't even think I'll be able to breathe let alone speak. "I'm so sorry for letting you down." My voice cracks at the end and he takes me in his arms.

"Never," he says softly into my hair. "Are you okay?"

I nod my head yes, because the last thing he needs is me complaining. "We have to get you home," he states.

"I have to get you to your sister," Michael says and I look up, seeing him walking toward us with Chase behind him. "Or she's going to chew my ass." My eyes see that his eyes are red and he looks as bad as I feel.

I walk from the courthouse by the front door instead of the back door, with Max and Matthew on one side. Chase and Michael on the other side.

We stop on the sidewalk as I take another look at Max as he nods to Matthew, who gives me a side hug. "It's going to be okay," he assures me, turning and walking toward the car that is there. Max follows him and I'm about to take a step forward when Michael looks at Chase.

"Hurry up," Michael urges. "Or else you'll be the one dealing with Jillian."

He nods at him and walks away. "Are you driving me?" I ask him and he just nods his head. It takes him two steps to stop in front of me. His hand comes up and he moves the hair away from my face. "Chase." I say his name, but he just shakes his head at me and pulls me to him. I've hugged him a thousand times since we've met. But this one feels different.

"Julia," he says, and all I can do is smell him. Everything in me settles. He lets go of me and I look up at him. "How are you doing?" His eyes never leave mine. I try to be brave, I try to pretend I'm fine.

"Like I'm dying inside," I say the truth, something about his eyes feeds my soul. "I don't know if I'm going to survive this." I wipe the tear rolling down my cheek. I've cried more tears in the last week than I thought was possible. "I could be a felon." The words taste like acid in my mouth. "I can't do my job as a felon." I put my hand to my stomach as it sinks with the thought that everything could be gone.

His hand goes to my cheek, where he catches another tear rolling down my face, before he moves his hand down and slips it into mine. It's like an electric shock going through me, as his fingers link with mine. "We are going to get through this."

He turns to walk to his car with my hand in his. "We?" I question when he stops to open my door.

"Yeah, we," he repeats, stepping up to me now. "There isn't time right now." His voice comes out in almost a whisper. "But later we need to talk." He steps with his chest against mine, pulling up our joined hands and he kisses my fingers. "If I don't get you to your sister…"

"I don't know if I can do it," I admit softly, the tears coming again. "I don't know if I can face anyone."

"You did nothing wrong. Nothing, there is not one thing that you did wrong and we are going to prove it."

I swallow now, not sure I can say another word, not sure I have it in me. Instead, I look up at him. "Thank you."

Both his hands come up to touch my cheeks right before he holds my face. "There is nothing you have to thank me for," he says, almost in a whisper, and his hands still on my face make my whole body heat. He's about to say something else when his phone rings from his back pocket. He laughs now. "That's twice now we've been interrupted before I can kiss you." His thumbs move over my cheeks. "There isn't going to be a third." I don't think I have any words left for a comment like that. To be honest, I want him to promise me that kiss. Maybe even dare him. The phone stops for a second and then starts up and I have to laugh. "Do you want to get into the car?" His hands fall from my face as I get into his car. He pulls out his phone and hands it to me.

"I don't think Jillian has ever called me in my life," he says and I grab the phone. He closes the door as I answer, pressing the red button.

Chase: I'm on my way, see you when I get there.
Jillian: Okay.

He gets in and looks over at me. "That was fast." He starts the car.

"I didn't answer her." I put the phone in the middle console, turning to look out the window. "If I hear her voice, I'm going to crack, and I can't show her." He doesn't say anything to me the whole ride there. My eyes burn from being up all night, my stomach tightens from the nerves or maybe not eating. My head throbs from everything that is going on inside of it. We pull up in the driveway and I see there are only two extra cars here. "How many people are in there?"

"I have no idea." He looks over at me as he turns off the car. "I mean, it's my family."

I laugh now, trying to push away all my feelings. "Only your family would have a party for someone who just got bailed out of jail." His jaw gets tight and I take a deep breath before grabbing the handle of the car. "Here we go."

I have enough time to close the door before the front door is swung open and I see Jillian. She stands there with tears streaming down her face. She runs to me and I see that her nose and eyes are both red. "Julia," she says, throwing her arms around my neck and I hug her as she cries. I push away the tears, knowing that if she sees me in tears, it'll be worse for her.

"I'm okay." I rub her back. "I'm okay." I look over her shoulder seeing Michael there, and if I know him the way I know him, he's freaking the fuck out. He's a tough guy to his core but if he sees Jillian crying, it's his kryptonite.

"We should get inside," Chase says softly from beside me and I feel his hand on the base of my back.

"You're a jerk." Jillian lets me go to snap at Chase, who just looks at her. "What took you so long?"

"We literally came right over," I say, laughing as Chase shakes his head.

"Can we get some food into her?" Max yells from the door. "She hasn't eaten all day."

Jillian puts her hand in mine as she pulls me away from Chase. I look over my shoulder at him, wondering if he is going to follow me in or just leave. "Are you okay?" Jillian asks, and I turn to look at her.

"I'm fine." I pretend and I know that even if I say I'm okay, she probably feels what I feel. It's the strangest thing with us.

"It's not fine," she mumbles when I walk into the house seeing Allison there with Dylan and Alex.

"There she is," Allison says, coming to me and hugging me. I feel her tears fall onto my shirt.

"Guys," I say, putting my bravest face forward. "I'm fine." I look at everyone. "Look, no bullet holes."

"She's in shock," Alex concludes and I can't help but laugh as Allison lets me go and pulls me toward the food they had catered. There is enough food to feed fifty people. "We ordered all your favorites," Alex says softly from beside me.

"Not you, too," I whine when I see she has tears running down her face. "I expected better from you." I point at her and she laughs. "Especially you."

"I know," she huffs outs, "I'm blaming the hormones." She throws up her hands and then I look at her shirt.

"You're leaking." I point at the round wet spots. She gave birth two months ago to their second son, James.

"Eeww," Michael says from behind me. "Get away from the food."

"Shut up," Alex tells him. "It's natural. I need to borrow a top, Jillian." She turns and walks from the room toward the bedroom.

I grab a plate of food and start to bide my time. Sitting at the table, no one sits with me but Jillian and I know they are probably giving the two of us our time alone. "Where is Mom?" I ask while I cut my piece of chicken.

"I didn't tell her," Jillian replies, her eyes down on her plate. "I didn't know what to say."

"True that," I say. "You could have just gone with, 'Mom, I better be your favorite because Julia is in the pen.'"

"Stop," Jillian says in her mom voice. "Stop pretending you are okay."

"I'm not okay," I admit to her, "but there is nothing we can do." She glares at me because there is nothing we both hate more than that saying. "I'm going to go see Mom tomorrow." I look over at her.

"I'll come with you," she offers. "We can get a cake."

"We can just write it on the cake," I joke with her as I move the food around my plate. "You look like shit, by the way." She looks up at me with her mouth open. "I have an excuse. I was in lockup."

"I stayed up the whole night," she tells me and I know she did. "I couldn't even fathom."

I reach out my hand to her, putting it over hers. "I'm okay."

"At least I didn't sit on a steel bench all night long." She looks over at Chase, who is sitting at the counter.

"What are you talking about?" I ask her.

"He stayed at the station all night," she shares, and my head snaps back to look at him. Seeing that he's wearing exactly what he was wearing last night and I didn't even notice. "He wouldn't leave if you were there, so he sat there all night."

"What?" I ask, even though I heard what she said.

"Him and Matthew." I turn back to her. "Chase wouldn't leave you and Matthew wouldn't leave him."

"All night?" I ask her and she nods her head.

"I think he threatened your lawyer also." My head spins with all this new information. "But Michael could have been exaggerating." Her voice trails off.

"But," I mumble, "why?" I don't know if I'm asking her the question or if I even want to know the answer, but I know that I'm going to have no choice but to ask him.

Twenty-Six

Chase

I SIT AT the counter, eating my food, with my eyes on Julia. We left her and Jillian alone to have their time, but there was no way in hell I was letting her out of my sight. Fuck that shit. The minute she got out of the car; I knew that she had put on her bravest face. It's like she went into protection mode to make sure Jillian was okay before she was. She didn't shed a tear, not one fucking tear as she comforted Jillian. She's a fucking warrior.

"If you stare any harder," Michael says from beside me, "your eyes are going to turn into laser beams."

"I'm not staring." I grab the water bottle and take a sip from it. "I'm looking." I smirk. "Intently."

"It's called creepy as fuck," Dylan chimes in from the other side of me. "You need to tone it down just a touch."

"Yeah, it's not like she is going to escape you,"

Michael says. "You've already locked her in." I can't help but laugh when I look around. "I'm going to ask you this one more time." I look back at him. "Are you sure about this?" I don't bother answering with words, instead I just nod my head. "I approve."

It's then that I laugh out loud. "Good to know." I put my water bottle down while I listen to Michael and Dylan talk about the upcoming road trip.

I sit here biding my time until she is ready. I look at my watch, seeing that we've been here for over an hour. I wait for Jillian to get up, leaving her alone, before I'm out of my chair, walking to her as she sits on the couch. "Are you ready to go?" I ask her and she nods her head.

She gets up and walks over to Jillian, whispering something in her ear. Jillian looks at her and then at me. "Okay, you promise you are going to call me if you need me." She nods her head smiling. I know the only way she is going to call Jillian is if she is bleeding and in dire need of a ride to the hospital, after she's already crawled halfway there.

We walk from the house side by side, my hand automatically grabbing hers as if we've always done it. I open the door for her, and when I get in, the only thing I ask her is, "My place or yours?"

"Mine is closer." She looks at me and I just nod at her. Neither of us says anything as I drive toward her house. I park across the street from where I was yesterday, just so she doesn't have to replay the scene in her head. We wait for the cars to pass before walking across the street. My hand slides into hers as we walk up the stairs to her apartment. She takes her keys out of her purse and I can see her hand shaking. She walks into her apartment and the light from outside is coming through the patio door.

I close the door behind me, and when I do, she snaps. She squats down in front of me and finally lets it out. The sob rips through her as she puts her hand to her mouth. I walk in front of her and squat down in front of her. I wrap my arm around her waist and stand with her in my arms. She wraps her legs around my waist and her arms around my neck. Burying her face in my neck as her tears seep into my skin, I walk through her house to her bedroom, going straight for her bathroom.

I look around and see that she doesn't have a bathtub. I walk over and set her down on the counter, right next to the sink, before I walk over and start the shower. She might not have a bathtub but her shower is huge with a glass door. I walk back over to her; the tears have stopped and she follows me. I push the hair away from her face. "Baby"—my voice comes out soft—"you are so strong."

"You waited for me." She looks up at me, her eyes searching mine.

"Yeah," I say, my fingertips touching her cheek and then going to her chin.

"Why?" she asks the loaded question. The same question I'm sure every single person in my family probably wanted to ask me today, but didn't. She puts her hands on my hips as I stand in the middle of her legs. "Why did you wait there?"

"You were there," are the only words that I can come up with, the only words that matter. My heart speeds up so fast, my mouth waters with the need to taste her. My hands shake as they trace her face.

"What does that mean?" She moves her face back and forth to feel my fingers.

"We need to get you in the shower." I avoid telling her what it means, not sure she's ready for me to give her everything. Not even sure I'm ready to admit that this thing with us is what dreams are made from. That this thing between us is what the fairy tales I read to my nieces are about. That this thing between us is forever. She's my forever.

I haven't kissed her yet, and yet I know. I pick her up and place her on her feet. She never lets her eyes linger from me. I bend down and rub my nose with hers, my lips getting so close to hers I can feel her breath on me. I pull her jacket off her shoulders, letting it slide to the floor by her feet. I bend my head and kiss her shoulder softly. "All night long," I say, moving the kisses up to her neck. "I pictured you alone." I swallow the lump that forms, pushing it back down. "I felt like I was missing a piece of me." I step away from touching her to pull the silky top over her head. Throwing it at her feet next to the jacket, she stands here in her strapless black bra. My hands go to the button of her white jeans, unsnapping them, the sound of the zipper echoes in the air. The steam from the shower now fills the room. I push the pants over her hips, squatting down in front of her slowly. Stopping to kiss her hip bone softly, before rolling her pants down to her feet. "Step out," I say, and she steps from her jeans and kicks them with the other clothes. She stands in front of me in her bra and panties and I've never been more turned on in my life. My cock strains against my pants to get out to her. My hands go to her neck. "If you weren't getting bailed out today," I say, "I was going to do whatever I needed to get to you." Her mouth opens in shock. "I didn't care, the only thing I wanted was to touch you," I say, my head lowers a touch, "make sure you were okay." A little bit more. "Make you know that I wasn't going anywhere."

I can taste her kiss when she puts her hands on my hips, gripping my shirt in her hand. "I was in a daze," she tells me. "I had no idea what time it was." She moves her hands higher up on my side, the T-shirt still clutched in her hand. "No idea what was going to happen." She moves the shirt over my head and tosses it on the floor. Her fingers move up my chest, the goose bumps fill my body. "I was numb."

When her hands go to the button of my pants, I can't help but call, "Julia." Her name is like a plea on my lips. She ignores me, my eyes watching her hands unbutton my pants. A little hiss comes from me when she turns her hand and palms my cock as she pulls the zipper down. I feel as if my skin is on fire. Every single touch is elevated, every single movement is one more piece of me being ready to be snapped. She pushes my pants open, stepping even closer to me as she pushes the pants past my hips and they fall to the floor at my feet. I pull down my pants kicking them toward the pile. She unclips her bra, tossing it to the side as she slips from her panties. She stands in front of me totally naked.

"Tell me." She looks up at me and all I can do is look at her, speechless. I've never in my life felt this feeling. I've never in my life wanted something as much as I want to taste her. I've never in my life wanted anything more than for her to be mine. "Why did you wait for me?" My hands go to my boxers as I take them off, my cock springing free. Her eyes move from the tip of my head down to my cock where she lingers for a second. She's seen me naked before, but even she must sense that this is different.

I move even closer to her, pushing the hair away from her face, tucking it behind her ear. "Why do you think?" I ask her and bend down and rub my nose with hers. "Why do you think I waited for you?" My lips brush hers and they linger for a second. "Tell me, Julia." I move my head left and right as my lips brush hers. "Do you not know why I waited for you?" My lips hover over hers and I can see her chest moving up and down. Her tongue comes out as she licks her lips, and I swear, if I were a bomb, this is when I would go off. "Do you know what you are doing to me?"

"Chase." She says my name as her hands roam up my chest. "Show me." Her tongue comes out and slides on my lower lip. We both attack each other, my arms wrap around her waist as hers wrap around my neck. Turning, I pick her up off her feet and walk with her to the shower, our tongues fighting with each other. It's the last first kiss I will ever have, because there is no way I'll ever let her go.

Twenty-Seven

Julia

MY HEART BEATS so fast and hard in my chest, I'm surprised it's not coming out. The thumping plays in my ears louder and louder each time I touch him, or he touches me. Finding out he waited outside for me all night long did something inside me I can't even describe. I've always known that people care. I've always known I've been loved. But that, that was something no one has ever done for me.

I thought I would be strong as soon as we entered the room, thought I would just brush it off. It's as if my body knew I was now in my safe spot and my knees gave out. It wasn't the first time I let my guard down in front of him, and just like before, he carried me. Now here I am in front of him naked, with every single nerve ending in my body on high alert. I've seen him naked before, but this is so much more. His fingertips touching me, his nose rubbing with mine, his lips touching mine. It's fucking everything I thought it would be. Maybe we both knew once we crossed this line, it would be over for us. That there would never be another person. That we would have the kind of love everyone around us has. That this whole time he was the one for me and I was just too scared to push it.

"Chase," I say as my hands roam up his chest. "Show me." My tongue comes out and licks his bottom lip. I think I hold my breath for a second, my heart stops beating at that moment, right before we attack each other. His arms wrap around my waist as I slide mine around his neck, getting on my tippy-toes. Our chests press together as our tongues go around and around. He picks up me off my feet, turning and walking us to the shower, our tongues fighting with each other. It's a kiss to end all kisses. I know that if this was my last night on earth and I could have anything I could ever want, it would be this kiss.

The warm water hits my back as I arch into him and he puts me down, our lips finally letting go of each other. Neither of us says a word, even if I could talk right now, the only thing I think I would say is *kiss me*. He picks up my loofah from the built-in shelf, along with my mango bodywash. He puts a bit on the loofah and then steps to me. "I'm going to wash it away," he says softly, moving to me and kissing my neck before washing me. I close my eyes as he moves from my neck to my shoulder and down my arm. His fingers slide in with mine and the slippery soap suds. He kisses my lips so softly it's as if it didn't happen as he washes the other side of me. He turns me around so my back is to him as the water runs down my arms. He moves my hair to the side and kisses the back of my neck. He moves the loofah from one side of my neck, all the way to the base of my back before turning me around, and I feel the soap run down my legs. My fingers tingle to touch him, my nipples are tight with need. Everything inside me is waiting for him to touch me, every part of me wants to be touched by him. Kissed by him, fucked by him. My toes tingle all the way up to my core, I need one touch, one stroke, and I think it'll be game over.

He moves the loofah across the top of my chest, the warm water running over me as he moves the loofah down. My eyes watch his hand as he washes over the swell of my breasts. The loofah rubs over my nipple and all I can do is put my head back and moan. He moves the loofah to the other one, but then I feel him suck in my nipple. My eyes spring open, seeing his tongue come out and rolling around my nipple before biting it. "Chase," I moan his name as he does the same thing to the other one. My hand comes up to grab his head, running my hand into his hair. He lets go of my nipple as he looks up at me, and now it's my turn to bend my head to his lips. I slide my tongue into his mouth and I was wrong before. This is the kiss I want to be the last thing I feel on this earth. The kiss is soft, it's delicate, it's filled with desire and need. He takes his time kissing me and I follow his lead as I feel the loofah wash over my stomach and right in the middle of my legs. I open my legs more for him as the loofah rubs back and forth, if he applied even an ounce of pressure, I would probably come in his hand. I want to beg him to come back with the loofah when I feel it move to my ass. I arch my back toward him and he lets go of my lips. His eyes are so dark they look black as he moves me to the shower stream, making sure that the water washes over me. He kisses and sucks my neck for a couple of seconds before the loofah falls to my feet and he slips his hand in mine. He walks me back two steps to the bench in the corner.

"Sit," he orders, and when my ass and back hit the cold tile, I don't even shiver because I'm so hot from his touch, it's a welcome feeling. He squats down in front of me, his fingers moving down from my hip to my knee. He picks up my knee and places my foot on the step, leaving me open for him. "My mouth is watering." His finger goes to my lips as he opens me up even more. "I would die," he mumbles, "just to get one taste." I feel his breath on me right before his tongue comes out and he licks me. His tongue moves through my folds to my clit as my ass lifts from the bench. "Tastes like heaven." His tongue moves side to side on my clit before licking down and sliding into me.

"Oh, God." I'm panting at this point and all he does is look up and smirk at me.

"Chase," I remind him, before he nips my clit and then devours me. He slides two fingers into me easily because I'm dripping wet. He pulls my ass forward a bit and I look at him.

"Chase," I call his name as he looks up at me, his tongue sliding into me.

"What do you want, baby?" he says between licks.

"You, I want you." My hands come up to pinch my nipples. "Inside me." His fingers move with his tongue now.

"Are you sure?" he asks, and I'm definitely panting now.

"Yes," I hiss and he stands up in front of me. I spring forward, gripping his cock in one hand, while my mouth swallows him. The girth is so big I can't wrap my fingers around it, I bob my head three times before he takes his cock away from me. "No." I swear I sound like a toddler.

He pulls my hand up, making me stand, while he sits, pushing his long hair back, the water holding it in place. He grips his cock in his hand. "You want me inside you?" I can only nod my head. "Then come and get what you want." I walk to him, the need to sink down on him so strong, but the need to have him over me stronger. Turning, I make my way over and shut off the water before heading back to him. His hand on his cock, he jerks himself off as he watches me.

I hold out my hand to him and he slides his hand in mine, without even asking any questions. He stands up, following me out of the shower. His hand grabs the towel as he dries me off, trailing kisses over my body as he does that. My hand goes to his cock the whole time as I work him in my hand. He stops drying me for a second to slide his tongue into my mouth. The kiss is fucking perfect, everything with him is perfect. He quickly dries himself off before I turn and walk from the bathroom, putting my arm behind me. He grabs my hand as I walk to the bed with him.

I've never brought anyone into my bed. It was a space that was just for me. A space that was only mine. I put my knee on the bed and he stops me by putting his hands on my hips. His chest presses into my back. He buries his face into my neck mumbling, "You still have time to turn back."

I look over my shoulder at him, my eyes staring into his. "There is nothing I have ever wanted more"—I bring my hand up to touch his face, his scruff making my fingers itch—"than to be with you right now." *And always,* my heart and head scream at the same time.

I move over to the middle of the bed, open my legs, and hold my hand out for him. He makes his way to me, fitting perfectly in the middle of my legs. He leans down and kisses in the center of my chest, right where my heart is. He put his elbows beside my face as he leans down and kisses me.

My hands rub his back as he kisses me. I can feel him hovering over me. My hand moves to the middle of us as I take his cock in my hand and rub up and down my slit. We've barely had any foreplay and I'm already dripping. I place him at my entrance and he slides into me. I let go of his lips to moan when he's halfway in. I feel so full. "Chase." I say his name in a whisper with my eyes closed.

"I know, baby." It comes through clenched teeth. "But if I go any faster, it's going to be over before we both blink." He puts his forehead on mine as he slides all the way into me. His balls hitting my ass once he does.

"This." I arch my back, hoping to get him deeper. "Is." I don't even know what this is, all I know is I need for him to move. "Please," I say, moving my hips from side to side.

He pulls out of me to the tip of his cock before he slams into me, both of us hissing out. "You fit me like a glove," he says as he pulls out and slams back in again. Our noses touching, our lips hovering over each other as we both pant out.

"Yes," I say when he moves faster than he was before. "Right there." My legs hitch over his hips. "I can't believe this." I feel my stomach get tight and the pressure building. "Already." I close my eyes and come all over his cock.

"So fucking tight," he says, his lips brushing with mine. "Mine," he says over and over again as the orgasm rolls into another one. My hips buck up and down to meet his thrusts when he plants himself all the way in me, and I feel him get bigger inside me. "Mine," he repeats, looking into my eyes, and my pussy convulses on his cock again. I don't have to say I'm his, because my body is telling him. I bring my hands to his face, holding it in my palms as I kiss his lips softly. His eyes close for a second before he falls on top of me. My legs and arms wrap him up as he turns us to the side and then he's on his back. I'm on top of him now, his cock still buried into me. Instead of getting up and off him, I sit up straight.

His cock is still hard in me. His hands go to my hips

as he smiles at me, my stomach flips for a whole different reason. A reason that I knew before, but now it's clear as day. I'm in love with Chase Grant. I've been in love with him this whole time, I was just pushing it aside. "What are you thinking about?" he asks as he lifts my hips off him before bringing them back down.

"I'm thinking about all the ways that we're going to have sex tonight," I lie to him, lifting myself off him before going down. I lean back as his hands go straight to my tits and he rolls my nipples between his fingers before pinching and then pulling. "Do that again," I say, my eyes closing halfway. He does it again and I come on his cock. "That's like four in five minutes," I joke with him.

He sits up, wrapping his hands around my waist. "I think we can do better," he declares, flipping me on my stomach and we do a lot better.

Twenty-Eight

Chase

THE ALARM RINGS softly from the side table. "That fucking thing." I hear her groan from beside me, and I can't help but laugh as I reach over to shut it off. I roll back to her, bringing her naked body to me. She wiggles her ass over my rock-hard cock. "I hate that fucking thing."

I laugh, burying my face into her neck. "I hope you are talking about the alarm and not my cock." I kiss her as one of my hands holds her tit in it and the other runs through her slit and into her.

"No," she pants out, "your cock is my new best friend." I finger her a couple of times to make sure she's wet for me. She tosses the blankets off us now, my hand lifting her leg as her hand finds my cock and places it where she wants it. I slide into her in one long thrust.

Fuck, every single time her pussy grabs my cock, and never lets it go, I could stay buried in her forever. "Yes," she pants as my hips move faster, her hand moving to her clit. "I'm so close."

"It's been one second," I say, laughing.

"I can't help it." She moves her hand even faster between her legs and I know she's almost there. "Your cock." She kisses my lips. "Is magic." She closes her eyes and moans out her release. I wish I could say I lasted longer, but I don't. The minute her pussy squeezes my dick like a vise, my balls get tight and I am right there with her. I let her leg go as it falls on top of mine. "If this happens every single time your alarm wakes me up…" I slip out of her when she turns around. "Then we should set that thing every hour."

I get out of bed looking down at her, my cock at half-mast. "We did do that every hour," I remind her and she rolls her eyes and shakes her head.

"No, we didn't." She gets up on her elbow and my cock goes from half-mast to full-on ready for her again. I've never, ever had sex like this. "We had three rounds the first time." She holds up her three fingers.

"Then we had a round in the kitchen." I hold up a finger.

"Oh, yeah." She smirks. "How could I forget? I've never been pounded while having my head in the fridge." I try not to laugh. I couldn't help it, she bent over and I was either going to eat her out or fuck her. My cock got first dibs.

"You bent over," I counter, "and your pussy winked

at me."

"Then you got me on the couch." She sticks one more finger up.

"That was your fault. You walked over to me, threw your leg over my hips, and sank down on my cock."

"You buried your face between my legs," she huffs, getting out of bed on her side.

"After you swallowed my cock." It's my turn now.

"Well, he looked sad," she says, walking to me. "So I wanted to make him happy." She walks past me and I slap her ass. She looks over her shoulder. "Don't tease me like that."

"When we have time," I say, "I'm going to turn that ass pink." Her eyes light up. "And you're going to beg me for it."

"Promise?" She holds up her hands and crosses her fingers and all I can do is shake my head. I follow her in the bathroom, watching her walk over and start the shower.

"What are you doing?" I ask her as she makes sure the water is warm.

"I'm going to see my mother today." She smiles. "I'm going to wash the smell of sex off myself." I take a step toward her and she holds up her hand. "What are you doing?"

"I'm going to shower with you," I inform her and she shakes her head.

I laugh. "This isn't how this works." I step beside her as she looks up at me, her mouth hanging open. "If you're in the shower, I'm in the shower."

"If you are in the shower," she says as I step even closer to her, "then it's going to be a long shower."

"We have to make it fast," I say, wrapping my arms around her. "I have to go home and pack." I hate I have to leave today.

"Nothing about you and sex is fast." She turns around, putting her head back. "The only fast thing is the way I orgasm over and over again." Her ass moves side to side on my cock, and she was right, it is not a fast shower at all. It is a very long one that ends with both of us rinsing off in cold water.

I step out of the shower before her, grabbing the towel and wrapping it around my waist. When she steps from the shower, I hand her a cup of coffee while I walk into the bedroom and get dressed. "How long are you gone for?" she shouts.

"Three days," I huff, finally finding my boxers and putting them on. "I have to go home and pack."

"What time do you leave?" She stands in the doorway wearing her bra and panties, with her hair wrapped in a white towel. I've had her over and over again and the need to have her again is fucking real. I open my legs, and she walks between them. I put my hands on her hips, leaning in and kissing her stomach.

"I have to be at the airport in an hour." I look up at her and she bends to kiss my lips. It feels like we've been together our whole lives, and in a way we have. She walks me to the door and her kisses leave me wanting so much more. "I'll call you tonight." I kiss her on the tip of her nose before I walk out of her apartment.

I rush and get to the airport with ten minutes to spare. I walk up the steps to the plane and spot Cooper sitting by himself. He is on his phone, and when I sit next to him, he looks over at me. "There he is." He smirks at me.

I ignore the smirk, putting my seat belt on as Dylan and Michael get on the plane at the same time. "Nice of you to join us," Cooper tells them and they just glare.

"It was Wilson's turn to get us," Michael huffs out as Wilson comes onto the plane calm, cool, and collected.

"And was late," Dylan cuts in, shaking his head.

"It's not my fault." Wilson holds up his hands. "Franny, she was, you know."

"Don't finish that sentence." I point at him.

"I'm going to throw up," Cooper says from beside me. "You know there is such a thing as too much sex."

My eyebrows pinch together and I shake my head. "There is not," Dylan says and Michael punches him in the arm.

"That's my sister," Michael hisses out.

"Also my wife and mother of my kids, so I think I trump you," Dylan goads, opening the shade and looking out.

"See what you started?" I mumble to Wilson as he sits in front of us.

The door of the plane closes and no one says anything when we take off. "So what's going on with you?" Cooper quizzes, and I just look over at him.

"You could maybe try to be a little bit more, I don't know, smooth in trying to get information." I laugh, shaking my head.

"What? I spoke with Dad, he said I should talk to you." I raise my eyebrows. "And then I spoke to Dylan." He points at Dylan, who has his head back and is sleeping. "He said you were busssh." He motions to his ears like they are exploding. "Then I spoke to that one." He points at Michael, who is also sleeping. "And he said you were like booom." He motions with his hands at my head exploding.

"We're going to be fine," I say, trying to convince myself also.

"Oh, there is a we." He turns to put his back against the wall of the plane.

"There is a we," I confirm to him. "Definitely a fucking we." I look down at my hands. "I don't even know when it happened but it did, and it's fucking great." I look at him now. "It's always been her."

He smiles at me. "You two have been thick as thieves since forever." I nod my head. "It was bound to happen." He doesn't say anything else to me nor do I to him.

After we check into the hotel, I fall onto the bed, and instead of calling, I FaceTime her. Wondering if it's going to be weird between us since we took our relationship to the next level.

She picks up after two rings. "Hello," she greets and the smile that fills my face when I see her on the screen is huge.

"Hi," I say softly, wishing I was with her. "I miss you. How was your day?"

She takes a deep breath in. "Well, I broke the news to my mother that her daughter is a jailbird." She laughs and I know it still hurts her.

"Was she okay?" I want to kick myself for not being there.

"She took it a lot better than I thought she would have." She smiles slyly. "I took Max with me and he was raging at the charges, so she didn't want to upset him more."

I throw my head back and I can't help but laugh. "You are just full of surprises."

She looks into the phone. "After last night, there is nothing that is a surprise anymore."

"Well, there could be one more surprise," I say and she looks at me confused. "We didn't use protection."

"Oh, that." She throws her head back and laughs. "I'm on the pill." She looks at me. "I've never been without one. So I'm clean."

"Same," I say and she rolls her eyes.

"You don't have to say same because I said it," she huffs. "It's whatever."

"It's not whatever," I say tightly. "Why would I lie about it?"

"I don't know. Also, I now know why I have never had sex in my apartment before." She shakes her head. "It smelled like a brothel in here today." I laugh now. "Thank God I didn't invite Max in." I can't help but laugh at her and all the doubt I had about it being weird between us is put to rest.

Twenty-Nine

Julia

"WE SHOULD DO this more often," Erika says from beside me. I look up seeing all the girls who have gathered in Jillian's house. The guys are on the road, so the grandparents are in town to take over babysitting duty. They literally live for this shit.

Franny showed up with four bottles of wine, which means we are probably all going to sleep here. Vivienne shocked the shit out of me when she walked in after Franny. She lives in New York, and if she comes to visit, it's usually for the weekend and not the middle of the week. Erika showed up with three bags of food. Alex showed up with two boxes of doughnuts and a box of specialty cookies.

We are all in the family room, the coffee table is filled with food. The bottles of wine are being passed around.

Franny and Vivienne sit on the floor with their backs to the couch. Erika, Jillian, Alex, and myself are all spaced out on the massive U-shaped couch.

My phone buzzes in my hand and I look down and see it's a text from Chase. I can't help the smile that fills my face.

Chase: I miss you.

"Who just texted you?" Vivienne asks from in front of me, looking over her shoulder at me.

"Um, no one," I say, trying to ignore the stares I'm getting. My hands start to sweat with nerves. It's one thing telling my sister we banged like bunny rabbits, but it's a whole different ball game with all of his female relatives. Especially his two sisters and sister-in-law.

"So you smiled like you just won the lottery for no one?" Franny rolls her eyes at me.

"Okay, fine," I say, throwing my hands up. "It's Chase!" I take the time to look at each woman in their eyes.

"Why do you sound like you're one second away from a freak-out?" Alex laughs at me.

"Because I think I am," I admit to them and Jillian sits up on the couch. I can already hear the wheels turning in her brain.

"I told you it was a bad idea." She points at me, her eyes glaring at me, her jaw clenched tight. "I literally said, you can't do that."

"I know," I huff out. "But I did and oh my God. The sex was the best I've ever had in my whole life." I shake my head. "Like over and over again he can make me orgasm in two minutes flat. Maybe even less. I mean, he has it all, oh my God."

"High five," Erika says, holding up her hand from the other end of the couch. "Cooper is that good, he just…" She sighs and smiles. "There was this one time we were on the…" She brings her glass of wine to her lips.

"Um," Franny says, raising her hand. "Can we not go into that much detail?"

I look at her shocked. "This coming from you, who wanted to draw us a diagram of Wilson's dick?"

"That is different, we aren't related to him. Please, for the love of God," Vivienne pleads, grabbing a wine bottle and just drinking straight from the top. "I've seen my brother's dick far too many times as an adult to count, and I don't think I can stand to picture it anymore."

"Yeah," Franny says, "and by the way, my picture wouldn't do it justice." She grabs her phone and we all yell NO! "I don't have that picture on my phone." She snickers. "That's a lie, I have a whole album of it," she declares proudly. "I'm just sending him a text to let him know I love his cock and all the things he does with it."

"He's on the ice," Vivienne says, pointing at the screen where they show him sitting on the bench next to Dylan. "I think he's a bit busy."

"Nah." She shakes her head. "He loves getting these texts. Gets him worked up and then when he comes home—"

"Can we focus on what Julia is going to say?" Jillian says over all the other side conversations. "I can herd kindergarten children easier than you guys."

"Yes, let's focus on Julia and the fact she banged my brother-in-law," Erika agrees, while she fake vomits.

"I'm going through hell right now," I finally say, my voice going low and the girls all look at me. Alex gets up from her side of the couch and comes to me, sitting next to me and holding my hand. "Like literally, I have all this shit going on and is it fair of me to drag him into all of this?"

The look on each face is indescribable, right before they all burst out laughing. "Like he's going to let you have a say in any of this," Erika says and it's my turn to look at her shocked. "I tried to leave Cooper twice." She holds up two fingers. "Now we have a million kids." I laugh at her.

"I tried to leave Michael." I look over at Jillian, my eyebrows pinch together.

"He knocked you up." Alex gasps. "You thought he was letting you go with half of him inside you?"

"What about you?" Jillian looks at Alex and laughs. "You left on a plane away from Dylan, how did that work out for you?"

"Amazing," Alex replies. "Thanks for asking."

"I didn't know exactly how dysfunctional this family actually was," Vivienne says, "until right now."

"You know better than that." Franny looks at me. "If he's in. He's in for life."

"I'm Cooper's second wife," Erika says.

"Yeah, we don't know what happened with him," Alex says. "Uncle Matthew is never going to live that down, just like my father is never going to live down he 'stole' my mother."

I put my hand on my stomach. "Listen, there is no amount of shooing him away that is going to work."

"Yeah," Vivienne says, "it's like a fruit fly. No matter how many times you slap it away, it always comes back."

I don't say anything else because someone scores and the talk turns to something else. Leaving me with my own thoughts. When he calls me later that night, he senses that something is off. "What's with you tonight?"

"We need to talk when you get home," I say, not even sure what we need to talk about but there are things that need to be said.

"Sounds good," he says and doesn't even pry to know what I want to talk about.

"That's it?" I ask him and he laughs.

"Well, I'm assuming if you wanted to tell me what it was, you would have just said it, instead of doing the whole secret thing." I can't help but close my eyes. "Besides, I get to see you and kiss the shit out of you."

The next day, I want to say I'm not waiting for the knock on the door but I'd be fucking lying. I wait for him while I sit on the couch, checking the time on the phone every ten seconds because it feels like it's been an hour. When I do hear the knock, I fly off the couch and run to the door. Opening the lock, I try to remain unfazed by him, but I fail miserably. He's wearing jeans and a black polo shirt. His hair is pushed back on one side while the other side hangs loose. His scruff is a bit longer than it was the last time and my fingers tingle to touch it.

The only thing I know is I smile and jump into his

arms. He catches me around my waist. "Hi," I greet him, wrapping my arms around his neck. He walks us into my apartment, kicking the door closed with his foot.

"Hi." He smiles and my head slowly moves down to kiss his lips. The butterflies already going nuts in my stomach. His eyes light up to a clear blue, and it's the last thing I see before I close my eyes and slide my tongue into his mouth. He moves to the couch, sitting down, and I straddle him. His cock strains through his pants and I can't help but grind on it.

I put my forehead on his when I let go of his lips. My hands leave from around his neck to touch his face. "Hi," I say softly as I kiss his lips again.

"Hi." His hands go to my ass as he pushes me more onto him. "We should get this talk over with," he suggests, rubbing his nose with mine.

"I should get off you, then." I say the words but nothing in me even makes an attempt to get up.

"No." He shakes his head. "I haven't touched you in three days." He kisses my jaw. "So you stay here."

"I can't really think when I have your hands on me." I've never been this honest before, usually I just skate around the subject, but with him, it's a whole different ball game. I don't even know if I'm in the game. "What is this?"

"You are going to have to be a little bit more detailed than that." He laughs and I sit up, my hands falling to his chest. I feel his heart beating under my right hand, and it's beating as fast as my heart is.

"Like, this me-and-you thing." When the words come

out of me, I want to take them back. "God, that sounds so needy." I try to make a joke out of it. "Obviously, it's not anything. We've been on like two dates. I mean, technically, I don't think we've been on any dates."

"We've been on more than two dates," he says, his hands moving to my legs as he rubs them up and down. "It's been over six years, surely it's more than two."

I roll my eyes. "Those didn't count."

"Okay, fine, so let's go on dates," he says without skipping a beat.

"Just like that?" I ask him and he smiles.

"Just like that," he repeats like it's not a big deal. He sits up a bit to kiss me. "It's that easy."

"It's really not that easy," I reply softly and he leans in and kisses my neck.

"Why can't it be that easy?" he asks, right before he nips my neck and I move my neck to give him better access.

"Because it's," I start to say but he moves up to my ear, sucking in the lobe and my head falls forward.

"I like you," he whispers in my ear, "a lot." His hands move up my legs to my hips. "You make me laugh." His nose lightly rubs my cheek right before he kisses me. "You make me crazy." I laugh at that one. "We like the same things." I don't even know what to say to that. "I especially like having sex with you."

I laugh at that one. "I like that also," I agree as his hand goes under my shirt, where he finds me without a bra.

"Is that what you had to talk to me about?" he asks as

his fingers roll my nipples at the same time. "Us dating?"

"Yes." I arch my back and he bends to take my nipple into his mouth through the shirt. The wet cotton sticking to my nipple.

"I would like to also say," he says, moving to my other nipple as he wets it also, "when I'm gone for more than a day, you wear a dress." His hips thrust up. "So I can slide into you easily."

I smirk at him. "Duly noted," I say and here in the middle of my living room, we decide we are officially dating.

Thirty

Chase

I SLAM THE door behind me when the phone rings in my hand. I look down and see it's Julia. "Hey there, beautiful," I answer and she laughs.

"Did you just send me flowers?" She laughs into the phone and just the sound of her laughing makes me smile.

"Who else would be sending you flowers?" I ask her and she laughs even harder.

"Sorry, scratch that, did you just send me the biggest flower arrangement I've ever had?" I can hear her sniffing. "I tried to count how many roses this is."

"It's five dozen," I answer her and she gasps.

"One for every orgasm you gave me," I joke and she howls in laughter.

"Don't expect me to send you any flowers, then," she

says, and it's my turn to laugh.

"Where are you?" I ask her, knowing she was going to call the lawyer to set up a meeting.

"Well, I'm unemployed, so I'm home," she replies, and even though her voice is light, I can tell there is a sadness there.

"Do you want to come over to my house?" I ask her, walking into the kitchen. "Actually, just come over."

"You went from asking me to telling me?" I can hear her moving on her end. "Typical Grant-slash-Stone-slash-Horton move."

"I'll make dinner, we can eat." I open the fridge. "And then we can—"

"Have sex," she cuts in. "I mean, I have to thank you for the flowers."

"In that case, pack a bag," I tease her. "I don't have work until tomorrow night."

"I saw you this morning," she reminds me. "And yesterday and the day before that and the day before that."

"Those days don't count and the one in there before, before really doesn't count because," I say. "It was half a day."

"Okay, fine," she huffs, "twist a girl's arm. Should I bring dessert?"

"I'm assuming you are coming with your sweet ass." She gasps. "Dessert is sorted, then."

"Goodbye, Chase," she says and she doesn't hang up. "See you soon." Then she hangs up. I put my phone on the counter, shaking my head. When she told me we needed to talk while I was on the road, I was shocked it took her two days. I full-on expected her to do it five hours after I left. I thought for sure she would tell me it was a mistake. There was nothing she could have said that would have stopped anything between us.

I grab some vegetables, putting them in a pan to roast. I coat them in oil and then salt before adding them to the oven. I turn the oven on and then walk to the bedroom, going straight to the bathroom to take a shower. When I step out, I slip on my black jogging pants and I hear the knock on the door. I run my hand through my hair, pushing it back away from my face. I open the door and see her standing there holding a bag in one hand and wearing her black coat tied at the waist. "Hi." I open the door wider to let her in. "Come in."

She walks in and stops in front of me, going on her tippy-toes. "Hi." I bend to kiss her lips. "Should I put my bag in your room?"

"Um, yes."

I smile at her as she walks around me and looks over her shoulder. "Are you not going to show me where to put it?" That look means she's up to something, so I follow her. "Should I put it in the closet?"

"You can put it anywhere you want." I stand in the middle of the room. She nods her head and walks over to the chair in the corner, putting it next to it. "I'll leave my jacket in here also." She unties the knot and the jacket falls open at the same time my mouth waters. She slips it off her shoulders, tossing it on the chair. She stands there in a little white top with spaghetti straps that is completely see-through. Her perfect tits with pebbled nipples asking me to bite them. My eyes roam down to her panties that again leave nothing to the imagination. I can see everything. "I hope you don't mind, I thought I would wear my pjs over." She walks over to me and my cock is screaming to come out. She turns around when she is in front of me. "You like the back?" She looks up at me smiling, knowing that I love the fucking outfit. Her hand goes to my face, then slides into my hair at the back of my neck, as I lean down and kiss her. My tongue slides into her hot mouth while my hands go to her hips to pull her into my cock. The little minx bends forward a bit and I snap. I pick her up and toss her on my bed, her laugh filling the room. But all I can see is the wet mark on her see-through panties when she spreads her legs for me.

I crawl on the bed with her and attack her mouth. We both need more than that. My tongue fits with hers as I hold her hands by her head for a second, before she moves and turns me to my back. She kisses my lips before moving down to my neck, sucking in my nipple right before biting it, making me hiss. Her tongue comes out as she trails it all the way to my pants. She kneels in the middle of my legs, her mouth sucking my covered cock, my hips thrusting up on reflex. She palms my cock, then moves frantically to pull my pants down, my feet helping kick them off, and she tosses them over her shoulder. "Looks like I get to have dessert first." She holds my cock in one hand as she licks the precum off it. "I win," she says right before she takes me into her mouth.

I want to say I'm the one winning but all I can do is close my eyes. She bobs up and down twice before trying to take it all down her throat, stopping three-quarters of the way down, her hand moving with her mouth. She looks up at me as she licks up my shaft, taking the head into her mouth again. She jerks my cock in her hand, sitting up, my head bends to kiss her, she slides her tongue into my mouth, her hand still moving up and down on my cock. She lets go of the kiss, but my hands come up and hold her face while I kiss her again. Her tits hanging right on top of my cock, she moves my cock left and right against her nipples. While I swallow down the moan that comes out of her mouth. Her tits slip from her flimsy top as she puts my cock between her tits, my hips now moving. She pushes her tits together making it tighter, my cock moving up and down. She frantically lets my mouth, leaning down to swallow my cock again. "Have I told you I love your cock?" she asks right before she takes it into her mouth. I sit up, moving her hair to the side so I can watch her suck my cock.

"Come here," I finally say, pulling her up and off my cock before I come in her mouth. She crawls up to me and now her tits are out of the shirt. With one pull, it's in two pieces in my hands. I suck the nipple that was teasing me into my mouth, biting down on it harder than I ever have. She hisses out and rubs her pussy up and down my cock. The wetness coming through her panties, my hand goes to her hip as I tear them away from her.

"You just ruined a perfectly good pair of pjs." She sits up on my cock as she moves to get it inside her, but I'm not ready yet.

"No," I say and she looks at me. "I haven't played with my pussy yet."

"Your pussy?" she asks, and all I do is push her down on the bed, her legs opening wide for me.

I grab her legs, pulling her closer to me, opening them up even wider. "Yeah, mine," I mumble, right before I suck her pussy into my mouth.

She moans when my tongue slides into her, "Fuck." I lick up to her clit, sucking before moving back to look at her pussy glistening. I take my forefinger and slide it from her clit to her pussy, slipping the tip in before going back up to her clit, pressing on it before going back down. I open one lip, my tongue coming out to fuck her with it. I eat her pussy as if it's my last meal. Her hips bucking up and down, her hands behind her head grabbing on to the pillow. I slip two fingers into her with my tongue. "More," she pants out. "Please more." I get up on my elbow looking down at her. My finger moving faster and faster in her pussy. Her moans are starting to get louder and louder. "Oh my God." She gets up on her elbows to watch me finger-fuck her. I slow down for a second, looking into her eyes as I turn my hand the other way, my fingers rubbing over her G-spot. She yells out when I touch it and I know it's a matter of time until she is over the edge. I move my fingers even faster. Moving my other hand to my mouth, I put my thumb in my mouth wetting it. I see her eyes get a touch darker, like if she knows what's going to happen. "Yes," she says, right before I slide my thumb in her ass. Her head falls back as my fingers assault her. My hand's moving so fast she yells louder and louder, her hand coming down as she rubs her clit around and around faster and faster. My fingers feel like they are being strangled. "I'm going to—" She doesn't say anything else because I feel her juices run down my hands. "I can't." She looks down at my hand, seeing it fuck her, as her juices keep coming out. I suck her clit into my mouth until she stops coming. I look up when her spasms stop, seeing her lying on the bed, her arms stretched out beside her. "What was that?" she asks.

"That was me having my dessert." I kiss her hip.

"I never came as hard as I did right now. I felt like it was pouring out of me."

"It was." I turn her onto her stomach and grab her hips. "The bed is soaked," I say and she looks over her shoulder at me; the question in her eyes. "I'll get to your ass later. I'm not going to last long," I admit, rubbing my cock up and down her slit before sliding into her. "Not after that." I slam into her. Her head falls down in front of her. "That was the hottest thing I have ever seen." I have to hold on to her hips even harder as I slam into her. Her pussy is even tighter than it was before. I slow down for a second, my thumb rubbing up and down her ass before sliding in.

She looks over her shoulder. "Don't tease me like that." I smirk at her as I fuck her pussy with my cock and fuck her ass with my thumb. "Chase," she hisses out.

"What do you want?" I ask her as I plow into her over and over again. Her eyes start to close when I know she's about to come again. "Tell me and I'll give you whatever you want."

"I don't know what I want. It's like every single touch lights me on fire."

I slap her ass hard. "Tell me what you want." She moans when I slap and thrust into her hard.

"I don't know," she moans, and it's almost a cry. "I need to come." I can feel it but I'm not ready.

"You came," I say, slowing down my thrusts, "not too long ago."

"I need to do it again," she says, trying to push back. I slide out of her and she moans in frustration, "No!"

"Get on your back," I say and my hand jerks my cock slowly. She opens her legs for me. "Tilt your hips back." I don't have to say anything twice. I rub my cock up and down her dripping wet slit and she is waiting for me to slam into her, but instead I move my cock down just a touch and push in a bit. "This what you want?" I ask her as she pulls her legs back even more. "If you don't tell me, I'm not going to move."

"Yes," she cries out, "fuck my ass." I smile at her as I slide in slowly. "Slowly," she tells me. "I've never." I stop moving, my cock halfway in her ass. "Don't you dare," she warns me and all I can do is look down.

I move my hand to her clit, stroking it in circles. "Take my place," I say, and she moves her hand to take over for me. While I slide two fingers into her pussy, my cock finally fills her. I don't move because the minute I do, it's going to be over. I've never felt more fucking tight in my life. Everything with her is on a whole different level, and I mean everything. "I'm going to move." She nods her head and I move my cock out and then back in again. Slow thrusts at first, my fingers working faster than my cock.

"Chase," she calls my name and I know why; I've hit her G-spot again. "It's there again."

"What is?" I ask her, going faster. My hips pulling out more and then slamming in again, my balls get tight and I come in her ass and she has no idea. It's all about her.

"The pressure," she says and I lick my lips, knowing what is going to come. "I don't," she says. "It's coming." I can hear the sloshing sounds when it starts to happen, my fingers curl up at once. She thrashes her hips up, and I pull my cock and my fingers from her at the same time I bury my face into her.

Thirty-One

Julia

I OPEN MY eyes but I see spots of white and black. My chest is heaving up and down as if I just sprinted a 5K marathon. "I think I'm dying. You fucked me dead." I open my eyes again and look over at Chase, who is on his back beside me. I smell the air. "Or I'm having a stroke." I've had some good sex in my life. I'll even admit that the good sex I've had was nothing compared to the sex we've just had. I mean, even before today he was number one on that list.

"You are not dying nor are you having a stroke." Chase doesn't move either, his head turns to look at me.

"Well, they say when you smell burning, you are having a stroke," I huff, taking another sniff of the air. "Do you not smell that?" I look over at him and see his eyes go big. "Or is it just me?"

"Oh, fuck." He rolls off the bed and runs from the room. I lift my head and I want to follow him but nothing on my body is moving. "Fuck, fuck, fuck." I hear him from the kitchen. The sound of crashing is next, followed by the sound of water being turned on and then a sizzle.

"Should I call 9-1-1?" I yell, but all he does is laugh. I hear his footsteps coming closer to the bedroom and then he enters. Naked in all his glory.

"Dinner is burned," he informs me and I laugh. "I forgot all about the vegetables I put in to roast." He shakes his head. "They are past the point of roasted and are officially charred."

"Can you get me my phone?" I ask him and he just looks at me. "It's in my jacket pocket." I point over to the chair that has my jacket on it.

"You can order food later," he tells me, walking to the chair.

"I'm not ordering food," I scoff at him, looking down at my naked body. "I want to text Erika to ask her if Cooper ever did what you just did." He stops moving, looking over at me, not sure if I'm joking or not. "Then I have to text Jillian about what just happened." I point at the bed area where we just had mind-blowing sex. "I should also text Vivienne and say she lied about anal." I shake my head. "Then I have to text Franny, because I feel like she, out of everyone, is going to understand this moment. Do you know she sexts Wilson when he's on the ice?"

He just stares at me with his mouth open, holding up his hand to stop me from talking. "One, I never want to hear sexting and any of my family members after it." He closes his eyes. "And two, can we not text any of the women in my family and tell them about the sex we just had?"

I roll my eyes. "All of a sudden he's shy." I get off the bed, standing for a second to make sure my legs can support me. "You are naked at every single family vacation."

He puts his hands on his hips, but my eyes go straight to his cock that is at half-mast. "It was one time and I was up watching the sunrise. How was I supposed to know the family would be gathering on the beach?" I roll my lips, walking over to him and look up at him. Fuck, he's sexy. Everything about him is sexy, from the soft curls in his hair to the way his scruff fills his face. From his blue eyes and plump lips, everything is sexy. Fuck, even his clavicle is sexy.

"It was not one time." I kiss his neck. "I think it was like five." I kiss him again.

"That other time, Vivienne said she bought me a swimsuit and it dissolved in the water. How is that my fault?" He bends to kiss my nose. "Now, are we taking a shower before we order or what?" He turns to walk to the shower, his pinky linked with mine as I move with him.

"Shower would be nice," I admit as I walk with him to the bathroom, stopping when I see the condition of the bed. The spot in the middle of it looks like I wet the bed. "We need to change the sheets." I smirk at him as I watch his ass walk away. "Also, there is no way I cannot tell people about what just happened." I throw up my hands.

"I mean, people might be able to tell."

"Julia." He says my name while chuckling.

"Chase." I walk into the bathroom and look in the mirror. "It shows all over my face I just had the best sex of my life." My cheeks are tinted pink, my hair is out of control. I have little red dots on my breasts and stomach from his scruff.

"You look just as beautiful as you did that first day." He stands behind me and puts his hands on my hips. "Shall we take a bath?" My eyes light up at that suggestion. "Bath it is."

"Are you coming to the game tonight?" Chase asks as we sit on the couch the morning after, having coffee while watching the news. Sitting beside him on the couch with my legs draped over his, Chase's hands across my legs while I'm in his T-shirt and he's in boxers. We spent the whole night together. Being with him is starting to feel like I've always been with him. Even when I woke up this morning in his arms again, it was like I've been doing it for all my life, instead of just a week.

"It's Saturday night," I remind him. "I haven't missed a Saturday night game since your cousin knocked up my sister." I roll my lips laughing.

"You aren't wearing a Horton shirt," he tells me and I just look over at him.

"Is that so?" I ask him and he leans forward to put his cup down on the coffee table, then reaches for mine, putting it next to his. He turns toward me now and my legs open in front of him as he lies on top of me.

"I believe that you said you were mine." I roll my eyes when he says that.

"I was two seconds away from an orgasm," I lie between my teeth. In all honesty, I was close to an orgasm but I was also his.

"Do I need to remind you?" He kisses my lips softly.

"Yes," I say and we both laugh. He pulls out all the stop remind me I am in fact his, over and over again.

That night at the game I don't wear a Horton shirt, instead I wear a Grant shirt, but with a twist. I put Dr. in front of it, making everyone laugh when they see me. But nothing is better than hearing him laugh when he finally sees it after the game. We walk from the arena with my hand playing with his hand that is wrapped around my shoulder. My head is turned to look at him as he smiles at me.

"This is going to be super weird," I say as he pulls up to his parents' house for Sunday lunch.

"Why?" He turns off the car and I open my door.

"Because we are kind of together," I say, not willing to put a label on whatever this is. We decided that we are going to be dating but I'm not going to ask anything else.

"Kind of." He slides his hand with mine. "Pretty sure you waking up with my dick in your mouth is us being together," he informs me right before the front door opens and his father is standing there. My face turns red thinking he might have heard what he said. I release Chase's hand as we walk in the door.

The sound of commotion is all over the place as Maddox runs through the hallway, stopping

to side hug me and say, "Hi, Auntie Juju," before running upstairs to the playroom.

I look over my shoulder at Chase, who is talking to Matthew about something, and I walk into the house. I've never felt like I'm walking on eggshells. I also don't know why I'm so fucking nervous. I've never been nervous coming to Sunday lunch. I also have never woken up with Chase's cock in my mouth before coming to Sunday lunch. "Hey," Allison greets when she spots me holding a plate. I walk over to her and kiss her cheek. "You smell good."

"Thanks," I reply, not telling her it's Chase's bodywash mixed with my perfume. "I'm hungry."

"Go grab a plate." She points over at the food. "Jillian is outside with the girls."

I nod at her, walking over to the food. "You ran off so fast." I hear Chase from behind me.

I'm about to say something to him when I see Cooper walking our way. "I heard you were wearing my jersey last night." He stands in front of the island looking at us. "But you then defaced it with dirt."

"No." I try to play dumb. "Who told you that?"

"I walked into my daughter's room today and she was adding it to her shirt." He glares at me.

I can't help but laugh at him, not sure what to say. "What can I say?" I shrug and look back at Chase. He has his hair pushed back and the way his eyes twinkle I know he's in a great mood. "She has good taste."

"You bet your ass she does," Chase booms out, laughing right before he leans over and kisses me, just like that. I'm expecting for Cooper to say something, but instead he just pffts out before walking away.

Sunday lunch is just like it always is. No one makes any remarks of us arriving together and then leaving together. I don't even get a snide comment from Vivienne when he slides his hand into mine, pulling me from the house.

He drops me off the next day on his way to work and the whole time my head is spinning. There is so much going on in my head. When he texts me he will be done by four, I stupidly say he should come over and I'll make dinner.

I take some salmon out and then roast some veggies. I've checked them every five minutes to make sure I don't burn anything, and when he knocks at the door, I jump. Opening the door, he just smiles at me, kissing my lips when he walks in. "Smells good."

"Um, thanks," I mumble and he follows me to the kitchen. It takes him about one second before he sees that something isn't right.

"What happened to you?" he asks and my hands shake.

"I'm just really fucking nervous," I admit and put my hand on my head, wondering if maybe I'm feeling sick or getting a fever.

"Why?" he asks, leaning against my counter.

"I don't think I've ever done this whole dating thing." I shake my hands, hoping the nerves leave me. "Like, usually I start to date and then it evolves into whatever." I can't stop myself from talking. "Or always it evolves into nothing." I throw up my hands. "But with you, all the work's been done already." He just looks at me trying not to laugh at my meltdown. "So it's like I've already liked you before I even dated you."

He folds his arms over his chest and I really want him to hug me right now. "It's almost as if it's past seven months and you haven't kicked me to the curb," he jokes with me. "Come here." He motions with his head to me. I walk over to him and he opens his arms, putting them around me, my hands going to his arms. "It's me and you," he says softly. I look down, swallowing the words that really want to come out. Not sure either of us are actually ready for them.

Thirty-Two

Chase

"OKAY, WHAT DO we have here?" I say, walking into the room. Cole, one of the defense guys, is sitting on the examining table. I can see blood running down the side of his face. "Ohh, stitches." I clap my hands. "My favorite."

"Fuck, bitch," Cole says, lying down, and I see he's cut open right on his left cheek.

"High stick to the face," I assess, walking over and putting on gloves. "Ten minutes, you'll be back on the ice," I say, grabbing the needle to numb him. "This is going to pinch," I say, just before I stick the needle right into the cut. He hisses as I stitch him up. "Three stitches, hopefully, no scar." I put tape on it to hopefully stop them from tearing open, but it wouldn't be the first time.

"Thanks, Doc." He gets off the table and heads back

out, while I clean up. I'm taking off my gloves when I hear the horn telling me the game is over. I hear the men start to come down the hallway. The sticks clacking together as they are put on the wall. From the sounds of it, we lost. I look up at the television screen seeing we lost by two. I wait forty-five minutes before I stick my head into the changing room.

"Cole," I call his name and he looks up. "You good?" He nods his head. "Who needs my help?"

No one pays attention to me, so I walk to my office grabbing my jacket and keys. I take my phone out and I'm about to call Julia when Cooper walks from the changing room. His hair is wet, his white shirt unbuttoned at the collar as he carries his jacket in his hand.

"Hey," he mumbles to me.

"How bad was it out there?" I ask him and he just shakes his head.

"Montreal will never get over us taking Dylan away from them," he says and I laugh.

"You got traded by New York and they don't give a fuck," I remind him and he flips me the bird.

"The last time we were in Montreal, the whole fucking floor shook when they scored." He shakes his head. "I will play anywhere but there."

"Good to know," I reply, unlocking the door of my car. "See you tomorrow."

"Yeah, say hi to Julia." I smile and nod at him. It's been over a week since we've made our couple debut or whatever the fuck you want to call it, and it's like if you see one of us, the other will be right there.

I get into the car, my head suddenly spinning. I knew dating Julia would be a big deal. The pressure of making it work just put more stress on us. I don't even know how she feels about me, I know she likes me but we never discussed it further. Being with her is effortless. We can be sitting next to each other without saying anything and it's okay. Neither of us pushing to make a conversation. She makes me laugh like no one else. She tells me exactly what she feels and why she feels it. She is so much fun to play games with, and even though it's only been two weeks, I feel like we were pre-gaming all these years. The last couple of days she's been more quiet than before. I have no idea what is going to happen, but I know that if she isn't in my life, I will not be okay.

When I look up, I don't even realize I'm parking in front of her apartment. I look up and see no lights coming from her place. I press the button for Susie Wong, putting my hand on the door, waiting for her to buzz me in. After two minutes I press the button again and still nothing. I grab my phone and call her. She picks up after one ring. "Hello." She sounds like she's out of breath.

"I'm outside," I tell her, stepping out a bit and looking up at her balcony. "Where are you?"

"I was surprising you at your house," she moans.

"I'll be there in ten minutes," I inform her, walking back to my car. "Maybe from now on we make plans on where we are sleeping."

"Duly noted," she says and I hang up, making my way over to my house.

Opening the front door, the smell of food hits me right

away. "Baby!" I yell, tossing my keys on the table at the door.

"In the kitchen!" she yells back. I step into the house seeing Julia with her hair tied up on top of her head. She's wearing sage-green yoga pants that mold to everything. My cock starts to stir while she bends down to take something from the oven. I walk around the counter in time to see her place the tray on the stove top. I can't help but smile at her as she takes off the oven mitts and turns to me. Her white crop tank top also molds to her, her tits fucking perfect, just like everything else on her.

"What are you doing?" I take two steps toward her and pull her to me. She gets on her tippy-toes and wraps her arms around my neck. "Hi."

"Hi." She puts her head back so I can kiss her. I bend my head and kiss her lips. "I made you dinner."

"You did?" I look over at the stove and see she took salmon from the oven.

"Did you eat?" she asks nervously as she moves away from me. "I should have told you not to eat." She laughs as she tries to cover up her nerves. "This played out way different in my head."

"You cooked for me?" I ask her, trying not to think that besides my mother, no one has ever cooked for me.

"Well, you were telling me how you didn't have time to eat when you left, so I don't know." She throws her hands up in the air.

"Come here, baby." I pull her to me, picking her up and placing her on the counter in front of me. My hands rub the sides of her legs as I try to calm her down and myself as well.

She opens her legs, letting me step between them. "You look hot when you dress up." Her hands come up as she plays with the button at the top of my collar that is open. "I remember once, but I forget when it was." My hand goes up to the scrunchie in her hair, letting it fall. "You wore this black suit." I push the hair away from her face. "Maybe it was New Year's."

My eyes go big as I take the phone from my back pocket, pressing on the side button. "Was it this?" Turning to show her the picture, her fingers graze mine as she grabs the phone from me.

"Oh my God," she whispers as she looks at my new screen saver. "Is this your screen saver?"

"Yeah." I smile, looking down at the picture. "It was from the last New Year's Eve party."

"We ended up being the only two single people there." She smiles. "Minus Vivienne, who decided she was going to spend the night in her hotel room ordering everything on the menu while she watched *Notting Hill* and *The Holiday*."

I throw my head back and laugh. "She went online and wanted to trade places with someone in London."

Julia's laughter now comes out, and she throws her head back. "Oh my God, and then your father found out that the guy lived with his parents."

"She was going to trade the brownstone in New York for a one-bedroom cottage in the middle of fucking nowhere." I shake my head.

"He was a sheep farmer. He lived in the barn." She

laughs continuously and I see the tears in her eyes from laughing so much. I can't help but stare at her when she stops laughing, she uses her thumb to wipe away the tears. "Why are you looking at me like that?"

My hand comes up to touch her face. "You are always beautiful, but when you laugh." I smile. "You are even more beautiful." I hold her chin in my hand, closing the distance between us. "The only tears I want to see coming from your eyes are happy tears."

"Yeah," she says softly. "Well, I have a meeting with the lawyer tomorrow."

I gasp out, "You never told me."

"Because I didn't want you to have to do whatever it is that you were going to do." She flails her hands in the air.

That's why she's been so quiet. "I'm going to call out of work," I say, shaking my head.

"No," she snaps. "I refuse to have your life revolving around this." Her head shakes side to side. "It's not even a formal meeting. It's to go over things that can happen or will happen. I think he wants to hire a private detective." She looks down at her hands. "I have no idea what this is even going to cost." I know if I say now she doesn't have to worry about it, she will only fight with me. So instead, I keep it to myself, for now. "But it is what it is and I can't change what is going to happen." I can see when she puts on a brave face. I know the exact moment it happens. She lifts her hands to hold my face. "Now, can I feed my man so then he can have the strength to do the nasty with me?" She laughs, trying to change the tone, and I let her do it.

"Why don't we do the nasty now and then I can eat?" I bite her lower lip. "Even better, I think I want to have my dessert before my main meal." My hands go to the top of her yoga pants as I rip them off her. She's wearing lace panties and I pull her to the edge of the counter, rubbing up the middle part. "Just like I like it." I squat down, pushing the material to the side. "Wet."

Thirty-Three

Julia

I FEEL LITTLE kisses on my neck. "Baby," he whispers and I sink more into the pillow. "Baby," he tries again. I lie in the middle of the bed on my stomach, where he left me about fifteen minutes ago. I was going to get out of bed, but I closed my eyes for one second and fell back asleep.

"Hmm," I moan as he sits on the bed next to me, on top of the covers. I feel him bend his head as he rubs his nose along my jawline. Even now, after I've been with him over two weeks, seen him naked seventy-five percent of that time. Had sex in so many different positions, had him slide his hand in mine. Kiss me softly more times than I can count, yet every single time he touches me, my stomach gets all these flutters. All. The. Freaking. Time.

"I made you coffee," he says as he trails kisses down

my jaw.

"Well, considering your dumb alarm woke me up," I mumble, not ready to stop him from giving me butterfly kisses.

"I thought my face between your legs was forgiveness enough," he teases, right before he kisses my neck.

I smile. "That definitely helped." Turning to my side, his arms drape across me. "Morning." He kisses my lips softly right before I sit up, holding the covers to my naked chest. "What time do you have to leave?"

"In about thirty minutes." He sits up. "What time is the appointment at the lawyer's?"

"Eleven." I avoid looking at him by leaning over and grabbing the cup of coffee. If he sees how scared I am, there is no way he won't show up. It's not that I don't want him there, I just don't want this scandal to touch him.

"I leave tomorrow for a couple of days. Then I have a shift at the hospital," he says and I look back at him, hoping he doesn't see how scared I am. "Pack a bag."

I smirk at him. "So bossy."

"When it comes to you." He kisses me before getting up. "You bet your fucking ass."

I shake my head and watch him walk into the bathroom. I get up and get dressed, us both walking out at the same time. He kisses me one last time before he closes my car door and I drive away. The phone rings as soon as I turn the corner and I think it's him, but instead it's Jillian.

"Good morning," I answer on the second ring.

"Why do you sound so chipper at not even nine a.m.?" She laughs into the phone. "Wait, are you in the car already. I thought the lawyer was at eleven."

"It is at eleven," I confirm. "I'm just leaving Chase's."

"Another sleepover." She snickers into the phone.

"Yeah, I went over to his house and surprised him with dinner." I know the minute the words come out of my mouth, she's going to be all over me.

"You don't cook," she reminds me. "You won't even cook for your nieces and nephews."

"That is not true." I gasp. "It's just easier to order in so I spend more time with them."

"Whatever you want to tell yourself." She laughs.

"I think I like him." I admit the words out loud for the first time. Putting it out into the universe instead of keeping it to myself.

"You think?" she scoffs. "You think?"

"Ugh, fine," I admit to her, because if anyone would know, it would be her. "I like him." I park my car and close my eyes. "Like a lot."

"Like, like like?" she asks and I nod my head, not saying a word. "Like eight months or nine months?"

"Like years," I admit. "I need you to tell me that this is not okay and I should walk away from him."

"Julia, let me ask you one question," she says softly. "How bad would it hurt you to do that?" I don't want to answer that question because I don't think I'm ready to admit that losing him or walking away from him will shatter me.

"I have to go get ready." I ignore answering her

question. "Max and Matthew are going to be here in an hour."

"Call me when you get out," she says right before she disconnects.

I walk into the house, going straight for my bedroom. Starting the shower before making my way to the closet, I grab a pair of black pants and matching shirt. I'm slipping on my ballerina shoes when my phone beeps.

Walking over to the bed I'm thinking it's Max telling me that he's on his way, instead it's from Chase.

Chase: Don't forget to pack a bag.

Throwing the phone down, I grab a bag, putting in a change of clothes. Taking one look at myself in the mirror I want to laugh that I look like I'm dressed for a funeral. As the minutes tick by, my chest gets tighter and tighter. I don't bother texting him back, instead I text Max.

Me: Leaving now.

I sit on the bed, my hands shaking just a touch as I see the gray bubble come up with three dots. Then the phone buzzes in my hand.

Max: Leaving now.

Grabbing my bag, I go out to the car, my head down as I walk. I try not to think about how my life has changed in the last two weeks. I try not to harp on things I have no control over. There are good days but then there are days when I feel like I'm drowning. But through it all, Chase has been my lifeline. I don't know how he knows when I feel sad, but he does. I stopped asking questions when I was on his couch and he was in the kitchen. My anxiety was starting to pick up, and all of a sudden, he walked over to me, pulling me into his arms. His whole body covered mine as he held me.

I pop open the trunk to put the bag in it and I gasp out. The baby bag is still in my trunk; with everything going on, I completely forgot about it. I put my bag next to it, picking it up and taking it out. The tears come without me even knowing it as I bring the bag with me, putting it in the passenger seat. I would love to take it to Penelope but I know it would just give her grandparents something else to hang over me. So giving it to the lawyer is the next best thing.

I put the address for the lawyer in the GPS, every single minute my breathing starts to come in pants. I pull up to the building finding a parking spot right away. I grab the bag and my purse, walking into the lobby. As soon as I step foot inside, I know this is going to cost a fortune, which makes my stomach turn even more. There is marble flooring all over, the lights overhead look like chandeliers. There are four double couches in the middle of the room, each facing black chairs lined against the walls.

I walk up to the reception desk and the girl smiles. "I have an appointment at eleven," I say softly. "Julia Williams."

She types something in to the big Mac computer on her desk before turning and smiling at me. "He'll be right with you," she says. "You can have a seat." I nod at her and walk over to the black chairs against the wall. I sit down, putting the baby bag beside me. My legs start to shake with nerves as I look down at my phone. My heart picks up and I can feel a panic attack coming. The doors open and my eyes fly up spotting Matthew and Max walking in.

The both of them are dressed in suits, looking at them you know that you don't want to fuck with them. It's this aura they give off. Max spots me right away and smiles as he walks toward me.

"Have you been here long?" he asks as I try to get up to give him a hug but my legs don't move. He bends down and kisses my temple.

"No, I just got here," I say and then Matthew looks around before turning to me and smiling.

"Hey, honey." He sits down in the chair in front of me. "You good?"

"As good as someone should be," I answer him honestly as Max sits next to me. "Um," I start to say and then look down at my hands. "I need to ask you two something."

"Anything," Max and Matthew say at the exact same time.

"You have to promise me," I start and Matthew is already shaking his head no. "You have to promise me you won't sink any more money into this." I look around. "I don't even know if I'll be able to pay you guys back for whatever you spent so far."

"Don't worry about that," Max says from beside me.

"Listen, I love what you both have done for me," I say, trying to be strong. "But I can't let you guys take this over. It's not your problem."

"Hey," Matthew says and I look at him. "You're family." He leans over. "Period."

I'm about to argue with them, but all the words get caught in my throat. "What's with the bag?" Matthew motions with his chin.

"It's Penelope's. The cop on the scene returned it to me the day after and I forgot all about it. I figured I can give it to the lawyer and they can get it to her."

"We'll get it to her," Max says, putting his hand on mine.

I hear the sound of clicking on the floor and my head slowly turns to the side. A woman wearing a black skirt and silky white button-down top smiles at us. "We are ready for you," she says and Matthew is the first one out of his chair.

Max gets up next and I start to stand, but my knees buckle. Making me fall back down and my hand goes out to stop myself from falling, hitting the baby bag, and sending it flying to the floor. It lands on its side and everything comes sliding out. Matthew flies to one side to catch me while Max grabs the other side. "I'm fine." I try to laugh. "My foot was asleep."

I lie and they both know I'm lying, but neither of them calls me out for it. "Let me get the bag," I say, bending down. Picking up the two diapers that are lying there in front of the bag. The diaper cream is not too far away. I start putting the things back in the bag when I pick up one of the T-shirts and a white envelope slides out to the floor. It's like the world stops spinning when I look down at the white envelope lying on the floor.

"What is that?" Max asks and I pick up the envelope, turning it over. My hands shake as if they know this is the missing piece.

"I have no idea," I say, my heart pounding when I see my name written on the front in Monica's handwriting. "But it's addressed to me." My hand moves over the block letters that are in the middle of the white envelope. "It's in Monica's writing." I look up at them, my heart beating so erratically as I hold my breath, tears running down my face. "It's from Monica."

Thirty-Four

Chase

I PULL INTO the garage at the same time Michael does. He gets out and stretches. "Someone looks tired," I observe, getting out of my own car, we are dressed alike in the team track suit.

"Yeah," he says softly. "Jillian was trying not to stress about Julia's visit with the lawyer today, but that didn't work." He looks at me. "How was Julia?"

"Pretending like it doesn't bother her," I admit to him, my stomach in knots thinking about how she just sat on the couch last night and stared off into the distance. She thought I didn't notice but my body was on high alert next to her. "I tried not to bring it up and instead I took her mind off it."

"How?" He puts his hands on his hips.

I can't help but laugh when the answer comes to me

right away. "Sex." The minute I say the word, his face grimaces. "You should have tried it."

"I did." Michael throws his hands up. "Obviously I'm not smooth like you, Casanova." His tone is aggravated at this point.

"I can give you some pointers, if you like." He glares at me while another car shows up and Cooper gets out, wearing blue shorts and a T-shirt with the team logo in the middle, his number in the corner.

He takes a second to look from me to Michael and then back to me again. "Why does Michael look like he's about to bite your head off?" he asks and I chuckle.

"He can't please his woman," I joke, but all it does is make his eyes go into slits. "I was about to give him pointers."

"I can please my woman just fine," Michael retorts, taking out his phone. I look over at Cooper, who is trying not to laugh as Dylan gets here.

He gets out of his car dressed in workout gear as he stands here looking at the three of us. "What's going on?" he asks, putting his baseball hat on backward. "Who is he calling?" He points over to Michael.

"No idea," I answer, looking at Michael as he holds the phone in front of his face.

As soon as the phone connects, he's yelling her name, "Jillian!" He looks at his phone. "I need you to tell my family that you're satisfied sexually."

"Oh my God," Dylan says, shaking his head. "What is wrong with you? I didn't even eat yet and I'm about to throw up." He puts his hand on his stomach.

"Shut up, you," Michael hisses at him. "Tarzan over here tells me I'm not satisfying you sexually."

"It's okay, Daddy," Bianca now says and I put my hand into a fist in front fo my mouth. "Mommy, tell Daddy he does satisfied good sexually." She emphasizes the word sexually. I'm trying my hardest not to laugh out loud, trying not to make a sound.

"Why am I not taping this?" Cooper asks, laughing as he claps his hands, not even caring Jillian knows he's with us in the room.

"Mommy," Bailey says, "did Daddy satisfied you? Yes or no?" Her voice goes higher on the yes-or-no part. "It's okay, Daddy, did you try your best?"

"I can't wait for parent-teacher conferences," Dylan blurts. "I thought it was bad last time when Cooper's kid drew this guy's penis." He points at me. "But this"—he points at the phone—"this is so much better. I can just imagine the girls going to school and saying Daddy didn't satisfy Mommy in the sex." He mimics the way the girls talk, hitting it right on the nose.

I have no words. I can't say anything. "Give me the phone," Jillian says to the girls, and you can hear her teeth are clenched together. "Are you out of your mind?"

"Yes!" we all shout at him as he looks at the phone.

"Chase w-was," he stutters. "I was just telling him everything is fine at home."

"It was before," she snarls, "it's not now. Goodbye, Michael."

"Love you," he says and all you hear is the beeping that the call has dropped.

"I can't believe this just happened," Cooper says when Wilson shows up. He gets out of his car in a track suit and carrying a plastic cup in his hand as he shakes it.

"What is this, a meeting?" He chuckles as he snaps open the spout for his cup, bringing it to his mouth.

"I was just telling Michael I could help him with pointers to help satisfy his woman," I explain, earning me another glare. "Since he can't use sex to take her mind off things."

"I heard." Wilson smirks at me. "High five." He holds up his hand for me to high-five him.

"No one is high-fiving anyone." Michael shakes his head. "That's like my sister."

"Well, if it makes you feel better," Wilson says. "I just satisfied their sister"—he points at Cooper and me—"very well, before I left the house." His face fills with a smile and he brings the cup up to his mouth again.

"That makes no one feel better," Dylan grumbles. "Like, not one person standing in this room right now feels better after that comment."

"Come to think of it," Cooper says, "I feel worse."

I can't help but laugh as we walk into the arena. I try to take my mind off Julia, but I'm checking the phone every five minutes because it feels longer. I'm in my office, going through the charts on everyone when I hear a knock on the door and look up.

"Hey." Nico sticks his head into my office. "Mind if we push the meeting up to say"—he looks at his watch—"in ten minutes?"

I laugh and nod my head. "Guys are on the ice, so

if something happens, they can call me," I say and he walks away, back down the hall in the direction of his office.

I take my phone out and send Julia a text.

Me: Thinking about you.

I'm so tempted to add I love you, but stop myself since I haven't even said it to her face yet. There have been times when it almost slipped out but I stopped myself, not sure if I should add something else to her overcrowded plate. I look down at the phone, wondering if she is going to text me back. I should have been persistent that I go with her. I should have just showed up and not told her. I tap my index finger on the desk, waiting for an answer but nothing comes up.

I grab my files and walk down the hallway to Nico's door. His door is open and I knock anyway before walking in. He took off his jacket and his white dress shirt is rolled up to his elbows. "Hey," I greet, walking over to the chair in front of his desk. We have these meetings once a week, where we go over everyone's injuries. Who is on the injured list, who got hurt, who is complaining of aches. No one runs a tighter ship than Nico, he knows what is going on in every single department.

"Okay," he says, grabbing a file off the top. "Let's get started."

I nod at him, opening up my own file as we go down the list from the name on top. "I think he's good to be on the ice." Nico looks up at me since last week I told him he needed more time.

"You sure?" he asks, moving his chair side to side,

waiting for me to answer.

"Yes," I confirm. "We went over a couple of things the other day and he was fine."

"That makes me happy," he states and the phone rings beside him. He looks down and then smirks. "It's your father."

"What?" I sit up straight. "He's supposed to be in a meeting." I look at my watch, seeing it's ten minutes past eleven. He said he was going to the lawyer with Julia. My stomach sinks thinking she went there by herself.

I grab my phone, texting Max.

Me: Are you with Julia?

"Well, well, well," Nico says, leaning back in his chair smiling as he answers. I have no idea what my father just said, but the smile goes away very fast. By the way his face turns, I know nothing about it is good. "What?" he says as he sits up. "Yeah, he's on the ice." He looks at me and he just nods. "See you in a bit." He disconnects, getting up, and I get up with him.

"What happened?" I ask him. "He's supposed to be with Julia." I take my phone out and I'm about to call my father.

"How close are you with Julia?" he questions and my body goes cold as ice.

"Is she hurt?" I ask as I take five steps to the door to rush out of it.

"That answers that question, but I need to get to the ice." He walks past me and runs down the hallway. "I'll explain later."

"Nico." I say his name but it comes out in almost a

growl. "Is she okay?"

"She's fine," he assures me, and for the first time since he answered the phone, I feel like I can breathe. "Meet us by my car in five," he says right before he runs off.

I walk toward the garage, the whole time my chest getting tighter and tighter. My phone in my hand not doing anything. I'm about to crawl out of my skin as I think about doing whatever I need to do in order to sacrifice myself for Julia. I will do whatever I need to do to take all her pain away. In this garage, while I plead with whoever is listening, I realize I'm way past in love with her. She is my fucking everything and without her I can't live.

I look up to the ceiling and laugh bitterly at the irony of it all. My father has said for years, once you find love, the real kind of love, not the bullshit puppy dog shit, it's going to hit you in the knees so hard you won't be able to stand. After it hits you in the knees, it's going to kick you in the balls so hard you won't be able to breathe. The only way anything will be better will be when you are beside that person. The only time you'll be able to breathe without feeling like the next breath will be your last is next to that person. The only time you will be whole is by being able to touch that person. It's like they are the beating of your heart. I laughed each time he said it. I never in my life believed it, until now. Until the thought that Julia wouldn't be here with me.

Seeing Nico go from laughing to serious and then hearing Julia's name, everything in me turned to stone. The thought something happened to her was literally too much to bear. The only thing that went through my head was getting to her. The only thing that went through my head was that I never told her how I feel. If anything happened to her, she would never know how much I love her.

Waiting for Nico by his car is agonizing. I take out my phone, seeing if Max or Julia texted me back but nothing is there. I look around when I see Nico rush out the door and unlock his car door. I get in as Nico gets in the driver's seat and the back door is opened. "Can we get going?" I say when the back door closes. I don't bother looking over my shoulder, the only thing I can do is stare out the window urging Nico to rush.

Thirty-Five

Julia

THE MINUTE I saw the letter with my name on it, everything in me stopped. I had zero idea of what could be in here. I waited until I was sitting in the chair before I opened the letter in front of Stuart, Matthew, and Max. My hands shook like a leaf on a tree during a windstorm as I opened the flap and took out the folded white paper. "Dear Julia," I read aloud, right before I cover my mouth to stop the sob from coming from me.

Max, who is sitting next to me, rubs my back. "Do you want me to read it?" he asks and I just shake my head.

"No." I take a deep breath in, trying to get my emotions in place.

"She's got this," Matthew says and I look over at him. "You got this."

I take another breath. "Dear Julia, I guess if you are reading this letter, something bad must have happened to me. I don't have to tell you how hard it's been for me, if anyone knows it, it's you." I wipe my cheek with the back of my hand. "I just want you to know how hard I tried to be the person you always said I was. I don't think I would have been able to do anything without you by my side." My lips tremble. "I hope you can forgive me." I close my eyes now as the tears just run down my face.

"Let me finish," Max says softly as he takes the paper from my hands. I listen to his words but I don't grasp any of it. "The last thing I will say," Max reads and I look over at him. "Penelope needs to be raised by a family who loves her. Who will keep her safe. I never contacted the father. But his name is…" Max looks up, his eyes going big as he passes the paper to Matthew, who jumps from his chair.

"What is it?" I ask him and then grab the paper from them.

Stuart claps his hands together, the smile on his face like the cat that just ate the bird. "Let the fun begin," he says, nodding at me. "I'll be right back." He walks from the room.

My head is spinning around and around as I read the letter over and over again, the tears just running down my cheeks. I use my fingers to trace the letters, knowing she wrote this for me. "I tried." I look over at Max, who is sitting beside me, his hand rubbing my back. "I tried so hard." The sobs rip out of me. "I was rooting for her so hard."

"You did everything you could have done," he tells me, and I know that I did.

"She wanted so much to be a good mom." I wipe the tears off my face. "She wanted to be so much better than her own mom."

The door opens and Matthew steps in. "Nico is on his way," he says softly as he sits down beside Max. "This kid's life is going to change and he has no idea."

"I can't even imagine what is going to happen," I add, looking around the table. "At the end of the day, this is about Penelope. She needs a fighting chance."

"She needs to get the hell away from her grandparents," Matthew declares. "From what Abigail said, they went to visit her once or twice."

I close my eyes, trying not to put it on myself, knowing there is nothing I could have done. My hands were tied. "Nico is here," Matthew says when getting up and walking out.

It takes maybe thirty seconds for him to come back in, followed by Nico. I look behind Nico and I'm shocked to see Chase right there, almost pushing his way toward me. He steps around and finally gets to me. I get up when he is close enough. He wraps his arms around my waist tightly, pulling me to him. He doesn't say anything to me. He just hugs me as tight as he can. He finally lets me go, and his hands hold my face, his eyes search mine. "Are you okay?"

"I'm fine." I nod my head as he kisses me.

"Um, sorry, but what the hell is going on?" I hear a voice and look over to see someone standing there in a track suit. His hair is still wet and I can only imagine what he is going through. I know right away this is Penelope's father, they have the same eyes.

"Why don't I take over?" I look at Matthew and then Nico, who just nods at me.

"Do you want to sit down, Tristan?" I ask him and he comes forward and sits down.

"Do I need a lawyer?" he asks and looks over at Nico, who sits next to him and shakes his head.

"Tristan, did you know someone called Monica?" I ask him, and his eyebrows shoot together and he shakes his head.

"Not that I can remember," he says, looking around at the men.

I reach for my file in my bag, pulling out the picture of her. My hands shake when I see her smiling up at me. "This is Monica," I say, turning the picture around and passing it to him.

"Sorry." He looks down ashamed. "I have no idea."

"From what she said, the two of you met at a party," I remind him. "You had just gotten drafted."

He huffs out, "I don't remember anything from that night. I was just so happy to be drafted I let loose." He looks at his hands. "There were girls everywhere." I can only imagine. "I don't know why this means anything." I can tell from his tone he's getting really fucking nervous.

I swallow down now, knowing what I say next or what comes next is going to change his whole world. "Two years ago, Monica had a baby girl." I look at him to see if he gets it. "We think she had your baby."

I can tell the exact time it sinks in as he gets up. "What?" He looks at Nico, who gets up and puts his hand on his shoulder.

"It's going to be okay," he assures him. "Whatever it is, we are going to be there with you every single step of the way."

"Where is Monica?" He looks around the table.

I was wrong, telling him he has a child isn't going to change his life, finding out he's the only parent this child has is going to change his life. "She died," I say, ripping the Band-Aid off. "Long story short. She didn't have that great of a relationship with her parents." He sits down now, his mouth opening and closing. "She was already in the system when she had Penelope, so we had to monitor her."

"Is Penelope," he asks, "is she?"

"She is alive," I confirm and he puts his head back as a sigh of relief leaves him. "Tristan, we would need to do a DNA test before anything," I say, and he nods his head. "Just to make sure that you are in fact the father."

"I don't know what to say," he admits, and I can only imagine what he is going through.

"I know it's a lot to take in, and I wish Monica had told you when it first happened."

"When can I do this test?" he asks.

"We have someone who can do it now," Nico says, and Tristan nods his head.

"Where is Penelope?" he asks, and my heart fills when he asks this.

"She's in the hospital—" I say, looking at Chase, who

cuts in.

"She had a couple of surgeries, but she's on the mend," Chase explains.

"I want to see her," Tristan says, getting up.

"That sounds great, but her grandparents have emergency custody of her and they won't let you see her."

"Fuck that," he says, looking at Nico and then at me. "This might be my kid and I didn't even know." He shakes his head. "She could have died, and I had no idea."

"We get the result in twenty-four hours," Nico says. "Why don't we wait for that and then we go to the next step?"

"Do you have a picture?" Tristan asks, and I nod, taking out the last picture I took of Penelope. I hand him the picture, and he grabs it, letting out a sob. "She's mine," he says. "She looks just like my sister."

Nico reaches over and puts his arm over his shoulder. "I want to know that when the test results come back, I can see her." He looks at me. "I'm sure there will be paperwork for me to complete."

"There will definitely be more paperwork for you to complete," I say, "She's in the system." I don't want to scare him, but he has to know. "So there will be follow-up."

"Whatever it is," he says, getting up, "I need to take this test." He smiles at me. "Thank you for finding me."

I smile at him, the tears blurring my vision. "Thank Monica," I say, holding up the letter in my hand. "She left this letter for me."

He nods his head. "Is she—" He looks around. "I'd like to pay for her funeral arrangements. If it hasn't been done already or if the state isn't taking care of it. I would like to."

"We got it," Nico says, not wanting him to continue. "We'll get everything set up." Nico looks at Matthew, who just nods as they walk from the room.

"I'll give you guys some space," Max says, getting up. "So proud of you." He kisses my head.

I watch Max walk out before turning back and looking at Chase. "I sure missed a lot," he jokes and I laugh for the first time today.

I pick up the letter Monica wrote. "She left a letter to me." My hand shakes. "Spilling all her secrets. She thanked me," I say between tears and a smile. "For everything I did for her." I cry and laugh at the same time. "She wanted to be like me." I shake my head. "She could have been like me."

He turns my chair to face him. "You have the best heart I've ever seen," he says, putting my face in his hands. "She knew with you in her corner, anything was possible." I just smile and he kisses my lips, tasting my tears.

"What is going to happen now, do you know?"

"Well, if Tristan is the father, then he can petition for custody, and since the letter says she never told him, the judge will most likely rule in his favor." I can't help but smile. "From what Stuart said, the parents were in it for the payday." I shake my head. "Not that I'm surprised, but if you take Penelope out of it, their case against me is very weak," I say.

"Can we get out of here?" I ask him and stand. He stands, looking down at me, his eyes shining.

"I'll take you wherever you want to go," he says without skipping a beat, slipping his hand in mine. "Anywhere with you." He brings our hands up to his mouth, kissing my fingers. "Oh, you won't even believe what Michael did," he tells me as we walk out of the room where my life finally came back to me.

Thirty-Six

Chase

"ARE YOU SURE about this?" I put the car in park and look over at her. The minute we left the lawyer's office, all she wanted to do was pass by and see if Penelope was okay.

"All I know is I have to see Penelope." She puts her hand on the door handle. "If I see Monica's parents, we'll leave."

"Okay," I agree, getting out at the same time as her. I slip my hand into hers as we walk into the hospital. We walk to the elevator and I press the number four. "I'll walk in front of you," I say and she chuckles.

"What are you going to do, be my body shield?" She looks up at me.

"Yeah," I say, bending to kiss her lips. Her eyes are still red from crying and so is her nose. The elevator pings and we take a step out.

I go on alert now as we walk closer to the room. "Wait here." I tell Julia to stand outside the door. She leans against the wall as I walk over to the open door. Only when I get to the entrance of the door do I see Abigail. She is sitting on the bed with Penelope in her lap. She is reading a book to her and she looks up and asks her something. Abigail just smiles at her, nodding. I stick my head in and look around. "Hey," I say and she looks up over at me smiling.

"Chase," Abigail says. "Penelope, can you say hi, Chase?"

"Hi, Ace." She waves her hand at me and I wave back.

"Are the grandparents here?" I look around seeing the room is very bare. It shows no one is spending the night with her. Usually, when kids are in the hospital, there is a cot brought in. There are food containers on the windowsills. There are changes of clothes everywhere. But this room looks like she just got here.

"They haven't been here in four days," Abigail shares. "I come after school and on my days off." She looks down and smiles at Penelope. "She's my favorite."

I walk out into the hallway. "Come on." I motion with my hand and Julia takes a couple of steps heading into the room. I stand at the door so I can keep an eye on the elevator.

"Mama," Penelope says when she sees Julia, and it takes everything in her not to collapse.

"She's not here," Julia says when she gets closer to the bed, sitting down. Penelope sits up in Abigail's lap and Julia bends to hug her.

"How is she doing?" Julia asks Abigail, who shrugs her shoulders.

"She's getting better every day. It's sucks she doesn't have someone here with her all the time." She looks down at Penelope, who is telling Julia to look at her book. "from what the nurses say is that her grandparents come in, make a stink for five minutes, and then leave." Penelope points at a cup on the side of them. Abigail grabs it and takes a Goldfish cracker from it. "Thank you." She holds it for Penelope who repeats, "Hank you." She puts it in her mouth.

"We should get going," I say, not wanting to push our luck.

Julia looks at Penelope. "I'll come back and see you," she tells her and Penelope just points at the Goldfish holder. Julia bends and kisses Penelope's head and then Abigail's. "Be safe."

Julia gets up and walks toward me, shaking her head. "It's okay," I say when we walk down the hallway to the elevator.

She presses the down button. "It's not okay," she says softly, "it's fucked up." She crosses her arms over her chest, stepping into the elevator when the doors open. There are four other people in there, so I stand next to her without saying anything.

We walk from the elevator toward the car and only when we are close to it does she turn on me. "It's fucked up," she says angrily. "This whole thing is fucked up to like the nth degree." She throws up her hand in the air. "Like it's kids having kids." I lean against the trunk of the car watching her pace now. "Fucking kids have kids," she repeats.

"The good news," I say and she looks up at me, stopping mid step. "Tristan comes from a great family." She cocks her hip at me. "And he has a good head on his shoulders."

She looks at me with her mouth hanging open. "Oh, yeah, he really has a great head on his shoulders, he couldn't even wear a condom."

"Okay, that was a lapse of judgment on his part," I admit. "But now that he knows, he's stepping up to the plate."

"He better," she huffs and walks over to the passenger door. "I need a drink," she declares and all I do is nod my head. I get in and look over at her.

"Where to?" I ask her, hating we have two places. Hating we don't just have one place where all of our stuff is.

"I have my bag in the trunk," she huffs, "so we might as well just go to yours." I nod my head, pulling out and making my way over to my house. I grab her bag from the trunk as we both walk into the elevator. My head is still on the fact I hate that we live in separate places.

I walk in and toss my keys on the table in the hallway. "I'll go put your bag away," I mumble. "You go get your drink." I walk away from her, going into the bedroom.

Making my way to the closet, I put her bag next to mine I use to travel. I look up, seeing just my clothes hanging up. Turning around, I walk out and go to sit on the bench in front of the bed. I'm looking at my hands, trying to think of the words to bring up her moving in with me.

"Hey." I hear her soft voice and see her standing there in the doorway. Everything hits me like a ton of bricks. I'm one thousand percent in love with this woman. I get flashes of our lives in the future and it shocks me. I knew what I felt for her was love, but holy shit, it's so much fucking more than that. "What's wrong with you?" she asks, and all I can do is shake my head, not sure how I can say it. Not sure what words would do justice for what I feel. "You've been quiet." She takes a couple of steps into the room. "Listen," she says, her voice tighter, and my body goes tight with the tone. "I know this is a lot to take in." She puts one hand on her head. "We can just pretend the last two weeks never happened and just be Chase and Julia again." She smiles but I can tell the smile isn't real. "Good friends."

"Are you out of your fucking mind?" The words just come from my mouth so fast I can't stop them.

"I have no idea." She puts her hands on her hips. "I mean, depending on who you ask, it's probably going to be a yes." She throws up her hands. "I have no idea. You've been really quiet since the hospital, so I kind of put two and two together."

I look at her. "And came up with five?" I ask her and she glares at me.

"I've never done this before, Chase, so what the hell was I supposed to think?" She stares at me.

"You are supposed to come to me and ask me." My

eyes stare into hers. "Ask me why I was quiet." My voice goes even lower at the end. "Ask me, Julia."

"Why were you quiet?" I swallow down the lump in my throat.

"There were two reasons." I hold up one finger. "The first one is because I hate we each have our own place." She opens her mouth to say something and then I hold my hand up. "After a long day out, I want us to have one place to go home to."

"But—" she starts, and I shake my head, and she looks at me shocked to say the least. If you would tell anyone I was thinking of moving in with someone two weeks in, I would tell you, you were out of your mind.

"I know." I open my legs and put my hands on the bench beside me. "Trust me, I know." She walks toward me, making my palms all sweaty. She stands in the middle of my legs looking down at me. My hands automatically go to her legs, while she pushes my hair away from my face. "That isn't even the craziest thing," I say.

"What's the second reason?" she asks in a whisper.

"I love you." The minute the words come out of my mouth, all I do is sigh. The truth finally out there, I don't have to be scared I'm just going to blurt it out at the most awkward moment. "I love you, Julia." I rub my hands up and down her legs. "The funny thing is, I don't even know when it happened."

I look in her eyes, hoping to fuck I'm not pushing her off the ledge, knowing it's been a whirlwind day, but also knowing I'm not sure I can hide it anymore. Not sure I'm willing to hide it anymore. "Chase." She bends to kiss my lips. Her tongue slides into my mouth, her hand palming my cheek. She lets go of my lips, standing up again, this time crossing her arms in front of her and pulling her shirt off over her head, leaving her in just her black lace bra. "When you walked into the house." Her hands move to her back as she unhooks her bra. "I was so scared that this would be it." The bra straps fall off her shoulders toward her wrists as she tosses it to the side. "I went into the kitchen and all I could do was look down the hallway to see if you were going to come back." She moves her hands to the side of her hip, where she pulls the zipper down for the pants, sliding out of them and her panties, she stands here in front of me naked. "When you didn't come back right away, I thought for sure it was because it was done."

"No—" I cut her off, not even wanting her to think that for another second more. "Not even close." She steps closer to me, my hands going to her hips, bringing her even closer to me so I can kiss her stomach. "I just didn't want to burden you." She grabs the back of my shirt, bunching it up in her hands, making it rise up and I help her shed my shirt. She tosses the shirt to the side with her clothes. "Stand up," she directs me, and when I do she slips her hands in the elastic of my shorts and boxers as she pulls them down. I kick them away from me. "Sit down," she says. I sit back down as she puts one knee near my hip and follows with the other, her hands on my shoulders as she straddles me. I can feel the heat from her pussy as she hovers over my cock. "I didn't know what I was going to do." She kisses me softly. "If you said it was too much for you." She moves her right hand off my shoulder, sliding it between us, fisting my cock.

"What would you have done?" I ask her in a whisper as she places herself over me and slides slowly down.

Our eyes lock on each other. "I don't know." She leans forward and kisses my lips as my hands grab her hips. She lets go of my lips in time to say, "But I know one thing," as she moves up and down on my cock. "I would have told you I love you." Her breath hitches as her lips hover over mine. "I love you, Chase." She moves her head to the side, kissing me again. Her tongue sliding in with mine, the love we feel for each other is all in the kiss. It's a soft and slow kiss, just like the way she is riding my cock. I move her ass up and down with my hands while her hands wrap around my neck, neither of us letting each other go. Our lips pressed together, my cock buried inside her.

"I love you," I pant when I feel her pussy squeeze me tight. "So fucking much." Her lips come back to kiss me.

My balls get tight as her pussy gets hotter and wetter, and I know she's right there. I know her body better than I know my own. Her head falls back just a touch. "I love you," on her lips as we both come together.

Thirty-Seven

Julia

One Week Later

I DON'T EVEN have a chance to say hello before I hear him huff out, "Where are you?"

"Hello, dear," I say, ignoring his question.

"Julia," he hisses, and I can even tell he said it with his teeth clenched.

"Yes." I know I'm pushing it; he's been gone for six days. The longest we've been apart since we got together. He left town the day after Tristan found out he was, in fact, Penelope's father. I guess the universe works in mysterious ways because he was about to go back on the ice but took another week on the injured list to deal with everything. From what my lawyer told me, the grandparents are fighting him.

"I'm on the edge," he warns and I just smile, the whole six days he's been a grouchy beast.

"I am at Michael and Jillian's house and I'm leaving right now." I get into my car. "I was thinking I would meet you at your place."

"I have a better idea," he says calmly. "I'll send you an address, meet me there."

"Ohh," I say, "are we role-playing?" He groans. "Should I go home and change into a special outfit? Can we play doctor?" I fake cough. "I think I'm sick." I fake cough again. "I need someone to take my temperature."

"Julia," he says. "It's been six days." His voice is tight. "And you want to push me?" I laugh. "I'm like a man living on the edge."

"Okay, we can calm down. You've gone longer without having sex." I roll my eyes. "So have I."

"Just meet me at the address," he insists, and I hear the beep come through.

"Where is this place?" I ask him, putting it in the GPS and seeing it's three minutes away from Michael and Jillian's place. "It's like right around the corner."

"I know. I'll be there in two minutes."

"Roger that," I confirm, hanging up the phone and making my way over. I spot his car parked in the driveway; a smile fills my face knowing in not too long I'll be kissing him. Everything with Chase has been at warp speed. From finally dating him to admitting I love him. Some would say it's a whirlwind, I say slow and steady wins the race. Even though I had no idea we were in a race to begin with.

I pull up to the curb, turning the car off, getting out, and putting my phone in the side pocket of my yoga pants. I walk toward his car and the driver's door opens. One foot comes out and I see he's wearing brown dress shoes with blue dress pants. He steps from the car and I see he's wearing a white dress shirt, the sleeves rolled up to his elbows. His hair falls in front of his face and his hand comes up to push it away. "Well, well, well," I say and he looks over at me, his blue eyes lighting up. I can't even help myself; I jump into his arms. His arms wrap around my waist as mine wrap around his neck. I can't help my legs wrap around his waist. "Hi." I smile big at him right before my lips smash on his. I let go of his lips and bury my face into his neck. "Hi," I say, smelling him.

"Hey, baby." He kisses my neck. "God, I've missed you," he mumbles and he squeezes me even tighter.

"Well, if you missed me so much, why are we here and not in a bed?" I unbury myself from his neck.

"Because I wanted you to see something," he says, letting me go as my feet unwrap from his waist and slide down his body.

He holds me until my feet touch the driveway. "Fine," I moan as his hand slips into mine. "Where are we?" I look up at the two-story massive house with a three-car garage on the side.

He walks to the door and I'm waiting for him to ring the doorbell, but instead he turns the handle of the big black door. "Um," I say as he pulls me inside the house. "You didn't even knock," I whisper-yell at him. I look to the right of me, where two French doors lead to an empty room and the left side looks like a dining room. He walks into the middle of the foyer of the house and I see the big winding staircase. Looking up you can see on both sides. Chase leads the way slowly through an archway that opens up to a huge family room, leading to the kitchen. The whole back wall has windows and you can see the pool. The kitchen has a huge island with eight stools. The family room has the only furniture there is and it has the same couch as Jillian. "What do you think?" He lets my hand go as he looks around the room.

"It's nice," I say, looking around. "It's spacious."

"I know." He puts his hands into his pockets. "The kitchen is what sold me on this place."

My head turns to him. "What sold you?"

"In the house in New York, we have this huge island in the kitchen."

"I know, I've been," I joke with him.

"I always fucking loved that island because it's where we all hung out," he shares with a smile. "It's the strangest thing, but we would just end up there and we would talk for hours. Especially Franny and me." I smile when he tells me the story. "So as soon as I saw it, I knew." I tilt my head. "That I wanted this house."

"You bought this house?" I look at him shocked out of my mind. "Like, this house?" I point at the floor.

"Well, you said you wanted to live with me," he reminds me and all I can do is stare at him, not believing what I'm hearing but also not as shocked as I should be.

"I meant like move into my apartment." I throw my hands up. "I never meant go out and buy a mansion."

Turning in a circle in the room with my hand up in the air. "Or, I don't know, move into your apartment?"

"I hate my place." His face does a grimace as he talks about it.

"It's because you haven't so much as put out a throw blanket." I fold my arms over my chest. "You have to put your own mark on it."

"Well, now we have this place and we can put our mark on it." He emphasizes the word our.

"Um, Chase." I swallow. "I'm even afraid to know how much this cost you."

"Trust me, we can afford it," he huffs.

"We can't afford it," I correct him. "You could afford it. I definitely cannot afford this."

"Michael bought Jillian a house." He shrugs.

"Jillian was carrying his child. My uterus is empty." I point at my stomach. "I literally just finished my period, so you can't even argue that point." I shake my head. "You can't argue any point. This is insane. Who buys a house without even talking to each other?" I ask him, and he is about to answer, but I just hold up my hand to stop him. "Okay, which sane person buys a house without asking the person who is supposed to be in said house?"

"I did ask," he says, and I'm not even prepared for the next words that come from his mouth. "Jillian came and checked it out. Along with Max and my father."

"My sister?" I shriek. "She came here and said to buy this house?" He nods his head. "She has been hanging around with your family too much." I put my hands on my head. "Chase, this is too much. I have lawyer bills.

I'm technically unemployed, there is no fucking way I can afford this house."

"Are you with me for my money?" he asks and I glare at him. "So what if I was already living in this house before we got together and I asked you to move in?"

"That's not the same thing." I close my eyes and pinch the bridge of my nose.

"If it makes you feel better, the penthouse is worth a lot more than this." He laughs as if it's still not millions of dollars.

"That does not make me feel better in the least." I cover my face. "I can't believe you bought a house."

"We bought a house." He walks over to the kitchen, where he grabs a manila envelope off the counter by the stove. His head is down as he walks back, handing it to me. "It's our house."

My hand comes up, taking the envelope in it. "Do I even want to know what is inside this?"

He smirks at me now and the fucking butterflies start in my stomach. "Probably not." He bends and kisses my lips softly. "But if you want, we can go see upstairs."

He slips his hand in mine as he pulls me toward the staircase. "The only room I had done is the master bedroom," he throws over his shoulder. "The rest you can do. Also, if you don't like it, we can change it."

I walk into the bedroom and stop right away. "There is a living room in the bedroom." I point over to the side where a loveseat faces two ottomans right in front of the big TV hanging there. "You know you're extra, when you have a living room in a bedroom." He laughs as I look over to the king-size bed. "This is your bed." I point at his bed.

"I figured if you saw I brought my stuff here, you would bring your stuff," he explains and even if I try to reason with his reason, I know that it'll be for nothing. I walk over to the bench where he told me he loved me for the first time. Where I made love to him, hoping he would know how much I loved him. "What are you thinking?"

He sits down next to me and I laugh. "I don't even know what to think. Like for one, wait until I see my sister." I shake my head. "There will be some heated words exchanged. You know she asked me to watch the kids while she went out this week. Probably here."

"She did," he confirms.

"Traitor," I hiss out. "Chase, this is." I try to think of the words. "This is just…"

He pulls me to him and I straddle his waist. "I love you," he whispers, right before he kisses me and then trails kisses to my cheek and neck.

"I love you, too." I move my head to the side, giving him more access to my neck. "But—"

"Shhh," he hushes, putting his finger on my lips and I throw my head back and laugh. "Pick your battles." I'm about to argue with him but his mouth crashes down on mine and he spends the night convincing me.

I SLIDE MY hand into Chase's as we make our way up the driveway to his parents' house. He opens the door with his empty hand and we can hear the chaos already. "How does it sound louder and louder every single time," Chase says, and I try not to laugh at him.

"There they are." Jillian smiles at me and all I can do is glare at her. "You look nice." She ignores my glare. "I like that top."

"No, you don't. You actually gave me this top because you hate it." I fold my arms over my chest. "Traitor."

"I don't know what you mean," she says and I roll my eyes. "Oh, wait, are you talking about the house?"

"You know damn well I'm talking about the house, Jillian." I put my hands on my hips as Chase stands behind me, putting his hands on my shoulders. "How could you?"

"I thought I was doing you a favor." Her voice goes a touch louder.

"A favor would have been you telling him it's a horrible idea and not to do it." The minute I say those words, she is the one who rolls her eyes.

"He already made the decision to buy the house, you think me saying no would have changed it?" She laughs. "Have you not met anyone in this family?"

I'm about to argue with her when my phone buzzes in my side pocket, taking it out, I whisper, "It's my work." I look over at Chase and then at Jillian, whose eyes go big. I press the green button, turning and walking outside where it is quiet. "Hello." I put the phone to my ear.

"Julia, it's Rosalind," she says, and I don't know why but I hold my breath.

"Hi," I finally reply.

"I'm calling with good news," she says and I just listen. "Once the grandparents were told the father filed for custody of Penelope, they dropped their case against you." I close my eyes at that news. "They knew pursuing a lawsuit against you while suing the father for custody at the same time would potentially weaken their custody case. They would be perceived as greedy and lawsuit happy which, apparently, they are. Once the district attorney found out they dropped their lawsuit, he dismissed all charges against you."

"Thank you for telling me," I say softly.

"I wanted to call and let you know. I'll call you tomorrow and we can talk about your return date."

"Sure," I say, stunned as she hangs up. Just like that, it's over. I put my hand in front of my mouth as the tears now come. I squat down on the front porch, the weight of the past month running through me when the door opens.

"Hey," Chase says, squatting down in front of me. A worried look all over his face, his hand comes up to hold my face. "What happened?"

"It's over," are the only words that I can pull out of me. "They dropped the charges and the case." He pulls me into his arms where I bury my face in his neck, and I sob even more.

The door opens and Jillian stands there looking down at us, her eyes go wide. "Oh my God, he did it," she says and I just look at her. "I can't believe he did it."

"Did what?" I ask her and then look back at Chase.

"Um," Chase says, and then looks at me before pushing me up straight but he stays down, going on one knee. "Not yet, but might as well since you can't keep a secret." He turns and looks at Jillian. "I was going to do this last night but the house didn't go over that well and I was picking my battles."

"Oh my God, oh my God, oh my God," Jillian says. "It's happening now."

"Oh my God, oh my God, oh my God," I mumble, thinking, *what the fuck is going on.* I also lean down and try to pull Chase up to standing, but he doesn't move, he only laughs.

"Julia Williams," he says with a huge smile on his face.

"No." I shake my head. "Immediately no." I glare at him. "Get up," I say as I hear more people coming to the door.

"Jesus, it's now," Michael states. "I thought it was after dinner." He throws his head back. "I'm starving."

"Chase," I say between clenched teeth. "It's not funny."

"Everything with you is funny," he says with the biggest smile on his face. "Every day with you is a gift."

"I just threw up," Michael announces, making me laugh while Jillian hits him.

"What is going on?" I hear Matthew from the back as he walks forward. "Karrie, he's doing it."

"This has to be the worst proposal of life," Chase says and I can't help but laugh at him.

"Oh my God, it's happening," Karrie gushes, putting her hands to her mouth, walking to the front. "Oh, my baby." She looks at Matthew. "All gone now."

"I'm not married," Vivienne reminds her from beside her. "So you still have one to go."

"Julia Williams," Chase says again. "Can you put me out of my misery and marry me?"

"We just started dating," I remind him and all the guys just laugh. "We technically just moved in together."

"He's getting the cow for free," Vivienne says. "Is no one going to mention that?"

"Vivi," Matthew and Karrie both say with clenched teeth.

"I'm just saying," she huffs. "Congratulations." She looks at us. "Now, I'm going to eat."

"Aw, congratulations, you two." Matthew comes out and gives me a hug first and then one to Chase.

"She didn't say yes," Michael says, laughing.

"She's living with him," Max says, looking at me and his face is beaming. "That's a yes."

"Show us the ring," Karrie urges, and I swear my head moves around seeing everyone fill the doorway, thinking this is some sort of prank.

"I'm dreaming?" I look at Jillian, who just laughs. "Also, I'm not talking to you."

"I didn't know he was going to do this." She rolls her eyes and I glare. "Okay, fine, I knew he was going to do it, I just didn't know now, now."

"Oh, put it on her," Allison urges and I look over at Chase, who just looks at me.

My heart speeds up and my stomach is flipping. I can't describe his look, but it's a look I see every day. It's that look he gives me, his lips form into a little smile and his eyes literally twinkle. It's a look that says I love you and I'm so happy you're here. He holds up the ring between his thumb and forefinger. "Chase," I say, the tears just pouring down my face.

He holds out his hand for mine and automatically my hand moves to his. He slides the ring down my finger and all I can do is crush my face into his chest. His arms wrap around me as our family members scream and holler around us. He bends his head and whispers in my ear, "You were made for me."

Epilogue One

Chase

One Month Later

THE FRONT DOOR slams shut and I hear her yell my name, "Chase Grant!"

"Oh, fuck," I hear from beside me as my father just looks at me. "What did you do?"

"I have no idea," I whisper to him before yelling back, "In here." I look over at my uncle Max, who is sitting watching the game with a beer in his hand, hiding the smile on his face. After dinner the men decided they would come over and help me hang my television. It made sense to just watch the game here instead of at my parents' house.

"I know that tone"—Michael just chuckles—"someone is in trouble."

"That tone," Dylan says, shaking his head. "That tone is one step after someone is in trouble." He uses his hand in the air for me to see exactly how high.

"Can't be that bad," Cooper says from beside them. "She didn't call him a motherfucker."

"Can't be that bad, she came home." Wilson laughs at his own joke before drinking a sip of water.

The minute she peeks her head into the media room, I can tell she's pissed and I'm not the only one. "Don't say anything," my father whispers to me. "Actually, just say no or yes." I look over at him confused. "Just deny, deny, deny."

"Hey, baby," I say to her softly and she just shakes her head.

"Don't you 'hey, baby' me, Chase Grant." She folds her arms over her chest and cocks her hip and even when she's mad my whole body lights up for her. "Is there something that you need to tell me?"

"It's a trick question," Cooper warns, not making eye contact with Julia. Instead, he just looks at the television screen now playing a commercial.

"Don't answer," Dylan mumbles, pretending to look around the room.

"Hey, honey, look how nice the television is," Max says to her and she ignores him.

"What happened?" I finally kick in and my father moans from beside me. His head goes back as he looks at the ceiling.

"Never ask what happened." He shakes his head. "Rookie mistake."

"I just got off the phone with my lawyer," she states, looking at me, then at Max and my father, who is now pretending that he is reading the ingredients of the beer in his hand.

"Okay," I say, still not sure why she's all bent out of shape. She was fine when she left to go visit the girls forty minutes ago. "Wait, why are you calling a lawyer?" I ask, confused as fuck now. I sit up on the couch.

"I called him because I never got his bill," she says, and all the men just shake their heads including me.

"Yeah." I knew this was coming. I mean, in reality I was hoping she would forget all about it, but pick your battles. Or as my mother says, wait until the second shoe drops. News flash, it just dropped.

"Yeah," she repeats. "That's all you have to say?"

"Pretend your chest hurts," Michael mumbles as he puts his hand to his chest. "I think something we ate is bad."

"You, zip it." She points at Michael, who pretends to zip his lips and throw away the key. "Did you pay my lawyer bill?"

"Yes." I laugh and see the glare back. "But this was like a while ago."

"What?" she shrieks, throwing up her hand. "Why would you do that?"

"Well, because you're his woman," Max now says like *duh*. "If he wasn't paying it, I would have."

"Just like that?" she says, and she looks at each guy who just looks at her.

"Just like that," Michael confirms. "It is what it is.

He's your man, what did you expect for him to do?" he asks her.

"I expected to pay the bill myself since it was my court case." She points at herself.

"That's not how it was ever going to happen," Dylan says and Wilson just agrees with him.

"Julia." My father looks at her. "Honey, we take care of our women."

"And when they don't listen, we kidnap them," Max says to my father.

"I didn't kidnap her." He smirks. "I tied her to the bed with handcuffs." Michael and Dylan roll their lips, trying not to laugh. "She loved every minute of that."

"Yup," Wilson says, "time for me to go." He shakes his head. "I never want to hear that my in-laws use handcuffs."

"You think that is hard?" Cooper says, getting up. "Those are my parents." He looks at our dad. "Never repeat that to anyone at any time. Ever."

Michael and Dylan are next to get up. "Remember one year when we found those handcuffs?" Michael looks at Dylan, then to my dad. "You said you found them on the street and were going to return them to the police."

"I lied," my father says, getting up. "Your father stole my sister."

Max just shakes his head. "Sure did." He slaps my father on the shoulder. "I'm going to go *steel* her right now." He laughs. "Remember when we were dating and you didn't know and I had a hickey on me?"

"What the fuck?" Wilson says. "I'm never coming to

any other family function."

"You had a sex tape." Dylan points at him. "Everyone saw your junk."

"Get out," Julia orders. "I need to speak to one man at a time, and when you are all together, it's like you share a brain."

She waits for everyone to leave before she looks at me. "You could have told me." She turns and walks from the room and down the stairs to the kitchen.

"I'm sorry I didn't tell you," I admit to her. I walk down the stairs looking around at everything she did in order to make this our home. The table at the door has fresh flowers she replaces every Saturday. The pictures of us taken during the years are scattered all around the house. The first picture we took together in Hawaii all those years ago in the middle.

"No, you're not." She snorts out, shaking her head.

"Julia, I don't know if you know this or not, but I paid your bail," I finally say and she looks shocked.

"What?" She hits the counter with her hand.

"Who did you think paid your bail?" I ask her and she throws up both hands, shaking her head.

"I was assuming Jillian, but I was so embarrassed I didn't really want to ask." Her voice goes low and now I walk around the counter to her.

Grabbing her by her hips, I pick her up and put her down on the island. Her legs open for me to step between them. "Baby," I say softly, "I would have begged, borrowed, or stolen to get you out of jail."

"I wasn't your responsibility." Her hands come up to

my chest.

"That's where you're wrong," I say. "That was when I realized I was in love with you." Her soft gasp makes me smile. "That night was the worst night of my life."

"You aren't the only one." She tries to make a joke but a tear runs down her face. "Is there anything else I should know?"

I chuckle. "I'm going to say no, but…"

"No buts, Chase," she huffs. "You already paid for this house. I can't even help pay for it since I'm still unemployed." After the charges were dropped, it took her a couple of days to come to the conclusion she needed to step back for a bit. She needed to reevaluate what she wanted to do.

"You know I'm a doctor, right?" I remind her and she rolls her eyes at me. "And you know I have a trust fund my grandfather left me. This house is paid for."

"That just makes it so much worse." She pushes me away from her but I just pull her closer to me.

"Is this considered a fight?" I kiss her jaw. "Because if it is, we have to have make-up sex."

"Well, considering I was really pissed at you." Her voice trails off when I suck her neck. "And—"

"Shh." I put my finger on her lips. "Just lie back." I push her back. "And let me make it up to you."

She lies back on the island. "Fine, make it up to me." She winks at me and I know in my heart that she's always been made for me.

Epilogue Two

Julia

Two months later

"WHAT TIME DO we leave?" I shout from the closet, trying to decide what to pack for the family vacation we do every year. This time we are going for the whole two weeks and apparently Wi-Fi is spotty, so this should be really fun. It's also the first time we go as a couple, which makes it so much more real. I mean being engaged to him is real but it's all been like a dream so far.

"Eight," Chase says, coming to the doorway naked. I get tingles everywhere when I see him naked. I just left him in the shower and we had sex less than two hours before that, yet I crave him. "What are you thinking about?" He pushes his hair back and I walk to him.

"I'm thinking." I kiss under his chin. "About how

I want to—" I'm about to say when we hear the front door open. "Are you expecting anyone?" I look over his shoulder and he just shakes his head.

"Hello?" Chase throws over his shoulder as the front door slams shut.

"It's me!" Vivienne yells. "Are you decent?"

"No!" Chase shouts and I shake my head when she groans. "What are you doing here?"

"I'm not going on vacation and I am staying here tonight!" she hollers up the stairs and Chase just rolls his eyes.

"I'll go deal with that." I kiss under his chin. "And remember the deal, no naked Chase for two weeks." I smack his ass before walking out of the bedroom.

I can hear the cupboards being slammed as I make my way down the stairs. Her luggage is at the door. "Hi," I greet when I walk into the kitchen, watching Vivienne find the booze. "It's in that one." I point at the one away from the fridge.

"I thought it was a universal rule to have booze on top of the fridge," Vivienne replies, walking over and grabbing the booze.

"It was until I almost broke my head trying to get to the bottle." I laugh at the night I thought grabbing a stool was a good idea, but it moved and I almost broke my face. I pull out the same stool, this time sitting on it while I watch Vivienne. "So what's going on?"

"I'm not talking to my father." She takes a shot of the vodka and hisses, then coughs. "That's disgusting." She points at the empty glass.

"Should I ask why?" I fold my hands in front of me, looking at her. Chase now comes in the room wearing shorts and nothing else.

"Why are you here?" he asks, walking over and sitting next to me.

"Wow, way to make me feel welcome." She glares at him. "Come over any time you want," she mimics what Chase told her.

"What did I miss?" Chase asks from beside me.

"Um, she's not coming on vacation and she's not talking to your father." I fill the blanks for him.

"Why?" Chase asks the same thing I asked.

"I bought a boat," Vivienne states and my mouth opens in shock.

"What do you mean a boat?" I ask her. "Like a rowboat or a canoe?"

"A three-bedroom, two-bathroom small boat," she shares and I can't help but laugh.

"That's called a yacht." I can't help but shake my head.

"You don't even have a license to drive a boat," Chase says.

"I do, too," Vivienne argues. "I got it last week after I bought the boat."

"How?" I put my hand on my head.

"I did the course online," she states proudly.

"That can't be safe." I look over at Chase, wondering if he is thinking the same thing.

"Okay, let's just backtrack for a bit," Chase says. "Start at the beginning."

"Well, I went away for Memorial Day, remember? With my friends to Miami and I loved it." She shrugs. "So I said, 'let me buy a boat and spend the summer on it and see how I like it.'"

"So you just bought one?" I ask, and when I think about it, this isn't even the strangest thing I've heard in this family.

"I'm going to be spending the summer on the boat," she says matter-of-factly. "And Dad forbade me."

Chase now laughs. "You're like old." She glares at him. "Older than me."

"Apparently, I don't know what I'm doing and it's not safe and blah, blah, blah." She rolls her eyes when the sound of the doorbell now fills the house.

"Grand Central Station," Chase mumbles. "It's like nine o'clock."

"It's five thirty," Vivienne says to him.

Chase yells, "It's open!"

The front door opens and then we hear steps. "Why is the front door open? What if I was a robber?" Max stands there with his hands on his hips.

"A robber who rings the doorbell"—Vivienne snickers at him—"that's nice of you."

"What's going on here?" He looks at Vivienne and then at us.

"I bought a boat," Vivienne cuts to the chase. "And I'm going to live on it all summer." She looks at me. "Can I use the guest bedroom?" I nod at her, and she walks to the stairs, stopping to side-hug Max before she walks upstairs.

"I'm sorry, did she say she bought a boat?" he asks, confused.

"Yes, and she's going to live on it all summer," I repeat and he laughs.

"Matthew must be going out of his mind." He claps his hands together. "Also, what the hell was she thinking? She doesn't even know how to drive a boat."

"She does now. She took an online course." Chase gets up. "Do you need me?" he asks Max, who just shakes his head. Chase bends to kiss my lips. "Love you," he says before walking away.

"Are you busy?" Max asks, coming into the kitchen.

"Not at this moment." I smile at him as he pulls out the stool that Chase just left. He sits and puts his hands in front of him.

"Why are you looking so weird?" I look over at him and he just laughs.

"I guess I'm nervous," he admits to me, laughing awkwardly. "I have something I have to talk to you about."

I sit upright now, thinking that he's come to tell me he's sick. My mouth goes suddenly dry and he must see I'm having a bit of a breakdown. "I have something important I want to do and I need your help."

"Anything," I say in a whisper.

"I know you haven't started work yet," he starts and I look down at my hands.

When all the dust settled, I just didn't have it in me to go back to work. I decided to take my own sabbatical and decide if that is what I wanted to do or not. The only thing I knew is I wanted to make a difference in their lives. "I just." I take a deep breath.

Max leans over and puts his hand on mine. "Well, that is what I wanted to talk to you about." He starts again, "The Horton Foundation does a lot of things for a lot of people." I nod my head, knowing his foundation works hand in hand with children's oncology. "I want to make it even better."

"I don't understand." I shake my head.

"I want to create a program under the Horton Foundation called Helping Hands. A program where people who are down on their luck or in the system, but can't find the help they need, can come to us and we help them. Whether it's finding them medical care or even a job or just helping and listening. We will have our resources and I'm rambling now, but…" He smiles when he says it, "I want you to run it."

"What?" I say, shocked.

"Julia, there is no one who will do a better job at it than you," he says with a huge smile on his face, and I can feel how proud of me he is. "We can make a difference." The tears just start to come now. "You will have free rein and all I will do is stand in the back and watch you flourish."

I put my hands in front of my face as I cry and he leans over, putting his arm over my shoulder, bringing me to him. "Why is she crying?" I hear Chase ask, his voice tense.

"I asked her to come and work for me," Max says softly. "She has yet to answer me."

I feel Chase beside me, putting his arm around me.

"You okay?" he whispers in my ear and I shake my head.

The front door opens and I hear Chase groan from beside me. "It's me!" Matthew yells and then walks into the kitchen. My hand moves from in front of my face.

"What are you doing here?" he asks Max and then looks at me. "Did you make my daughter-in-law cry?"

"Why are you here?" Chase asks him from behind me now.

"I bought a boat," he announces and we can't help it, the three of us just burst out laughing. I look up at Chase who bends down and kisses my lips.

"You okay?" he asks as his eyes look into mine.

"Yeah," I reply and then I look over at Max, leaning in. "I'll take the job."

THE END

For Julia & Chase

Made For You

Vivienne

I did the last thing I ever expected to do.
I bought a boat.
A beautiful boat that was all mine to spend the summer on.
Only thing I was looking forward to was the calm being on the water brought me.
A place where I wasn't a hockey dynasty princess or the only single girl of the family.
What I wasn't looking forward to was the broody man in the boat next to me.

Xavier

I was at the top of my game two years ago.
Then it all came crashing down.
I hung up my skates and vowed to never play again.
I was good at hockey, but hockey was bad for me.
I planned to spend my life on my boat with my dog.
Alone. Happily alone.
Until she came along.